JOHN

JOHN

NIALL WILLIAMS

BLOOMSBURY

First published in Great Britain 2008

Copyright © 2008 by Niall Williams

The moral right of the author has been asserted

Bloomsbury Publishing Plc
36 Soho Square
London WID 3QY

www.bloomsbury.com

Bloomsbury Publishing, London, New York and Berlin

A CIP catalogue record for this book is available from the British Library

Hardback ISBN 9780747594369

10 9 8 7 6 5 4 3 2 1

Trade Paperback ISBN 9780747595816

10 9 8 7 6 5 4 3 2 1

Typeset by Hewer Text UK Ltd, Edinburgh
Printed in the United States of America by Quebecor World Fairfield

All papers used by Bloomsbury Publishing are natural,
recyclable products made from wood grown in well-managed
forests. The manufacturing processes conform to the
environmental regulations of the country of origin

To the Memory of
Stephen G. Breen (1955–2007)

I

1

The sun rising, a bell is rung. On the narrow bed inside the cave the
old man hears the bell but does not see the light. He has not been
sleeping, but lying wakeful in almost a hundred years of memory.
In the cool of the cave he rises to sit upright; his feet find the leather
sandals. It is another morning. This one is cold. There is a wind
from the sea. Storms have been foretold, and it was advised he
move from the wooden hut on the hill. They were not wrong, he
thinks, the storm is near.

Within the sound of the wind is the slap of sandals on stone.
Papias is there. 'Master,' he says.

The old man stands. The youth holds out his arm stiffly, as if it
were a rail, and the blind hand alights upon it. Together so, they
move out towards the wind.

At the entrance of the cave the man's robe flaps sharply and his
long hair blows about. He pauses Papias an instant, as if he can see
then the thin crack of light unlidding the darkness in the east, or the
pale spread of dawn on the broken surface of the sea. The wind
blows at him. His face is long and composed and ancient; his eyes
are open but unseeing. The blindness came to him there on the
island of Patmos in the second year of his banishment, in the
aftermath of vision, now a long time ago. But the things he had
seen in the world are not forgotten, and on the rocks above the
shore it is as though he views the dawn.

Papias waits. The old man is thin and vulnerable to the wind. His
legs are not steady. He is a frail assembly of bones. Waves ride in

3

high and collapse further up the stones. The air is full of the excited noise of the sea, and in standing facing it the old man may lose all sense of time and be returned to the beginning. It is dark still. He steps towards the sound of the waves on the stones, and Papias puts out his arm in case the old man will fall forwards. But he doesn't. He stoops down and feels for the water. He lets its iciness flow about his wrist and then cups a handful and brings it to his face.

'The storm,' he says. 'The storm comes.'

'Yes, Master.'

The bell rings again. They go towards it across the shore. From the darkness other figures appear and move wordlessly in the wind to a place above in the rocks. They are in number near thirty. As light breaks and reveals great heaves of black and purplish cloud rolling in the sky above, the men wait. They watch Papias lead the old man up the rough stones. The one that holds the handbell places it on the ground. Where they stand, exposed, the wind shows them little mercy. It comes at them like a paring knife, as if to test if anything in them not hard and true remains. It whistles and blows. Their robes slap. There is not light enough yet for them to make out one another's faces.

John arrives among them. They look upon him with reverence and greet him with the quiet gladness of those who are afraid each time they see him that it may be the last. Some are young and others old, but none as old as he. He takes their greeting kindly. Then, in that place on the hill, he stands and holds his hands out from his shoulders, parcelling a portion of the half-light and the wind. The men bow their heads. The Apostle's blind eyes gaze forwards into what only he can see. By the rock where once lightning struck and where, with his head pressed against the stone, he had the revelation, he kneels now. The others do likewise, shadows faceless in the half-dark. The wind whirls about them.

They pray.

The storm proper arrives by mid-morning. He is back in the cave and sits on a large stone just inside the entrance. He sees the storm through its sound. He sees the swirl of cloud descending out of the bruised heavens. Darkness contends with the little light and makes nothing of the day. The sea is up and crashing. High swells surface in mid-water and ride imperious to the shore, dragging back rocks that had once been surrendered.

The wind howls. Papias asks his master to move inwards out of the gale. But he will not. He is like a watcher on the deck, attendant, expectant. Salt skins his face, embeds in a thousand wrinkles. He sits, crouched forward as if he might miss something, as if in the contention of earth and sea and air is a message in a language just beyond his understanding.

'My Lord,' Papias hears him say, but nothing more.

The island is sheeted in rain. Vast, urgent thunder rolls across morning. Still John does not move from his place. When the bell rings at midday, Papias asks, 'Master, will you stay and not risk the weather? Will I tell the others to come here?'

'No, I will go.'

And as before, he rises and takes the youth's arm and goes out across the foreshore, where the stones are slippery and treacherous, and up the rock steps to the small gathering. In the wild elements there they pray again. Lightning fingers the sea. Their faith holds them, but they look to the old man in their centre as to a mystery. Some have followed him for years, through Troas, Apollonia, Samaria, other places, desert lands where he came preaching. Whether because of the conviction of his manner or that he spoke of what he himself had witnessed, they left their lives aside like old garments and followed.

Now they stand in the storm bowed and praying. When they have finished, and the rain beats down still, one of them, Matthias, loudly asks, 'Master, tell us, is it a sign?'

He knows he is not to ask. He knows that all have the same question in their minds all the time, but that none utter it. For there is an unspoken understanding that the Apostle does not want to be asked, because for him everything may be a sign; because he was a witness of Christ and because he had the vision on the island years

5

ago, he may see into everything. Or nothing. The vision of the revelation came and went, and there had occurred nothing since. At first the small community of disciples had expected other visions to follow. Even while the words of the revelation were being scribed, they imagined another coming. They looked at the heavens as if they might see evidence of an aperture, a sky portal thrown open and the first fierce angels descending. Every storm, every sudden change in weather might carry meaning. A flock of seabirds, a heavy catch of fish, these might be portents. The world became burdened so, and the old Apostle with it. He felt their hungering and grew quiet, like the sea exhausted by storm. In time the disciples understood and did not ask. It was to be a test of their faith. They understood endurance.

But this morning, standing in the storm, rainwater dripping from his black curls, Matthias asks again, more loudly, 'Master, will you tell us, is it a sign?'

The others look up and then look down quickly, as though the blind man can see them. Their faces, their beards, run with rain. The noon is dark, the day ruined, above them the un-forgiving sky.

'It is a storm,' John says at last and then steps blindly away down the rocks before Papias, who scrambles after him.

Inside the entrance of the cave the Apostle sits again. Papias brings him a cloth for his face, another he lays on his shoulders. John says nothing. He tilts his face slightly upwards, where the wind meets it, and he sits there, his bones locking, aches of age arriving. He remains wordless, witness of the storm's urgencies, his brow furrowed deeply, as if engaged in an impossible act of translation.

The storm does not lessen. It brews and boils on. The day stays dark. All about the island rain-wind scours. The small community of fishers that live on the eastern shore remain in their homes and wait.

Then, when the short day is falling into night and fresh lightning crackles, the old man stands. At once Papias comes to his side.

'You stay,' says John.

'No, Master, please.'

'Stay. I command it,' he says, and he goes out of the cave into the driving rain.

His footsteps know the way. His sandals do not slip as he makes his way down to the sea. The wind and rain is a hurly-burly, the heavens unpacking torrents and gales and all manner of broken weather thrown out in the dark. The old man feels the thin framing of his body, how his joints ache, how the very bones of him resist movement. He has walked ten thousand miles, more, preaching. He knows that at his great age he should long ago be dead. He knows that already of the twelve there are few remaining. He has heard of crucifixions, stories of torture and stoning. He has heard from boatmen landing on the island how the persecution of the Christians has continued until it has seemed he has lived to see in a hundred years the vanquishing of the faith that gave his life meaning.

He goes down to the sea and along the shore, where the tide is high and the rocks rattle like bones. Blindly he finds the stones that are the steps and returns for a third time that day to the Rock of Revelation. He does not want the others about him now. To go truly he has to bend forwards and feel with his hands the way. The cold of the rain-wind is bitter, the sea in the night loud. There is no moon nor stars, as there have been none for him in many years. He clambers higher, then loses his footing and slips. His skin is thin and bleeds easily; the salt air tells him of the wound at his ankle. He climbs on until he comes at last to the flattened rock itself.

John stands in the storm. He has no fear of any kind. He has outlived all manner of pain and been near enough to death to kiss its face and walk away. He has lived for a purpose and believes he knows what it is. He remains, awaiting the coming.

And so now, at his great age, he stands and opens his arms to the wild night. It whirls about him. Not twenty feet away Papias watches silently. Rain comes and goes and comes again. The old

7

apostle's arms tremble and waver, his long white hair blown back, and the flesh of his face weeping the salt rain.

'My Lord,' he cries out, and raises his hands upward to the utter dark. 'My Lord, your servant waits.'

2

Later, sleepless, in inconsolable dark he thinks of the beginning.

The day was blue and still. We were to be out in the boat fishing on Lake Genesareth, but I did not go that day. When Father came to call for me, I was already gone. Fishing was dull and tiring. What did I want of the family business, catching fish and drying them for sale in the narrow storeroom at Bethsaida? I was proud and stubborn. I left the house as if pulled on a cord, and walked that day as others before many miles through the dust to the place by the river where small numbers gathered to hear the teaching.

This day was no different. I was gone before James and Father had woken. I walked out in the cool of the early morning and across the unrisen dust of the street. It was a long journey. The sun rising thinned the blue of the sky until it shimmered.

On the road there was no one. No birds flew. For sound there was only my footsteps, the soft crush of sandals in sand. Brilliance of light. The low hills and folds of the desert unshifting in the windless day.

Remember looking upwards at the sky. Remember wondering what a day this was, and thinking of them waking now and going out on the lake with the nets. Remember thinking of the disappointment my father would feel seeing my bed empty.

But I walked on. That blue morning crossing the distance between one life and another, though I did not know it yet.

The Baptist was a thin figure with long hair. He seemed to eat not at all. From long speaking his voice was strong, his words compelling. He spoke of the Messiah coming. From scripture he quoted Isaiah: 'I am a voice in the desert, crying out, "Make the Lord's road straight!"' This man spoke, it seemed, all day and night, untiring. From him the stream of words that washed over those who sat by the riverbank, in some manner comforted by the vision of one so flowing.

I sat by the side of Andrew and listened.

The sun was hot, the river shone. Soft dazzlements crossed the current. I watched the water moving in light. I watched the heavens blue in the water. Remember. I turned my face upwards, imagined flight on such a day as this. What height I could reach into the blue, and what it might be to see from above. Imagining when the Baptist made louder his voice and cried out, 'Look! Behold! Here is the Lamb of God!'

Andrew turned first.

I looked around behind and saw you walking.

The storm continues for three days. The disciples come to the Apostle's cave. They pray the prayers he has taught them. Prochorus asks, 'Master, will you teach to us from the Revelation?'

John does not answer. They are unsure if he is with them or not.

Prochorus carries the copy he himself scribed in the Greek language. Matthias nods purposefully to him, and he begins to read from it.

'After these things I looked, and behold a door was opened in heaven, and the first voice which I heard was as it were of a trumpet speaking with me, which said: Come up hither, and I will show you the things which must be done hereafter.

'And immediately I was in the spirit: and behold there was a throne set in heaven, and upon the throne one sitting.'

Father's eyes. His face when I told him.

'Jesus, son of Joseph?'

'Yes, Father.'

'You are going to follow Jesus, son of Joseph?'

James beside me. I had brought him the next morning to see for himself.

'Both of you?' Father said.

Mother by the table, arms crossed on herself. 'Zebedee, be quiet.'

'He is your mother's cousin, he is Salome's cousin. And you think he is the Messiah, he is the Christ? And what of the family? What of the fishing? I am old. Who is to care for us in our age?'

'We must go.'

'Why? Why must you go? You are young. You are rash and stubborn. I am your father. I know because it is my rashness and my stubbornness. But why? Are there not others who have gone? Why must you also? Both of you? I need you here.'

'God will care for you,' James said.

Father's fist hard on to the table. He would have broken things. He would have lifted the table and thrown it against us. He would have nailed shut the door. Mother came to him.

Father's eyes. How they looked upon us, sorrowful.

And knowing.

As if he knew, the years ahead, the suffering, but could not save us from it.

Father.

His last look as we went. *Knowing.*

When we returned from Cana, illumined, excited, witnesses of the signs, proclaiming, Barnabus met us at the road and told us, 'Zebedee is dead. Your mother is gone to live with a cousin.'

O Father. O Father, look down upon me.

'Master? Master, surely you will teach us now,' Matthias says. He is a thin, dark-bearded figure of thirty. His hands he holds cupped in front of him, his head angled forward. His manner is honeyed with humility.

'Is the storm passed?' John asks.

'It is passing, Master,' Papias says.

'Master, the teaching?' Matthias presses forwards. 'We wait for your teaching. If you do not teach us, what are we to think? We are weak and you must give us answers. You have answers for us from on high.' He has stepped forwards to stand directly in front of the old man. 'Tell us,' he says. 'Tell us, O holy Master, what the Divine sees for us.'

There are looks and frowns. The cave air is clotted with disapproval, but Matthias is unperturbed. 'Tell us, O wise and holy Master,' he asks, 'how long are we to live here on this island in banishment? Tell us his plan. How are we to continue to wait and pray here, Master, if we do not know?'

'Matthias! Cease, be silent,' an elder, Ioseph, says.

But others, Auster, Linus, Baltsaros, move slightly forwards and Matthias continues: 'How does it serve to be silent? Are we not human? Is it not of man to seek to know? How can this be wrong if it makes stronger our faith? That we might better serve by knowing, surely this is truth. Is this not the truth, Master? All want to know what only you can tell us. How long more? How long more will we wait for the coming?'

'Brother,' the bald figure of Lemuel says, 'it is not for us to ask.'

'But it is. It is for us to ask and for our master to tell. How long? How long more are we to live on this barren island? I am not alone in asking how a life here, far from all, serves the Divine. I am not alone in asking, only in asking aloud. I am speaking the truth for us all. Surely there is a sign for us. Surely he has told you and you can take us from this darkness.'

At this, Matthias drops to his knees before John. He reaches out and takes the old man's hand and places it upon his own head.

'Behold, I touch the hand that touched the Christ,' he says. 'Of he that has seen. When will you guide us into the light of his presence? Master, tell us.'

'Matthias! Enough!' Ioseph steps forward, puts his hand on the other's shoulder to draw him back. But Matthias pushes it off.

'Does the Lord speak to you still, or is he silent?' he asks.

The sea sounds at the cave's entrance. All watch the old apostle's face. It is impossible to read what thoughts travel there. His mouth is tightly closed, his lips thin. As if in deep communion, or scrutiny for something precious lost, there is a deep furrow between his brows. His breath through the long, straight nose is inaudible. He has such stillness as do the dead. His long white hair falls thinly in serene compose. But within him may be thunders and lightnings. None can say.

Matthias holds his hand firmly. He will not let go until he has his answer. 'Is he silent to you?' he asks again. 'Does he speak to you?'

The slightest thing now may be a sign. There is turned on the old apostle's face such study and concentration as to note each quiver of muscle, each infinitesimal flickering of nerve, and such as may betray the truth of his response. His blind eyes are open and clear as sky. His lips press together and then – is he going to speak? The disciples dare not make a sound. Those who know they should admonish Matthias and leave do not. Those who so desperately hunger for an answer allow themselves to lean ever so slightly forwards.

John's tongue touches his lips.

Beside him, the youth Papias stands.

'I am the servant of the Lord, Jesus Christ,' he says. 'As are all of you. Because we were called. I heard the calling, and I have undertaken the Lord's work until he comes again.'

The elder disciples nod, comforted even by so few words.

But Matthias asks, 'Will he, Master? Will he come again? Will we see him with our own eyes? And when will he come? Is there a sign?'

'Matthias!' the scribe's voice calls out.

'Be calmed, Prochorus,' says John. He raises his brows as if so he might lift the weight on his spirit; his voice is quiet and firm. 'He will come again, Matthias. You will see him with your own eyes. As will I. The Lord has told me so himself.' He pauses, as if the saying aloud of this has renewed him in some way, as if he has traversed some shadowed terrain in himself into a naked light. 'He will come again,' he says simply.

'Soon, Master?'

'The hour grows near,' John answers. He withdraws his hand and holds it in the other.

The hour grows near.

3

The storm passed, a boat lands. It brings news of the outside world, and Papias carries this to the cave.

John sits outside on a rock, his face to the pale sun. He hears the footsteps of the youth and interprets their heaviness.

'Papias, you may tell me,' he says.

'Master, it is sad news. The boatmen say the persecution continues.'

'This is not their only news.'

'No, Master.'

'Tell me.'

'They say there was news of a new Christian martyr. He was one who had travelled, it was said, as far as the Caucasus Mountains to preach the word of the Lord, and had preached to the Scythians and from there went to Byzantium, then to Thrace and Macedonia, down the Corinthian Gulf to Patros in Greece.'

'Tell me.'

'Aigeatis, the governor of Patros, became enraged at his preaching and ordered him brought before a tribunal, where he was asked to renounce the Christian faith. But he would not.' Papias pauses. He studies his master's face, for it shows something he cannot explain. It is as though what he is telling is already known, or has to the old apostle been foretold. 'The governor Aigeatis ordered him to be crucified, Master,' he continues.

'Yes.'

'Do you know already, Master?'

'Tell me.'

'They say he was scourged and hung upon the cross, that he hung there for three days in suffering. The people came around him, and in his suffering he cried out to them to love the Lord Jesus. For three days he would not die. He was scourged further while he hung on the cross, but yet did not speak against our Lord. The boatman says his last words are reported, "Accept me, O Christ Jesus, into your eternal realm." '

Fear and sorrow and awe pause Papias. He thinks of the agony of the martyr and his own intolerance of pain. He thinks of what it would be to have the ropes bind his arms to the cross, of the muscles tearing, and the wounds from the scourging crying out. He thinks of the thirst, and the sun burning, of the hunger and the anguish and how all such would be relieved at once if he were only to renounce. He blinks himself out of such thoughts.

'The boatman says the martyr's name . . .'

'Andrew,' says John.

'Yes, Master.'

Andrew, the first. The fair-haired. Brother of Simon Peter. His father, Jona; his mother, Joanna. Andrew, who believed before I did. Who saw Jesus walking and jumped to his feet at once. That blue morning. We ran to be up with him. The first words our Lord spoke to us, 'What are you looking for?'

I, too timid to answer.

Andrew asked, 'Rabbi, where are you staying?'

'Come and see.'

How he ran back for Simon Peter, shouting, 'We have found the Messiah! We have found him!'

The beginning.

The day being dry, the old man walks out on the island with Papias. The youth gives his right arm. He does not speak unless spoken to. He believes himself honoured to be attendant on the Apostle.

The place is mostly rock, the wind cool. Sea sounds and seabird calls fill the air. They take a route up from the shore, the old man in his white robes frail and shaped thin by gently pressing wind. The youth is dark-haired and strong. White clouds cross swiftly above them, freeing and capturing the sun.

While to the others the island of their banishment has become smaller with time, to John in his blindness it has become boundless. In the dark in which he walks it is a landscape endless as eternity. He has seen it years previous, but forgotten the exactness. Now it is only the dark place where he is waiting for the light. He has Papias guide him up across the weathered rock face, past the low dwellings of the other disciples, and away on to the higher ground, where there is a view of the open sea and the island's perimeter. It is the highest point.

Whether the Apostle knows this exactly Papias is not sure. Whether he brings them there to the closest point to heaven on purpose or it is an assigned place and the Lord has communicated this to John, Papias does not enquire. In the holiness of the Apostle he believes completely. He believes all things John does are for a reason, and that this will be revealed in time. In recent months Papias has heard others in the community murmur doubt about the old man's memory and cogency. Matthias is not the only one to question. Others, too, are grown restless and impatient, the ascending columns of their prayers thinning at the base. Papias hears, but says nothing. He tells none of this to the old man, for it seems a betrayal, and his own faith is still absolute.

When they reach the high point, the wind blows more vigorously. John's hair is taken back, his white beard laid against his neck. His blue eyes look about, as though they had sight.

What is happening in his mind? Papias wonders. What sights does he see? His master is like a cave full of secrets.

The sea below is white-capped and the seabirds hover and cry. There is a ship on the horizon sailing west. John stands without a sound.

It is as though he expects something to happen here, Papias thinks. It is as though at any moment a door might open in the heavens above him. Papias looks up at the blue and the white clouds crossing. For the old apostle he anticipates what it might be that is shortly to happen. He pictures a brilliant light; he imagines music of trumpets, and all manner of white horses, winged and golden shod, beating down in majesty out of the upper realms. Papias sees an order of angels swoop from the entranceway of the Eternal and flank the incandescent light. He anticipates a bliss divine. Upon the head of this ancient man he foresees a white fire alight and all grow radiant in such dimension as to blind with whiteness and make men fall to their knees as the Christ descends to be once more, there, by the side of his beloved disciple.

While they stand, Papias sees it so. In the furnace of his youthful faith he forges this perfect image. He imagines it will be at any moment. He is certain this is what his master awaits.

John says nothing. He attends the wind.

An hour, two hours pass. The silence is absolute. The old man's ankles ache. The bones of his legs are brittle and full of pain.

Clouds come from the east, darkening.

Nothing happens.

When he fears that he will fall, John reaches out to allow Papias to support him. He leans on his arm, but says nothing.

He stands there on top of the island. To the north is the risen darkness of Mount Kerketeus, clouds gathered upon it. Together the Apostle and the youth wait.

When the bell rings noon, they come back down for prayer.

'It is written,' Matthias says that evening to a small gathering in the narrow confines of his dwelling, three sides of timber planking against rock. He holds open the scroll of the Book of Revelation. ' "And when he had opened the fifth seal, I saw under the altar the souls of them that were slain for the word of God, and for the testimony which they held. And they cried with a loud voice, saying: How long, O Lord, holy and true, dost thou not judge and revenge our blood on them that dwell on the earth?"

'Amen,' Auster says, and nods toward the thin, flaxen-haired figure of Linus.

'Amen,' say the others.

Lambs all of them, Matthias thinks. Lambs that can be led.

He turns on his heel, spreads open his hands. 'How long, O Lord? How long? Yea, I dare to ask. While Domitian reigns there continues persecution. The crucifixion of the apostle Andrew is only one of many. The soul of the slain. I hear him crying out. We will be slaughtered from the earth and none care. We will be forgotten.'

'But Matthias, ours is not to question,' Cyrus says. 'Ours is to wait and keep the faith. ' "*Yet that which you have, hold fast until I come.*" '

'But so, too, it is written, Cyrus, "*Behold I come quickly*",' Matthias replies.

Cyrus nods. 'This is true,' he agrees. 'We believe our Lord is coming, Matthias.'

'But why does he wait?'

The lamb can't answer.

'How many crucifixions does our Lord want? Five hundred more? Five thousand? How many more crucifixions will mark the roads of Domitian's empire while we sit here?'

The lambs don't bleat. 'Recall,' Matthias says, 'the Apostle himself wrote: "And behold there was a great earthquake, and the sun became black as a sackcloth of hair, and the whole moon became as blood; and the stars from heaven fell upon the earth, as a fig tree casteth its green figs when it is shaken by a great wind.

' "And the heaven departed as a book folded up." ' Matthias does not need to read; he knows the words. ' "And every mountain and the islands were moved out of their places; and the kings of the earth and the princes and tribunes and the rich and the strong and every bondmen and every freeman hid themselves in the dens and in the rocks of mountains. And they say to the mountains and the

19

rocks: Fall upon us and hide us from the face of him that sitteth upon the throne, and from the wrath of the Lamb. For the great day of their wrath is come, and who shall be able to stand?" '

He pauses, his face flushed, and he looks at each. They are a small gathering, chosen, asked from among the others to come to debate the way to truth. They are mostly the younger of the disciples. Their beards have no silver, their faces are unlined. They have come in recent years, many by choice, to be in the company of the Apostle, to await with him the coming. But time has worked on their faith, the nothing that has happened each day since eroding mountains.

' "The great day of their wrath. The great day of their wrath is come, and who shall be able to stand?" ' Matthias continues. 'But tell me, where is this wrath? When is this day? This I ask you. Tell me if you know. Tell if it is only poor Matthias who does not understand. Take him from his ignorance. Is it to come while we sit here on Patmos? Verily, is this the intention of the Divine? Tell me, tell me Baltsaros, Linus, is it the intention that we wait on till old age and weakness come? Is this what you think Cyrus, Auster? Or' – Matthias raises a finger as if to arrest a thought, as if there passes in the air just then a solution hitherto unconsidered – 'might it be, might it be that we are to go forward to meet it? As an army on a plain is emboldened by the approach of another legion, should we not make the great day happen ourselves? Should we not show ourselves willing to the Divine?'

'It is a vexing question, Matthias,' says the high voice of Phineas.

Bald-pated fool of a lamb, eyes too close to each other for clear thought.

'But how can we know?' Phineas whines. 'Only the Apostle has seen the Lord, and he commands we abide here.'

The others nod and voice agreement.

Lambs indeed.

Baltsaros says, 'We are all grieved, Matthias, to hear the news of the apostle Andrew. But his place is assured at the table of our Lord in heaven. His work was complete. In that we can rejoice.'

'Rejoice because every day we are less, not more?' Matthias arches his eyebrows. 'Truly? Truly? Well, I cannot rejoice. What work for God do we do here? Are we not the same as those dead? What keeps us here in banishment? An edict from Rome? Because if we leave this island we will be persecuted and crucified? Consider this: perhaps this is our destiny, and we hide from it here, are cowards. I do not rejoice in the death of Andrew, I grieve and anger. As should you all.'

Aware of how incautious are his words, he stops. He must bring the lambs back into safe pasture.

'Forgive me my weakness, my brothers. Pray with me that I may know the way to truth,' he says, and before them kneels down and bows low his head.

A brilliant stratagem. As though I ask them to show me the way. These lambs that think they are lions.

Matthias closes his eyes. The seeding is begun.

4

And the beast coming up out of the sea having seven heads and ten horns, and upon the horns ten diadems. The beast that was like to a leopard, and feet the feet of a bear, and mouth of a lion.

And the seven vials of the wrath of God. The sore and grievous wound that fell upon the men with the character of the beast. The blood poured into all the sea, wherein every living soul died. The rivers and the fountains made blood. The sun afflicting men with heat and fire so all were scorched and blasphemed. The vial that was poured on the seat of the beast so his kingdom became dark and they gnawed their tongues for pain. The sixth vial that was poured into the river Euphrates and dried up the waters. And from the mouth of the dragon, from the mouth of the beast, three unclean spirits like frogs. Spirits like devils working signs. And the seventh vial poured on the air, and a voice out of the temple saying, 'It is done.' And lightnings and voices and thunders, and a great earthquake, and the great city divided into three parts, and every island fled away and the mountains not found. And falling then the great plague of hail.

Did I see such things as these?

Did I?

Did those words come from me?

I remember not.

Was there a vision so clear?

When Papias reads it to me, it seems familiar yet strange.

Dear Lord, remember your ancient servant. Have pity. Pages in the book of my memory fall away.

Did the angel come to me truly?

Did I see such vision? And then was blind?

But Jerusalem fell. The mountain Vesuvius opened with fire. Nero's Rome burned. Such things did happen.

And yet you did not come.

Papias reads to me: ' "And I, John, who have heard and seen these things. And after I had heard and seen, I fell down to adore before the feet of the angel who showed me these things." '

But now I am afflicted, Lord, and cannot remember.

My spirit thirsts for salvation.

John kneels in the rock chamber and confesses. Papias is gone to see what fish have been caught. The old apostle's head is bowed. The news of the death of Andrew has struck him like many blows. Though the crucifixion may have happened a long time ago and the news taken this time to travel, it is to him as though yesterday. Cut as wounds into his mind is the history of the suffering of each of the twelve. Accounts he has heard. Each of these return him to one moment on the road.

They were passing through Phrygia and the country of Galatia when they met a traveller in purple. He was a wizened creature, humped, with ragged beard. Sun blazed upon them. 'O Christians!' he called out, his head tilted upward, his rheumy eyes aswim. 'Come, buy from me!' He had a wife and a loaded ass, gestured with a long-nailed hook hand for them to pause. The Apostle and his followers had nothing to trade. And when he discovered this, the traveller spat into the sand. 'Ye are not worth spit,' he said, and waved his wife to stop unloading the goods. 'Ye will be dust soon,' he muttered for consolation, glare-eyed, blister-cracking his lips. 'Ye're heads will roll like the son of Zebedee,' he said with undisguised glee and turned away.

'Wait. Tell us,' John called after him.

The traveller stopped, looked back over his hump. 'For what profit?' he asked.

'I am a son of Zebedee,' John said and walked forward. 'Tell.'

And for the pleasure of pain, for the tale he could carry to the towns of Phyrgia and perhaps trade upon it, the traveller turned. 'I saw myself the head of James, son of Zebedee, cut from his body by order of Herod Agrippa. I saw the blade rise, the hair pulled back, the eyes wide like moons.' He came closer. 'I heard the bone snap,' he said, clutching his hooked hand to his own throat below a blister-smile. 'The head, it rolled,' he said, and rolled his hand in a tumbling fall. 'The brown eyes stared till dust blinded them.'

John fell to the ground and cried out. And then bowed down and scooped a handful of dust and pressed it into his mouth to keep from shouting out with sorrow. The wild lamentation that lacerated him he could not release in weeping, for the others of his followers he believed he could not show the feeling of abandonment by the Lord. Instead the wolf of grief he took inside himself and let it roam and savage freely.

In repeated dreams after came the sight of his brother bowed before the blade the traveller told. In such dreams always John stood among the assembled witnesses; powerless, he saw James refuse to deny the Christ and his prayers growing louder even as the blade rose in the air. Forever since, though blind, he sees still; he hears the terrible crack and sees his brother's head fall away.

Now, with news of Andrew, all such returns to him. The loss is so great as to be unutterable.

John kneels and confesses. He kneels so long on the bare rock of the cave floor that his knees lock, and the framework of his bones entire is turned solid. First he aches, and pain is everywhere. And then, slowly, slowly, he passes beyond the condition of pain, into an inner terrain where by himself he himself is forgotten. There, these his ancient hands held together, this his bowed head with white hair, are no more present to him, and he is become instead like an element or a timeless feature of that place.

He is away, and out of this world.

Water sounds. The cave where he kneels speaks with the sound of a thousand invisible streams.

★　　★　　★

On the far side of the island, Papias goes to visit one of the poor families of fishers that live there. On the eastern shore there is a small scattering of houses that existed before the Christians arrived. At first mistrustful of the band of men who were brought and released on to the island, the fishers grew to understand they offered no threat, and then to warm to them because they were hated by the despised Romans. Finally, some among them were converted by the stories of the Christ, Jesus. The kingdom everlasting was explained to them, and gave solace in the hardships of island life to those who felt abandoned on that bleak edge of the world. When sons and husbands drowned, the Christians were told and asked to come and pray.

So now, the youth Papias.

In the days after the storm one of the fishermen, Xantes, did not return. Then his broken boat washed up at the feet of his wife, Marina, who was watching from the shore. She went back to the house and held her two small children and said not a word. When the others came to tell her what she already knew, she did not weep. They said it was only his boat and Xantes might have lived. There was no body.

For the following three days there was none, and it was presumed destroyed on the rocks or eaten by the creatures of the sea. The fishers sent word to the Christians, and old Ioseph, feeling ill, had asked Papias to go and pray with the woman.

It is a morning bitter with cold. Grey seabirds claw on the rocks and do not fly. Dull oaten-coloured clouds travel the sky. Mercilessly the wind beats at the sea. While Papias hurries, he looks out at the small scars of white surf, the unsailed waters. His sandals are worn, the soles thin. His garments are dirty from the walls of the cave. He wishes it weren't so. He is honoured that Ioseph has asked him this first time, and he wants to appear as he imagines a holy man should. I should be clothed in light, he thinks, then chastises himself for such vanity.

'You bring the Lord,' he says under his breath into the wind. 'You are clothed in the Lord.'

He crosses up over the bare, smooth stone at the top of the island and descends toward the fishers' dwellings. In his haste the edge of a rock gashes his ankle. He cries out but does not slow down. He is thinking of the prayers he will say. He is thinking he is engaged in the most important business of life.

He has been told the house, and knocks on the rough timber of the door. There is no answer and he knocks again. The third time he knocks and opens the door. Inside in the dark sits the woman Marina and clutched against her, her two small children.

'I come to pray for your husband's passage into everlasting life,' Papias says, the door light framing him.

The woman does not move. Her fair hair is coiled on her head and tied with a headscarf, her dark eyes distant. Lain at her breasts the infants sleep.

'I bring the love of the Lord Jesus,' Papias tells her.

She turns to him. She is twice his age. Her face, planed with light, is sadder than any he has seen.

Walking swiftly in the sunlight that day. The dust.

The knowledge that all my life had come to this moment.

Andrew running back to tell Simon. 'The Messiah, we have found the Messiah!'

My eyes not moving from you as you walked forward. My mouth open, as if I had eaten the world. As if the world were round like a ball and I had taken it inside me and could not yet know how I might breathe again.

'John, son of Zebedee,' you said. 'Come.'

Some moments as clear as water. Your hand held out.

A lifetime ago.

Knowing. Knowing in that first moment: I believe. I will follow you.

Andrew running up with Simon Peter. The smile in his face. How he wanted to laugh out loud with delight. As though this was a great victory. You turned to Simon and said: 'Your name shall be Cephas, Peter.'

And Andrew wanted to laugh with delight.

But gravely Peter looked at you, and bowed then and was changed already.

'Come.'

That road in the sand. The three of us just behind you speaking not at all.

The blue of the sky. The light. As if something had opened and we had walked right through.

I remember.

A feeling of light, of lightness.

And knowing. When I looked in your face. That was like no other face, and your eyes that were like no other eyes. Because of the kindness and the love. And the suffering.

'Come.'

Walking that dust road away from the river, we, your first disciples. The first time any had followed you.

So we felt chosen.

And the light and the blue of the sky. And the three of us just behind you speaking not at all.

Each of us already thinking: this is what is to be.

As if already it were written.

My Lord.

I remember.

5

She says not a word. She sits with the infants against her in the dark.

'I bring the word of the Lord,' Papias says. His Greek is perfect, but the woman shows no sign of having understood. Fearful for the children catching cold, he closes the door against the bitter wind. The little windowless room of the dwelling is darkened. This dark she has been sitting in, he thinks, and goes across to a rough board on the far wall to seek a lamp. His hands pat where rats are, and he bangs with his open palm on the timber several times. There is no lamp. The room is darker than the cave.

'Have you no light?'

He cannot see her eyes, only the outline of her head and the lumpish shadows of the infants. He moves closer. There is a stool with lambswool and netting; he lifts these aside and sits. He is close enough to make out her face now. Her eyes stare as though sightless, and her demeanour is of one thrown back from drowning, a straw of strength remaining.

Grief has exhausted her, Papias thinks, the good news of the Lord will be a salve.

'I am come to pray with you for the salvation of your husband, who has gone to eternal life,' he says.

She makes not the slightest movement or response, but stares on into the darkness between them. The air of the damp dwelling is close and bitter with brine. Behind him Papias hears the rats returned to the board table against the wall, scrape, nuzzle, and gnaw. He must concentrate hard to remember the order of prayers he rehearsed. Then from the unseen he smells something foul rising. It seems to thicken in the air as if the grief itself is spewed and lumpish and vile. It sickens him, the foulness, and he blinks away from beginning and scowls. The wind laughs at the door, a dry rattling. The stillness of the small room presses upon him; he feels the strangeness of it as if he is entombed, and though he has ready the words to begin, he cannot begin. The foul air, the windowless dark, the staring eyes of the widow, and the rats running down the board hungry and dissatisfied and hunting meagre nothings in the blind underfoot, these all undress his courage. He feels the wound at his ankle smart, and he makes a small noise with his sandals to keep the rodents at bay.

Still the woman stares, the children unmoving upon her breast.

A cold ooze slides on to Papias's forehead. His lips dry. I am lost, he thinks. I am not prepared. The counsel he is to give, the comfort he is to bring, are taken from him into the dark as insubstantial things. He tries to begin a silent prayer, to ask the Lord to be with him.

But the woman reaches forward and the thin bones of her fingers grasp his wrist. 'I am with demons,' she says. 'Death comes from me.' And she pulls his hand across the dark to alight on the cold infant nearest, and at once Papias knows that both children are dead. The cold of the flesh is appalling and he stands up and pulls back his hand. He cries out and rushes to the door to pull it open. The wind meets him. The light of day blinds and spins his head, and he staggers some steps to where he stumbles and bends down and voids himself on the rocks.

'Papias is not returned, Master, from the fisher's widow. I will care for you this evening,' Prochorus says.

'I need no care. You may return.'

'I have brought some bread and fish pottage.'

'Have them yourself with my blessing.'

John hears the other cross the cave to the small table and place a bowl there then return. He hears his knees crack to sit. There is the small puttering sound of a flame for the lamp.

'Shall I read with you, Master?'

'My thanks. No.'

They sit. At the mouth of the cave the wind noises. It is as if they are deep within a shell cast back by the tide whose memory is captured. John's breath is slow and thin. Next to him, the other is more restless. Prochorus is sixty years. His head is bare but for two thin ridges of grey hair above his ears. His beard is a wisp. The long fingers of his hands seem destined for fine work, and he can scribe with either one, but without instrument or papyrus they seem lost for purpose and move about on his thighs, his forearms, smooth the nothings on his pate. At sixty years he retains this energy in his body and would prefer any chore to sitting with the old apostle in silence.

'The pottage is good,' he offers.

'Prochorus, there is no need to stay. Nothing will transpire.'

There is a sigh released through the nose, there is the sound of fingers spreading on the knees and the slight friction of the cloth as Prochorus rocks very gently back and forth. The stool rhythms his restlessness.

'Should we pray, Master? Perhaps I should pray with you?'

'Pray as you return from here, Prochorus. I thank you for your intentions. I will see you at the dawn bell.' John offers his hand. But the other returns it to him and says: 'I am staying here until Papias comes.'

'Very well.'

John sits perfectly still. He has an ability Prochorus cannot fathom, to simply be. To sit in the turning of time as though nothing of him is diminished by it, as though he may wait for ever. His patience is beyond patience, is beyond any quality nameable in the vast vocabularies of the four languages Prochorus knows; it is a quality he has never seen in another human. For in the old apostle's constancy is a stillness that is not reposed or serene, no portion of him sleeps nor idles, but all is instead attentive, expectant, and indefatigable. From him there is not the smallest movement. *Patior.* Prochorus thinks of the Latin verb, to endure and to suffer.

The younger man folds his arms, his hands cup his elbows and he rocks forwards. He looks about him into the halo of light the lamp throws against the cave. The water sounds run, and here and there high in the roof glisten thin streams. He looks at them. He looks at the patterns of their descent, where they pool into the dark. Hunkered forwards he studies the cave floor, the beaten arc of path the years have made, elsewhere the sandal-printed dust. A place near the entrance where Papias lights small fires from what fuel can be found on that treeless isle. He rubs his palm across his beard, smoothes with right forefinger his right eyebrow. He tries to listen to the sound of the wind, to interpret in it music or messages, but hears only the howling and the loneliness.

Night is fallen; Papias is not returning. Prochorus is staying until the dawn now. He looks to the old man. Should he ask him will he be guided to the mat on the floor for sleep? Does he sleep at all?

They have sat for hours, John moving not the slightest. Prochorus himself is weary. When he is not active, heavy soft sponges of drowsiness descend on his brain. But he will not leave the old man; he will not sleep unless John does. And he decides that he cannot ask or disturb the Apostle in his meditation. Instead Prochorus blinks his eyes; he opens his mouth wide and hears his jawbone crack in its socket and holds a hand against it as if in admonishment. His head grows unbearably heavy. He feels it nod forwards as if in agreement and straightens himself and shakes it once to throw off the sleep that nests on stillness. He should get up and move about. He should put out the lamp perhaps. But he does neither. The sitting is intolerable prison now, but he cannot escape it. He considers it would be weakness and fault to move now. He must offer it. The old Apostle may be in communion such as he himself has never known. He it was, after all, who came upon John years earlier in their banishment, when the lightning had passed and the Apostle lay collapsed on the great stone. Prochorus had thought him struck by lightning in the temple of his head. His eyes were blind and he was speaking quickly, so quickly that at first it seemed he spoke in no language the scribe understood. Prochorus

31

asked him if he had been out in the storm, if he been struck, for the rock was blackened. John did not answer but continued as if in tongues. His hand he reached on to Prochorus's shoulder, and the younger disciple led him to this cave nearby as their shelter. It was there, in the days and nights ahead, in fevered fits and starts, in long streams of words, and longer pauses, in a voice loud and strong and often angry – his hands flying out into the air about him, his blind face to the cave roof – that the Apostle dictated his revelation and Prochorus wrote it down.

It is the event of Prochorus's life. It is as close as he has come to the presence. Though years later he does not forget an instant of it. Not the hairs that stood on the back of his neck as he wrote, nor the chill in his blood, nor the sense he had as his stylus moved on the papyrus that the words would last the lifetime of the earth. He believed.

He knows it by heart. In the small hours of night, to keep awake now he mutely recites verses. Beside him, John is as before.

Some moonlight is uncovered by the wind-dragging clouds and falls at the entrance. Prochorus looks; he wonders what it might be to be visited just then by seraphim. Would he give his eyes for such? Would the dazzlement singe his brain? Although not an ancient, he is already an old man himself now. Perhaps there is nothing more for him. He wonders how each is chosen. How as if from a great constellation a hand sweeps through stars and selects one. He wonders at the destiny God has chosen for him, and if perhaps again, now, this bitter night, the Apostle will catch fire and speak.

'Let it descend' is his prayer. 'Let it come again, now, Lord.'

The wind whips up from the shore where Papias crouches to his knees over the stones. His head sings. His eyes blur with sudden tears. He feels struck in the pit of his stomach and retches violent, vacant gulps. The sea wind salts his face. From the corner of his mouth it pulls aslant a thin drool. He cries out a sound none hears. He stands upright and looks back at the widow Marina's dwelling, where the rough door opens and bangs with invisible traffic.

When he collects himself, Papias goes back inside. The scene is unchanged: the widow and the infants motionless upon her. The door opens and closes the light so she appears as in a series of identical portraits, each painted a grievous grey, each with a wild, implacable suffering.

'The children must be buried,' Papias says, softly. 'They are gone to the Lord.'

The widow shows no sign of understanding. Her eyes stare, as if across the room she keeps demons at bay.

Gently Papias leans down and places his hands on one of the children. The flesh is cold and scaled with something rough he cannot see. He goes to lift the child off the mother, and the moment the weight shifts she lets out a scream and grasps the infant to her.

'The children must be buried,' he says again. But the mother will not let go the child and shakes her head back and forth, and would be weeping if she had not wept herself away already, and so instead makes a kind of moaning crying and clings to the dead. Papias pleads with her. He tells her he will pray over the children. He tries to lift the first from her again, a girl it is, but the mother will not let go her hold. It is wretched and ugly and intolerable, and still the door bangs and opens and bangs and opens behind him in the wind.

'O Lord, help me,' Papias cries. 'Stop, stop, let go!' He wrenches the infant from her then, and then the other, and rushes outside into the ravaged light of day.

The girls are as nothing in his hands, weight of shells, no more. The lower side of one child's face and down her neck is spread a greenish scaling; the other wears it about her mouth like a lumpish paint. Papias looks up to the sky and wails. He holds the infant girls in the wind as if in offering, as if he believes that from the sky now will come a miracle. He draws down into the deep well of his faith and brings up this clear pure stuff that believes in the absolute bridge-way between man and God, that between earth and heaven is constant traffic of beseech and grant, that somewhere in all the lands stretching from Judea into Asia Minor, and even to Rome and Gaul beyond, there occur visits of the Divine, and the sick are sometimes restored. He holds the infant girls aloft in the wind. Ioseph has baptised all on the island, and will have dipped these children in the water; there is no fear for them. But still Papias finds himself asking. His faith tempts him to think of a personal favour. He looks at the girl with the ruined skin of her face and he closes his eyes. When he opens them, it will be gone; it will be cleansed away and he will feel the returning breath. Papias prays for it. He asks that it happen now. In a fever of belief he tells God that he will not succumb to vanity but keep the curing a secret. No one need know.

The wind beats at him. His eyes are shut to the dull grey hood of cloud, the obscured face of the heavens, but at any instant he expects to feel the blaze of illumination. His youth demands it, a visitation fierce and rapturous and violent.

Salt air swirls. Sandflies find the gash at his ankle and embed in blood. Gulls downed and raucous make urgent angry business with their wings. But Papias pays them no heed. The girls in his arms, his praying is absolute and aloud now. The Greek ascends into the air like a white ladder pressed up into the invisible, all about it the soft, exhausted collapse of the sea in the stones.

'Now, O Lord, come and make these, your children, live!' Papias cries. He tilts his head to allow the imminent radiance to blind him. That, he would gladly accept. Gladly he would be as the old apostle, his master. He has heard of so many healings, so many accounts of miracle, of leprosy cleansed, lameness righted, and even, yes, the dead rising, that he does not doubt the power; what he doubts is only his own worthiness to be its conductor.

The children lie along his arms, his hands cupping their heads. Across the sand floor unseen scuttles a crab. It delays on ochre seaweed, makes small pinchings of sideways motion; it is the size of a man's hand. What food it finds in the slime of the weed is insufficient, and it comes forward, pincers purposeful and elegant, across the shifting undulations of the sand. Minute twigs, like fingertips, the crab squeezes for small life. The blown bits of dwellings and boats from the sea, briny insect-loaded sea wrack, soft crumble harvests of rot alive with maggots, pieces of cloth run away in the wind, sheltering hard-skinned sea slugs, all that the storm undressed and shore-scattered like a bounteous god the crab considers on its route. In low observance it finds a plenitude and yet progresses onwards, as if a little of each is allowed only, or its lot is to be unrestful always on land. The crab crosses shingle and grit, finds brief meaningful pause in the under-place of a rock, scuttles on.

The crab arrives at Papias's foot before it knows it. The force of the youth's stance has embedded him, and sand thinly covers his sandals. The level is blown next to his ankle, where in the wound sandflies cling and suck and buzz, emboldened by the man's stillness to believe him dead or dying. Some, giddy and sated, fly up and hover briefly about the lifeless girls, land inquisitive, explorative, then flee the wind, back down to find the warm blood of the ankle they have forgotten. Black-shelled, sea-creased in an exquisite pattern of five arcs, ignorant of the world above, the crab lies motionless; it pinches a full careless fly, an ooze of white pulp, then senses the something in the sand below it.

Papias knows nothing of this. His voice is hoarse from praying against the wind and he has stopped now to wait. He imagines more prayers will only annoy; he has asked and his entreaty must travel whatever vast distances, through what realms lie ranked and assembled the saints and all the orders of angels up and on to the throne itself. He must attend. The girls grow weightier in his outheld arms. An ache pulls at the top of his shoulder. But Papias will not yield to it. He fears the slightest movement may disturb the ladder, may off-centre the miracle. Suffering is the currency for salvation, and he intends his arms to fall away before he surrenders the girls to death.

In the thin sand covering Papias's right foot a featureless ant is paused. Sweat, salted and savoured with longing, has fallen. The ant moves upon it and the crab pinches and catches sand and skin both. A flake of toe flesh is peeled. The sand shifts, exposing a small wound, and the crab sidles closer, till it lies along the line of the foot facing the five toes.

Papias feels the claw and the sharp announcement of intent, but he does not move and he does not open his eyes. His arms are agony. His head is bowed forward.

The sky darkens. Gulls and petrels dance upon the breaking waves. Effort and strain make the youth hot.

Papias cries out. For an instant, no more, he tries to endure the pain, tries to hold the girls in his arms and see if, now, at this moment of agony, at last the light is to descend. He looks up into the merciless grey, then cries and drops to his knees, laying both infants on the sand. Then he crouches forward, his two hands pressed into the damp grit and his forehead lowered to it, and he lets from him a long loud cry of no words, a wailing plaint that goes on and on, issuing freely from the place where his faith has been pierced.

Dark is fallen. Papias stares out into the sea. He has missed returning for the evening bell and prayer. A wounded part-moon is un-covered in the sky.

The bodies of the girls are before him.

It was for me to do this, he thinks. It was for me and not another to come today.

Wearily he rises and goes by the dwelling and finds a heavy stick there. With this he breaks the shale and opens a hole. In time he kneels and claws the dirt free, then is himself inside the pit, scrabbling at the dark below when he had imagined such light from above. He finishes and climbs out and goes inside the fisher's hut. It is dark. The shape of the woman Marina is where Papias had last left her.

'We must bury the children,' he says. 'I have prayed for them. They are with our Lord in heaven.'

She rocks back and forth slightly in her sitting. She says nothing.

Papias goes outside and lifts the infant girls one at a time and lays them into the pit. The wind is gone. Night is tranquil and ink. He stands bowed and prays again and does not look up into the sky. He scoops the dirt with both hands and lets it fall.

He returns to the hut.

'A mouthful of your water, please,' he asks. But Marina does not move, and he pats the dark blindly till he finds the water pouch and drinks.

'I have demons. I have death,' the woman says.

Papias lowers the water.

'My husband first, then my children. Who I touch dies. Now you,' she says.

6

Afraid that he is forgetting, John remembers. Afraid that age invents memories, he goes into the vastness of his mind to find the true.

Six stone water jars. Or eight?

Six. Our talk at the table. Nathaniel and Philip joking, something about under the fig tree.

Dusty from the long walk to Galilee. Andrew leaning to me: 'We will see the sky opened and the angels of God ascending and descending upon the Son of Man. He has said so.'

Yes.

Drinking the wine freely all of us, excited. Chosen.

At the wedding they were not expecting us. They did not know you had disciples, Lord.

Your mother: 'They have no wine.'

'My hour has not yet come.'

That look. As if you did not wish it to begin.

We fell silent. A bird flapping high in the awning.

'They have no wine.'

Because she knew it would be now. Now would be the first sign. There in Cana.

But you did not speak; you looked to your mother's eyes.

I thought to say we would leave and get wine. I was the fastest; I could run and bring wine from a cousin of Nathaniel not far.

But the look in your mother's eyes. As if she pushed you with her eyes: Go, now, begin.

The bird flapping high above. Not escaping.

The six stone water jars, empty.

I did not need a sign, Lord. Already I believed.

Your mother turning to the Architriklinos: 'Do what he tells you.'

The moments after, I remember. Your mother touching your sleeve. Walking from you. My puzzlement sitting next to you. Across from me, Nathaniel and Philip and James. Andrew pushing to see. None of us knowing what to do.

Your face. The light in it. The knowledge.

'Fill those jars with water.'

The buckets being brought from the well, the water clear falling into them.

'It is only water,' Andrew whispered.

More buckets brought. More water.

Your face unperturbed and considering each of us. Your sad smile of knowledge.

'Now draw some out.'

The heads of us turned to see.

Not I. I knew. I heard the Architriklinos cry, 'It is wine!' But already you had stood.

'Come.'

Philip could not stand; Nathaniel took his arm. Your mother was watching us leave. The music was playing.

You looked at the awning; the bird flew free.

The angel descending has golden wings. From the fore rank of seraphim, seated blissful in divine light, it has come, its form majestic, its purpose sanctified. Rising resplendent upon its summons, and laying broad the full glory of its wings, it had paused momentarily before flight, in manner as one elect and upon the rim of high heaven prepared. With single beat it met the hallowed air, fanned to the seraphim ambrosial farewell and flew beyond the gathered company of the prophets and the saints and the martyrs of the Almighty, beyond Isaiah and Elijah and Moses and all the faithful departed. To the furthest frontier of the celestial it arrived effortless, was as a flaming comet passing, lustrous, sublime. From its prominence at heaven's gate it considered amassed the stars below, myriad assembly of creations, carpet of illumination, then plunged headlong. Wings enfolded rearward, feet as one, it fell like God's arrow. Past the illumined belt that girdles paradise, and the supernal glow that radiates beyond, past the black and the blue, the lesser worlds of empty space, fathoms numberless of uncreated nothing wherein the cries of the undeserving perish and reach no further, past all the angels flew.

It made descent beyond purgatory and paused not to pity or preach, not to tell of those elsewhere bound in chains by the burning black waters of the Styx, the Acheron, the Lethe, whose agony was promised everlasting. It passed as lightning, swift, strict, missioned; came to that outer region where the sun burned white brilliance of fire, made melt any. But here the angel was scorched not and came itself as silvered light, in form formless, in speed absolute. And so appeared in hovered pause above the placid shelf of planet Earth, within its sight all lands and seas that were, all from Asia to Judea and to the north as far as Gaul and Brittania. Its wings it extended then; feathers slight fell, drifted below as marvels; then, in brief quiescence considered the beauty and perfection of creation, what rivers and mountains, what seas.

From all, the angel chose the island, and lifted and lowered its wings mightily and swooped invisible down.

Now, here, at the entrance of the cave, it comes. Appears from within a great illumination, a thousand lamps large, dazzling to human sight. In accompaniment is a sound, sweet, melodic, music without playing. He folds to him his golden wings. He comes from the light and is clear and beautiful to behold, face becalmed, demeanour serene, as though journey from the ranks of seraphim in heaven to the place beneath is not arduous or lengthy.

'Prochorus,' the angel says.

The man bows low to the ground, then drops to his knees.

'Prochorus,' the angel says again.

The scribe cannot believe the angel knows his name. Then he believes it and believes his reward is at hand, believes when he rises that he will assume eternal form and begin his own ascent. His being is filled with gratitude and surrender. Upon his face is a look of transport.

Then he feels himself shaken. A hand touches his cheek.

'Prochorus!'

And he opens his eyes and sees Papias standing there.

'Wake, Prochorus, wake. Where is the Master?'

The angel is gone. There is only the looming face of the youth.

'Prochorus, the Master is not here.'

The scribe is curled on the floor. Chastened by the vanity of the dream, for some moments he cannot stir. It is as though, returned to earth, he is made of weightier stuff and will not be able to stand. But the look of Papias is wild and urgent, and Prochorus presses against the burden of disappointment and rises.

'How long have you been asleep?'

Prochorus does not answer. He crosses the cave with the lamp to where the Apostle had last been sitting. He looks into the empty space in puzzlement. Papias comes to his shoulder. Neither of them say what crosses in their minds. Neither say that perhaps the Apostle has been taken from them.

'Go, wake the others. Call his name. Quickly, quickly,' Prochorus says.

The dawn is near to breaking. There is a chill wind. Papias hurries away across the rocks, while Prochorus stands and cups his hands and calls after the Apostle. His voice travels nowhere. The sea sighs back at him and he feels unwell. He calls again, and again. He goes some way along the upper ledge of the scarp and stumbles and falls forwards, and fears then the blind apostle has plunged off the edge to death in the rocks below. The thought is as a sickness and he lets out a cry.

Across the darkness the other disciples come. Shades against the blued blackness of the predawn, they announce themselves like seabirds by calling. Their master's name is cried over and over.

They assemble and disperse, assemble again. None admonishes Prochorus for sleeping when he was to be watching. The business of finding the Apostle is too urgent. Even the elder, Ioseph, is with them now, and with him the wheezing, anxious figure of Simon.

'Where might he be gone? This is not good. This is not good.' Simon wrings his hands.

Ioseph is swift and decisive. 'Two along the upper rocks,' he says, 'two to the eastern ledge. Linus and Prochorus go above to the meeting place, either side of the pathway. He may be fallen. Simon stay here. Papias and I to the foreshore.'

'I am more nimble, I will go with him.' It is Matthias, who appears out of the dark.

'Very well. Simon, remain here by the cave lest he come.'

'But why is he gone?' Papias asks.

'Go,' Ioseph says. 'Hurry.'

A dull daylight greys the island. The figures of the disciples clamber away, calling. They are like ones abandoned in the dark. Across the air no seabirds fly, and the bleak sky above the island seems lidded closed. Matthias moves quickly, his thin figure light. He stops calling. From the foreshore he considers the ledge above them, the fall that would be fatal. Papias is behind.

'Do you think he is perished?'

'Papias, are you unwell? Your face is pale.'

'I am . . . I may have taken ill in the night. Do you think he is perished?'

Matthias looks at him in the thin light. He does not answer. He thinks: What will it mean for them if the Apostle is gone? Without him what will be the hope for their faith enduring there in banishment on the island? What if he is simply wandered out in the dark and fallen to death? What if he has simply succumbed to the fate of the aged or infirm? A mere human ending. It will mean nothing; his power will fade away. There will have been no sign, no miracle. They will feel cheated; they will hunger for a new master.

'I will go the southern shore,' Matthias says. He points in the opposite direction. 'Can you walk that way?'

Papias nods.

'If you find him and he . . .'

They look at each other, then away. They do not say. Matthias's impatience is clear; the old man cannot be left alone; that is what their living has become, minding him on an island. He shakes his head at the thought of it, then he is gone up on to the large rocks, where a man falling from above would be broken like a shell.

Papias prays as he walks. He scans the upper shore, the grey sand where gulls stand curious over spews of seaweed, the smoothed salted stones. The morning is bleak and cold. His eyes are rheumy, blurring the middle distance so a blackened mound of algae, or rockweed might easily be the figure of a fallen man. Papias fists an eye, the other blinks into the bare wind. Is that him? His sandals quicken on the sand, sinking some and making jagged twists of his prints. His heart races, his prayers are stopped. He runs lamely, wound in ankle smarting, pushing back with his hands parcels of the air, wavering his head to and fro and blinking for vision. The black mound, is it the Apostle's white garment sea-spoiled? Did he fall blindly into the sea? Papias clambers on to the first of the rocks, his ankles angled over and slipping, his body pitched forward so he feels for balance with his hands. He progresses, and then stands, fists his eyes again, and sees that the mound is not a man but a large, dark fish haloed with flies.

Momentarily, Papias sits, sighs relief. A needle of pain presses in above his left eye. The fish is of great size and without wound. It lies on one side with mouth pursed and flat incurious eye, its scales lustreless beneath the leaden sky. How it arrived so far up the rocks, what ailed it, age or disease, are not apparent to Papias. It seems to him a strange portent, and for a moment he delays on lunatic logic: the fisher gone, a fish in his place.

He looks at it, waves away flies: is it living still? Is it beached and in need only of return to water? It may be, and is briefly puzzling for reasons he cannot shape, but Papias cannot delay. He steps back, the flies return. He scratches at his face and moves back down the rocks again, hurries limping once more along the grey sand.

*　　*　　*

43

My soul longs for you.
  Each day, each night.
  I have loved you with my life, Lord.
  As the vine for water, my soul thirsts for you.
  Come, Lord.
  I have remained.
  Come for me now and take me to you.
  This is my prayer. Now, Lord.
  Now.

Further along the shore Papias finds the footprints. The parting tide has left a virgin floor of sand, and upon it in the curved pathway of the blind is a pair of barefoot prints. Heel-heavy, stagger-stepped, by the white salt frill the prints make a route towards the water. Papias hurries after them. His head is still needled, his stomach unwell. Is a fever establishing in the caverns of his body? Warm droplets glisten on his brow, fall like stars past his eyes. The prints blur in the softened sand and sink, vanished into the shallow pools and low waters of the tide. Papias feels his heart drop. The Master is gone into the sea, he thinks, and without reason he thinks again of the large fish, the symbol of the Christian, beached on the stones, and steps himself into the first skirting wave. The water is shocking with cold. It seizes his ankles like ice manacles, burns his toe wound. He is gone, he thinks, gone; and with utter grief he scans the waves coming toward him and thinks he will fall into them and never rise such is his loss and guilt and regret.

He wades forwards and scans sideways into the sea, his vision smeared, and grief delirium not far. Gulls raucous wheel and hang overhead. Long, ragged ribbons of weed are in the tide and twine about him. He presses further into the freezing waves, peering down at what touches against him, half expectant to see floating and dragged there the drowned apostle.

Papias sees what may be the white head. It is some way out, in the high, rolling waters. If it is a man, he is to the point of his depth and faces the waves that come higher than him, making his head vanish in the foam.

Now, Lord.
    Now.
    I am here to meet you.
    By water. As in the beginning.
    Come now.
'Master! Master!' Papias calls. His voice is carried away, but in the expiration of another wave he sees clearly now that it is the Apostle deep in the sea. Papias calls to him again and wades forward. The water is ice against his chest, his breath is crushed. But he pushes on; John is thin and weak and will drown in moments. What madness is this? Why has he blindly gone into the sea? Is his mind overthrown? He must be saved. Unevenly the sand floor falls away, and suddenly Papias is deeper and loses footing and drops beneath a wave, wide-mouthed and gulping. He cannot swim; he paws wildly at the sand glitter and a long, slimed scarf of weed that enwraps his neck. His life bubbles furiously; kicking and flailing he sinks to drown.

In blind underwater his eyes are bulged O's of astonishment that it will end so. He calls out another grey bubble, is by a wave rolled upon himself so his garment swirls as a sea flower, and his white legs are strange stamens, loose and long and darted through by silvered fish in that fish-full sea.

Kicking done, a sandal falls free, spins, floats, sinks, heels into the home of sea lice and sea worms.

Papias is taken out by the hungry tide; the one who came to save, drowned. His eyes are open, white and pinked as scallops, his fingers pale starfish, all his body a bountiful island of feed. Underwater, the motion of the waves is soothing, is as waves of sleep coming, one after the other, each taking him further. He lets go, lets go of rescue, of struggle, of overcoming the sea. In the same instant, as if his life departs from him like a ship and he watches it go, Papias feels float from him the service of the Apostle. Floating from him are the years he has followed the Master since he heard the Christians were banished on Patmos and came himself in a fisher's boat to be baptised and stay. From him go the years of prayer and attendance and faithfulness, dissolving goes the night he has spent, the woman Marina, her dead children just ahead of him now on the journey into the everlasting. All sails into the deeps. Papias lets go, is dragged down by the undertow, wave-spun, his chest crushed for last air. A briny nothingness takes him. His brain is dulled, a sea cabbage, his final expression empty surrender.

The undersea sounds constant pounding. As though all is within a great ear, pulse and thrum, susurrus, the ceaseless sighing. Fish, silent as death, slip one direction for another. On the sea floor a shell moves minutely. Black weed waves funereal slow. The body of the man sinks unevenly, feet down, head up, as if to foot off water sprites or land walking in the afterlife. It is as ascension in reverse, slow, deliberate, hands outwards, hair fanned, garments waving even with heavenly majesty, but in descent. This floating sinking is for ever, a journey not many feet but enduring out of time, the sea's small mercy before the body touches bottom and does not rise.

But then it does.

It defies the laws of death and dominion of the sea.

It surges upwards, past waterweed and fish shoal and bursts headfirst through the waves.

Papias does not feel the hands that grasp him. His eyes are away, his mouth agape. He does not know how the drowned return, how life is measured, cut, or granted, how in the vastness of the sea the blind apostle has found him. Has he pulled back the tide like a cloth? Has he *seen*? Papias has no mind to ask. Lifeless, he does not feel the fierce strength in the old man, but is fallen against the Apostle's breast, is cradled there, where the sea seems to withdraw from them. What daylight shines, what air enwraps them, are all unknown to the drowned servant; what prayers may be said, what words called up to the very gates of heavens, unheard by him.

He is held in the arms of the Apostle.

Then brusque life returns. Violent air like fierce light is thrust into the flooded chambers, and Papias is convulsed. He gags and his head shudders. John holds him. The sea about their waists. With brief flickering the eyes of the drowned open. Papias sees where he is.

He opens his mouth and speaks a spew of seawater.

'Praise God,' the blind apostle says.

And Papias turns to the grey swirl of sky all about them, as if he might see just then, the sight of the Lord himself departing.

7

'His mind is lost,' Matthias says. 'In his blindness he does not know day from night. He wandered out and did not know where he was and could have perished in the sea. This is the truth. Prochorus, tell me, is this not the truth?'

They sit inside the open doorway of Matthias's dwelling of skin and sticks, planking and rock. Iron light falls, the sea beyond rough.

Matthias offers a dried fig, gnaws on its aged wrinkling when it is declined.

'You have known him, Prochorus. He is no longer the same man. You cannot say so. And yet we follow what he says. Answer me this: if he says we must all walk into the tide and drown in the morning, what shall we answer?' Matthias's hooded eyes seek the scribe's, but Prochorus looks away.

'I tell you this. We do nothing here for the Lord. This is not what God wants of us, Prochorus. He spoke to the Ancient many years ago, but does he now? The others will not ask this question, but they think it. I know they do. You do, too, don't you? You must wonder where is the one singed with fire that dictated the revelation? Where are the revelations he promised were at hand?'

The fig requires harsh chewing to find flavour. Matthias works it, pursed in his cheek, fingers out seed caught in his teeth. His voice is clear and unafraid; he has calculated what he is to say and has chosen now, and Prochorus, with whom to begin.

'Consider,' he says, and draws another fig from the pouch, offers it, is declined, eats. 'Consider this: Jesus of Nazareth was a man. He was the son of Joseph the carpenter. A Galilean. As a child he was a child. He did not cure the sick, raise the dead. He was as you or I, Prochorus. There were no signs. Nothing. Why so, if he was the Son of God? Why, if the Son of God, and his cousin is dying of a snakebite, his aunt lame, why not lay a hand and heal? Why not begin God's work at once? Illness and hurt were always present, why wait? Why play with other children and live an ordinary life if Jesus was the Son of God?'

Prochorus is uncomfortable on the timber stool. He feels flushed. The sweet smell of the fig on Matthias's breath is turning his stomach. His face is parched and stiff from the salt wind.

'Answer me, Prochorus. Why?'

'I need water. I am thirsty.'

'There is only one answer,' Matthias continues, the water in a pouch behind him. 'The Son of God would not play with children, would not learn the trade of carpentry. For what? For what purpose learn to plane wood? No, these are human things, Prochorus. Listen to me. Listen.' Matthias's lips are thin, his face a thin triangle climbed with black beard. 'The truth is, Jesus was as you or I.'

'Jesus was the Christ.'

'But first he was a man, *then* God descended upon him. Just as he had on the Baptist before him, and before him on David, and on Moses, and Elijah, and so on into ancient time. The Lord descended upon him and he *became* the Christ and was no longer the carpenter. God came upon him so that Jesus might do his work. It is the truth; I know it, Prochorus. And answer me this, why would the Son of God allow himself to be scourged like a man, to be spat upon, humiliated, and hung to his death on the cross?'

Matthias leans forward; the zeal of his words carries him. His brows are brought together in a deep furrow. Impatiently he waves a thin-fingered hand in the air as if warding off a bird.

'What was to gain by that? How many more followers might we have if at that moment he had shone forth with blinding light? If he was truly the Son of God and had been able then to strike,' he fists a hand, smacks it to the other, 'if enemies and unbelievers were made to fall to their knees then, and he proved himself the Almighty?'

He draws his stool closer; his voice is throaty now with passion. 'Think, Prochorus, what would have been then. Think of how he may have thrown off the cross like a stick, how he may have risen in air clothed in light and all would have seen and believed. *Believed*, Prochorus. Think of it. All would have believed, and for all time. We, his followers, would not have been persecuted. Despised by the world. We would have been honoured. And would the Son of God not want that? Would he not know that by showing himself then and not hanging on the cross all would have known it to be the truth: that Jesus of Nazareth was the Son of God? And none could deny it. His followers would have out-numbered Roman legions. So why, Prochorus? Why then did Jesus not do this? Did he want us to suffer? To be hated? Flogged at the walls of synagogues? To be banished by Roman emperors to live on such a barren rock as this?'

Prochorus does not answer. He palms his bald head. His brow is bubbled with sweat, a furious itch is on his cheek and neck. He works at it. He wants water, but has not time to ask before Matthias says, 'What is the answer? How can it be explained?' He taps his fingertips together, a tent in desert wind. 'My learned friend, I will tell you. Jesus of Nazareth was not the Son of God, but a man like you or I. When he reached the age to be useful to our Lord, God descended upon him so that he might do his works. Christ did not come *in the flesh*, but in spirit. And so, too, God *departed* from him and left Jesus before Calvary. And Jesus knew this. He was again a man. He cried out as much. The power of the Lord, the spirit, had gone from him, as from all of the prophets. He suffered, he died on the cross, Prochorus. He could not shine forth or throw off the cross, because he was as you or I then and could do nothing. Do you see?'

The light in the hut is low. The wind is gone away. There is curious stillness, on the damp sand floor a converse of flies.

'I need water,' Prochorus says.

The other does not move. His eyes are fixed on the scribe.

Prochorus works the itch on his right cheek. 'Matthias, a drink,' he gasps. 'Water.'

'Water, yes,' Matthias stands and from a table behind him lifts the water bag, holds it. 'You are learned, Prochorus. You are knowledgeable, able to discern truth. I respect you. That is why I have spoken.'

The scribe's hand is reached out, the water not yet given.

'As the Lord visited Jesus, Prochorus, so, too, he can visit himself upon others. You know this. We are not meant to remain here. It is not the Lord's intention. We who follow him have been chosen, and are free from sin, and must not live uselessly here in banishment. Prochorus,' Matthias whispers, '*I know this to be true.*' Then he gives the scribe the water bag.

Prochorus drinks. His eyes are already fevered, the side of his face red with rash. And whether because he sees this or he judges he has risked enough for now, Matthias says no more. He sits on the stool, tents his fingertips. No wind at all blows.

I hated them for wanting always a sign. 'What sign can you show us?' Always asking. 'Go on, a sign, a sign!'

I did not need a sign. I believed.

You know I did.

We went up to Jerusalem when Passover was near. A dry season. In the temple precincts the animal sellers, the coin changers changing the denarii and drachmas to pay the temple tax of a half-shekel. Calling out their rates to those approaching. Oxen in the passages, sheep, cages of doves. Noise of trading. Hot sun. The long journey we had walked to come there.

When we come to the temple, something will occur, I thought.

On the long walk up the hillsides you did not speak. You walked swiftly. I was by your side.

When we came, they had already heard of you. Their murmurs we heard: 'That is him! That is Jesus, the one who did those things. They follow him. Look!'

And some called your name, and others asked did we want strong oxen, fat sheep, cheap rates for coin changing. They pulled at your sleeve. I struck one in the face. James another. He kicked a table of coins. Spilling in the sunlight. The cries of the animals, the sellers waving their hands. James with his hands about the neck of another.

Because we had imagined it otherwise. Because we had walked that long walk up the dry hillsides, thinking, Behold, the Son of God comes to Jerusalem.

And we, the chosen, alongside him.

But no glory was in this. Dirt and noise and fighting. A man pulling me back, striking me.

Another standing before you offering a jewelled brooch, pulling at your garments. Thinking because we were your many servants that you were wealthy.

You bent down to the bedding of the oxen and entwined the straw and reed to make a whip of cord. Raised it in the air.

The only time I ever saw your anger.

James and I and Philip and Andrew wild with fighting, furious as beasts.

You were ashamed, I thought. Of them. Of us, too. And knelt down in that deserted passageway of the temple.

To repent.

For the glory of the Father could not be won that way.

In two days the sellers and the coin changers would be back. You knew that. You knew and knelt and knew already the history of what was to come.

The merchants went running to the chief priests and the elders and told them of you, how the people would not be able to pay the temple tax if there were no coin changers.

And the chief priests came and asked, 'What sign can you show us, authorising you to do these things?'

I confess, Lord, I, too, wanted a sign then. I wanted them struck down, made lame, prostrate on the ground before you.

You placed your hand on your chest. 'Destroy this temple, and in three days I will raise it up.'

We did not understand then. No more than the priests. I looked at the temple walls. I expected you would make them fall by raising your hand. Such was my belief.

Such was my love.

'Master?'

'Papias. I hear in your voice you are recovered.'

'I have brought a bowl of lentil pottage. Master, will you eat?'

'My thanks.'

It is mid-morning. John sits near the cave entrance, his white head tilted back, brown blind eyes open to the weak sun. There is a little wind. Before him the island prison is stilled and empty, bleak rock and brooding sea.

The young disciple carries a small wooden bowl, places it in the Apostle's hands, sits by him while he eats. Papias has told none that John was in mid-sea when he found him. For in the aftermath of the rescue he was not sure himself what he saw. He has said only that he came upon the Apostle wandered down by the shore. He has not said he himself was drowned and found by his blind master in the deep waters, for the puzzle of what happened is too profound and unclear in his mind.

'Your foot is lame?'

'It is a small thing, Master.'

'I hear you limp.'

'It will be soon healed.'

John spoons the pottage, the lentils long soaked and thick and savoured with fish tails and herbs.

'I have been weak, Papias,' he says. 'I have surrendered to impatience.'

'You are our master. If you are weak, we are weaker. You are the beloved disciple of the Lord himself.'

'Do not call me that. I am no more beloved than another – all are beloved.'

Papias purses his lips, does not ask the question he wishes to, what the Apostle was doing in the tide. He is filled with restlessness, wild birds of the unasked, the untold. His hands tap softly on his thighs. He studies his wounded foot, raised lips of scar, sand-gristled. He wants to tell of the woman Marina and her dead children and her belief she is with demons, but feels a cloud of guilt over it. He did nothing wrong; he stayed with the woman, he prayed for her, he prayed for her children safe passage to heaven. But still, in him is guilt and restlessness.

'Tell me of the sky,' the Apostle says.

'The sky, Master?'

'Yes. Tell me.'

'There is cloud. White cloud. Moving slowly. And some blue in the east. Pale. Very pale.' Papias does not know what else to add, whether there is something of significance he misses. The old man says nothing. He sits, face angled to the light, silent.

Is it this sky or another in memory he sees? Papias wonders. In his blindness does he remake the world as it was once? Where does he go in the long silence of the days here on the island? Papias is too young to have known him in his vigour. The Apostle was already blind when the youth sailed to Patmos, and so he has not seen the strong figure of the fisherman, the muscled, brown-haired figure who in his own youth had walked into Jerusalem by the side of Jesus Christ. But he has heard a thousand stories. *Boanerges*, Jesus had called the sons of Zebedee, Sons of Thunder, for their temper and strength. Papias had heard of them in preachings from wandering Christians who came in from the desert lands beyond Antioch. He had heard of the twelve, the followers of the Galilean, and how one was little more than a youth; this one loomed in Papias's mind. To be of that age and see the Christ, what would it have meant? Would Papias himself have known? Would he, too, have abandoned his family, the fishing business, to follow? He had listened to the preachings carefully, the stories they told beneath a held awning on sticks, of the signs at Cana, the healing of the royal official's son, and come back the following day to hear more. In dazzling sunlight he sat cross-legged and heard from the blistered lips of the Christians' accounts, grossly detailed, of the scourging of

Jesus. Blood spatter, lacerations, spearings, stones thrown, all were vividly painted. Thin arms out-spanned, head thrown back, one with ragged twist of dusty beard and eyes baleful and prominent, made alive the agony of the crucifixion, the nails driven, the pulp of hand bursting, the raw torment when the cross was risen up and the Christ hung.

And these things the youth John witnessed, Papias had thought. When he lay in the cool of the night after, images of the preaching took possession of his mind. For the three days the Christians remained he went to listen. He heard the glory of the resurrection told – John running first to the tomb but waiting at the entrance, as if he did not need to see to believe. The Christians told it like a triumph, though the flies sheltered beneath the canopy and crawled on their faces, though some passing called out at them to be gone, or derided their telling with pulled faces and mocking gesture.

'What of John after?' Papias had asked the skeletal Christian. 'What of the Son of Thunder?'

'To John was given the care of the Lord's mother, Mary. And he was attentive to this until she rose to heaven in glory. Then he travelled in his ministry, as do we, telling the good news. And for this he was imprisoned and stoned and flogged, but escaped and continued. He passed through lands as many as stars, through Phrygia and the country of Galatia, Mysia, Bithynia, through Pisidia into Pamphylia, was in Thyatira and Amphipolis, Thessalonica, saw fifty men crucified on the road out of Sepphoris.'

The Christian, warming to his topic, continued, the naming of places a kind of conquering.

The boy Papias had sat, mesmerised. It was the best story he had ever heard. In it he believed utterly. When the Christians left, ragged caravan of a donkey with pots and water bags, mat rolls, rattle and hum of murmured prayer, Papias missed the theatre of their conviction, the quality they bore of being *touched*. He watched for others, pricked his ears when stories circulated of Christians driven out, of crucifixions, stonings, of how they were beggars and would steal even the mat you sat on. When others came, as they did – now three thin and wizened near ghosts, one, whose face was bubbled with leprosy, now a sprawling family, men, women, a blind child – he went and listened.

'What of John, the youth?' he always asked, 'who sat at the right hand of Jesus?'

And so, frayed patchwork of Christ's history was his. From numerous tellings, expansive, exaggerate, or spare, Papias learned the life story of the Saviour, but more, assembled, too, the image of the fearless beloved disciple.

'Where is he now?' he would ask. 'Where is John, the youth?'

He was now an Ancient, he was told. One said he was imprisoned in a pit in Rome, to be fed to the lions, but the Lord God came in a chariot of light and saved him and slew all that attended. He had gone into the east another recounted, into strange far lands on the furthermost edge of the earth to preach the resurrection. He had cured a thousand, it was told, made see the blind. He had plucked a spear from his side and tossed it from him as a dove that flew into the heavens. He walked the world entire as living witness and could not be killed, the Christians said. Ten thousand miles were in his feet, dust of all creation.

One, Nuri, a rag of man, sag-fleshed, slit-eyed, said he himself had touched the Apostle's robe. He held a bone of arm towards Papias, outstretched claw of fingers, in invitation for the youth to leave his life and join them. Beneath the pulsing heat, blue canopy of sky and scorched light, Papias had considered them: the smallest of tribes, their two goats, their road-worn apparel a badge of their poverty, the watery pink of zeal in their eyes. He had read more books than all of them, had clean robes and a room of his own next to his parents, whose love he had as an only child. The claw wavered in the sunlight.

'Come with us,' Nuri said, hacking the words like pits from the thin gully of his throat. 'Come and follow the Lord.'

The others, who sat to listen or stood about momentarily to eye the curiosities, looked then at Papias as at a spectacle. He felt their eyes upon him, the sudden ringing in his ears as though his head was inside a bell. He had not expected it. Nuri was a shrunken and unseemly messenger if from God. His skull was reclaiming his face. His lips, part eaten by some long-ago disease, were dried crusts, quivering now as he waited for the answer.

'He has called you. Will you come and follow the Lord?' he asked a last time.

In the distance of the village a donkey brayed. The spell broke, and Papias shook his head and walked hotly away. There were jeers at the Christians and jokes in the aftermath of intensity. In the evening they were gone, empty circle of printed ground when Papias returned to it the following day, in its centre, stick-drawn, the sign of the fish.

For a time then he kept himself from others who passed that way.

But always there was a prompting. In night visions he would see the Christians flogged, the crucifixions rising one after the other along the roads of his dreams. He saw the outstretched hand hanging in air before him, and sometimes the white-clothed figure of the Christ himself, pacing away over desert sands toward immutable destiny. But these yet did not sway him. He awaited a sign, and believed he was sent it when one day two years later he heard that the apostle John, himself, the Son of Thunder, was banished in exile on the island of Patmos.

Papias sailed there and was baptised, and because of his youth and devotion, became the attendant of the Apostle.

These things he thinks now as he sits by John at the entrance of the cave and tells of the sky. His is to serve the Master, he tells himself, and in doing so serves best the Lord.

But as he sits and the clouds move swiftly across the blue, Papias also thinks of the two children he has buried beneath the stones, and the woman Marina who believes she is a harbour for demons and death.

8

'Master, it is Prochorus. He is ill with fever. The side of his face is imprinted with blister.'

Danil, a disciple of sixty, brings the news. It is late afternoon. Light is thinning.

'He speaks in delirium. We must pray for him.'

John stirs from reverie, angles to Danil his head, then rises quickly. 'I will go to him.'

'No!' Papias does not mean to startle but he does. 'I will go, Master, let me.' He wears a pink desert flower of guilt and concealment on his cheeks.

Danil looks at him, astonished that he would tell the Apostle what to do.

'It may be catching,' Papias says to him and twists the hand that touched Prochorus's face to wake him. 'Let me go only.'

John does not pause. 'Lead me,' he says.

They go down the rock face to the stones of the foreshore. Seabirds whirl above them. A bright wind hammers silver out of the sea. The Apostle's robe is blown against him, so he seems thinned to nothing, a pale sliver of light traversing the stones. They come along by the hardened sand, the smaller gulls dancing before them, printing the virgin ground.

'Here, Master,' Papias says, and they turn where the shore bends away and stones have been lifted to make a pathway upwards, towards two huts, part tent, part boat, perched on the edge. The old apostle is surprisingly nimble, his feet sure, his head high, and he moves with silent purpose and fixed demeanour, unencumbered, it seems, by blindness.

When they arrive on the cliff top, three of the other disciples, Simon, Lemuel, and Meletios, are knelt outside praying. They stop when the others approach, rise and go towards them.

'He is worse with every moment, Master,' Simon says. 'Ioseph is with him.'

John stoops in the doorway. The inner darkness is no darker to him. He does not see the ravage of black blister that spreads on the scribe's face and neck, the yellowish complexion of his forehead. By his side, Papias sees these and must draw his hand sharply to his mouth to obstruct the vomit, then spin gagging out into the daylight.

Ioseph rises from his place by the bed mat and touches the Apostle's hand. 'He will not take water, Master,' he says. 'He speaks wildly, cries out, then is silent but for convulsions that seize him. He is shaken as if by a force, then released like a creature thrown aside. His blister climbs and bubbles. He is fevered hot as fire. In instants he returns to himself, speaks for you to come, then is lost again.'

John approaches. He feels downward with his right hand, is guided by Ioseph, and so finds the rough timber stool. His head is upward, his eyes far away, as though watching in the infinite dark for the descent of most slender light.

The other disciples gather behind, silent, watchful, expectant of miracle and afraid it will not come. They have testament of many healings, have preached the same countless times – leprosy, lameness, wild contagions of the blood – death itself they have preached undone by faith. But never have they witnessed it. Their stories are their creed, and by these they have stood in marketplace and hilltop telling to the crowd until so many imagined damaged figures were made whole that the world entire could seem cured by this Saviour. The disciples recounted it with greater or lesser detail each to their own fashion. But in each of them, in the disparate corners of lands where they were, the telling was informed not by

59

evidence. They had seen no curing themselves, only told of those told to them. Now they hold their breaths in the hut – to keep from the fever, and lest they obstruct by human weakness the coming of the power.

It is so. John bends down his head to Prochorus and whispers his name. The scribe does not move. He lies with shallow breath on the ledge of death. John lifts his right hand, thin fingers moving toward the other's brow.

'Do not touch him, Master!' It is Papias, flushed and wide-eyed in the doorway. 'Do not touch him, Master.'

Simon cannot help himself from moving slightly back, but not John. There is a fragment of delay, no more; John's hand reaches and finds the face of Prochorus. His fingers feel the broken skin, the fury of heat, the clam and ooze, a quality waxen and lifeless in the flesh. He lays his palm against the flamed cheek, bows his head, prays.

By the entranceway the others kneel. Discovering a shallow in their faith, they breathe through cupped fingers. The time is like a dark metal beaten thin. It stretches outwards to where it must give beneath the blows. For nothing happens. Swiftly the afternoon is taken by evening into the sea. A lamp is lit. And still the Apostle is bent down over the scribe, his hand upon the face. He prays in silence, moves slightly back and forth on the stool so its joints sing thinly.

And still nothing happens. How often is it to be so? To the ten thousand prayers they pray these years on the island what answers come? No miracles have attended them. No signs that they are cherished, or that the long suffering of their faith is considered, that their sacrifice is measured and in the hereafter will be rewarded.

There is nothing. There is darkness and wind off the stars. There is the same sea sighing in chains of waves. What invisible drama plays, what passes to and fro in the columns of air above them, none knows, but the disciples think: perhaps the time is arrived at last. Perhaps the bald scribe who had attended the Apostle in his revelation is himself to reveal the Lord.

The time is beaten away, and is as nothing. No hours are measured.

The knees of those kneeling ache, the damp of the ground travels through them. Night saddles their shoulders with cold. On the bed mat Prochorus tosses and wrestles the unseen. John says his name, but it does not still the scribe. He kicks at a beast that stalks toward him.

This, your servant, Lord.

If it be your will.

Before the dawn the wind turns about and comes from the sea into the dwelling. It makes flap the canvas sides; bestirs papyrus, dried seaweed, fistful of seeds; rolls the wooden beak-cup from table to floor. The disciples are statues in half sleep, half prayer, otherliness. The wind touches them on their stooped shoulders, passes to the Apostle, who turns towards it, inquisitive of what fills the dark room where the scribe is dying. His hand is laid on Prochorus's forehead. The fever is there still. The prayers, the herbs brought and crushed, tinctures dribbled on his lips, poultices applied, all have wrought little change. Only that the patient is grown calm. Several times in the night he woke and whispered with cracked voice what could not be understood. Now the wind whirls into the hut. The lamp is out. All are in blue-black shade and do not know at first that then Prochorus opens his eyes.

John feels it.

'Prochorus,' he says, and leans down. He puts his head close to the other's lips.

What the scribe says is not heard by the others. The Apostle listens at the swollen, blistered mouth. To Prochorus he says then, 'I tell you, Jesus is the Christ, truly he is the Son of God.' And leans slightly back as though he is newly aware of a task ahead of him and the enormity of it, as though he sees suddenly the frailty of faith, of Christianity itself. John sits upright. He raises his voice in the wind.

' "The wind blows about at will," Jesus said to Nicodemus, in Jerusalem. "You hear the sound it makes but do not know where it comes from or where it goes. So it is with everyone begotten of the spirit. If you do not believe about earthly things, how are you going to believe when I tell you about heavenly things? No one has gone up into heaven except the one who came down from heaven – the Son of Man. And just as Moses lifted up the serpent in the desert, so must the Son of Man be lifted up," the Lord said, "that everyone who believes in him may have eternal life in him." Yes, the Lord said, "God loved the world so much he gave his only Son that everyone who believes in him may not perish but may have eternal life." '

The Apostle pauses. He has preached the scene many times in far places. He has remembered often sitting in the starlit night when Jesus spoke the words for the first time, when the lemon trees were in bloom and the air sweet.

He leans close to the scribe. He touches with his fingertips the eyes, discovers that Prochorus is dead.

Anger and grief course through him. John stands up, a pale figure before the dawn, and when he speaks there is violence and hurt in his voice. The other disciples are gathered at the doorway, Matthias now among them.

'The light has come into the world, our Lord said, but men have preferred darkness to light,' he cries out, 'because their deeds were evil, for everyone who practises wickedness hates the light and does not come near the light for fear his deeds will be exposed.'

His chest heaves. It is not clear if he knows that Matthias is there, or whether he thinks there are others, too, who no longer believe as he has told him. He stands and is a glimpse of his younger self, fierce and loyal and resolute. His lips quiver with anger. It is as though he sees in the landscape of his blindness a vast temple begin to crumple, and he throws out his hands to hold it up.

Abruptly he pushes forward and knocks a stool. Papias steps quickly to his side, offers his shoulder for his master's hand, and they go past the others outside to where the dawn is not yet risen and the wind gone elsewhere.

9

The scribe is buried in a mound on the cliff top, his face towards the east. Stones are piled above him, their soft clack a doleful music. The disciples stand and pray. John is not with them. He has told Papias to leave him, and his absence is felt but not spoken. Old Ioseph leads the prayers. Matthias stands by his side with two others, Auster and Linus. The ceremony is short, Ioseph's voice thin with grief. For each there is a sense of betrayal of which they cannot speak. How has this happened, that their scribe has been struck down like this? That one who gave so much of himself to the service of the Lord has been visited by this plaguey death? Why has he been taken from them? The air above their heads is crowded with questions. The death threatens the unspoken belief they have in being chosen, in being set apart. Not because they have imagined themselves free from dying, nor because they have taken as a sign the great age of the Apostle and believed they, too, will outlast all perishing until the dawn of the Second Coming, but because Prochorus was not old. Because his role in their community was to record, and the taking of him seems an act full of portent, as if their tongues have been pulled out. All have expected the Apostle to have further revelation, and for Prochorus to be on hand to write it down. Now his death seems a wilful silencing. The disciples voice no protest. Some of them, bowed, mute, with vigilant rigour tour the inner rooms of their souls and find evidence against themselves — jumbled furniture of doubt, unbelief, false piety, pride — and leave to begin atonement.

Among them Papias harbours the greatest guilt. He fears he brought the sickness to the scribe, but has told no one. He has no sign of it on himself. When the disciples leave the burial mound, he hurries away down the rocks to the shore. His face is white, his eyes glitter like fish scales. Arriving on the soft pebble–and–shell floor of the departed tide, he slips and sinks in haste, his sandals are unfooted as he steps forward into the shallow waves. There, grey corona of gulls turning above him, he bends and dips his hands in the salt sea and rubs them hard together. Again and again he dips and draws the water and scrubs the invisible from his hands. The waves are against his calves, his robe darkly stained to his waist. Against the backs of his legs and beneath his feet he feels the suck of the out–flowing sea. His actions are uncalled for. He has already tumbled entirely in the waves since visiting the fisher's wife, but nonetheless scrubs now at his hands with a wild passion for absolution. He knuckles one palm then the other, presses his fists through the cold surface of the sea and holds them there as if manacled. The gulls wheel, waiting to see what strange fish may appear.

By the time Papias is done, his hands are as red as if hell–burnt. He comes from the sea shivering, and Matthias is standing nearby watching. Two paces behind him stand Linus and Auster.

'Young Papias,' Matthias says, 'what troubles you?'

'I did not see you there.'

'You were occupied intently.'

Papias turns back to look at the sea, as though a plausible reason may be written there.

'How cold your hands are,' Matthias says, stepping closer and for an instant taking the reddened fingers in his own. 'Are you suffering some ailment?' Matthias's voice is soft and comes about like a velvet cloak. His eyes are darkly inviting. 'Papias, tell me,' he says, and lets go the hands.

'No. No, I am well. It was something from the cave, something on my hands,' Papias tells him, tells the others behind him, folding his arms so the evidence is tucked beneath them. He feels the lies multiply like flies around a rotted fish. 'I was foolish. I thought it might be . . . I thought there might be disease.'

'You are upset by the death of our dear Prochorus.'

'Yes.'

'Indeed are we all. He is a grievous loss.' Matthias looks to the others and nods towards them. 'But he is now in everlasting life, therefore why should we mourn? Don't you believe so, Papias?'

'I do.'

'What does the Ancient say? What does he say about the death of our scribe?' Matthias is close enough to kiss Papias on the cheek, the cloak tightly enwrapped.

'The Master has not spoken of it.'

'Truly?'

'Truly, he has not.'

'Not of Prochorus. Nor of me?'

'No.'

'You find no comfort in that, I am sure. I find no comfort in it. Indeed it is troubling that he has not offered us wisdom.' Matthias looks out into the sea. 'He is himself perhaps unwell. Have you remarked it?'

'The Master?'

'Yes.'

'No, I have not.'

'You may have other concerns. Let me ask you, Papias, do you think the Lord God wishes us to remain here?'

'The Master says so.'

'Indeed.' Matthias considers the sea a moment longer then turns to face the youth. He smiles and says, 'Does the Lord speak only to him? Curious if one blind old man was to be the only ear for the heavens.' Slowly he shakes his head. He places one hand on the other's shoulder. 'Did not the Lord speak unto Moses and say, "Speak unto *all* the children of Israel and say unto them: You shall be holy"? So it is written in scripture, Papias. Yes, dear brother, surely there is more discourse between heaven and earth than to one Ancient. The Lord does not speak to only one. But we will

65

talk again of this, you and I. I can see you are anxious to be elsewhere. Perhaps Linus will attend to the Master and allow you . . .' Matthias throws open his hands. 'Go wherever it is that presses on your mind so.'

'No, Matthias.'

'O, yes, I insist. It is small charity to attend to yourself, Papias, that you may better serve. You are free, I relieve you.' He turns to those behind him. 'Linus, go and serve the Ancient, our beloved apostle.'

'He does not like to be called that,' Papias says quickly.

Matthias spins about as if stung. 'Truly?'

'Yes.'

'And why not? Is he not the Beloved? Was he not the one our Lord Jesus loved the best? Who sat at the right hand? Who laid his head upon his breast? Surely he was the Beloved? Or am I mistaken? Does my memory go? Or is it his? Who does he say he was now?'

'No. No, his memory does not.' Papias's cheeks burn. Matthias's eyes are dark. He is close. His gaze seeks entry to secrets. Behind him at two paces the short, squat figure of Auster watches, and on the near stones Linus, fair-haired, slim, tall but stooped, shoulders curved forward as if to hide himself from the slight wind.

'Linus, go,' Matthias says over his shoulder. 'Attend him. But do not call him the Beloved.' He does not take his eyes from Papias. Stones click the other's departure toward the cave.

'Young Papias, you are weary,' Matthias says. 'Weary from troubles and grief. I read it on your face. Your cold hands burn red.' He shakes his head slightly, as though there is an unfair balance he would set right. 'Go, go and be at peace.'

Released, Papias begins to turn. But the cloak is still about him. 'But Papias, know that if you have concerns, if the Ancient appears' – Mathias pauses to consider the word – 'diminished in his faculties, exhausted, if you consider him too greatly taxed by his duties, come and let me know at once. Do this. I will assist you in all things. Do you understand me?'

Papias nods to be free.

'Go then, and may God bless you.'

At last he hurries away along the sea-washed stones. The day is calm but dull. Weak light is smeared. Grey waters stir restlessly. He descends to the eastern shore and across the large rocks. Seabirds scatter and return to stand behind him. Places he clambers on hand and foot. The rocks rise toward a short cliff as if the sea has broken them from the land and abandoned them. Papias makes his way upwards. In crevices are feathers or twigs or small bones decaying in sunlight and sea air. Sometimes in the rock gaps are clear falls to still pools below. His reddened hands cling to pull his weight upward across a flat-faced slab. He kicks into a smallest ledge, goes cheek-printed against the rock and hauls himself head and chest over, then climbs atop. He stands a moment, looks up at the fringe of green and the ragged thorn bush that leans aslant from the cliff edge. A powdery ground is at the top. The sea now well below him, he considers at once the route onwards and does not look down.

He does not see Auster following.

At full stretch Papias can reach the cliff top. Briefly cruciform, he clings either side of him to the rough face of the island. His fingers scrabble. Ground falls away. There is no hold. He should go back down and around the long way. But then he will be seen. Instead he scratches at the dry dirt and pebbles above him. There is nothing solid. An error now and the fall would break his back on the rocks below. Papias feels the rashness of the plan, how guilt skews the mind. His toes are pressed in the tight mouth of a thin ledge, his heels in the air. But he won't go back. He is not sure he could. He hangs there some moments, a cross of conviction. With breathy whisper the sea below collapses upon itself. Sounds of soft breakage and gull cry and the beating of his own heart: these things Papias hears. He hands away loose dirt, its click and clatter marking the distance down. He tries a claw of cliff top, but there is no support in it. It gives easily. Ache knots in his calves. For a moment there crosses his mind the thought of letting go, of stepping out of his toeholds and falling headfirst, the brief bliss of flight, his robe aflutter and the perfect calm of a mind cleaned of all concern. It is a moment only. Then he is returned to the faith that there is something for him, that there is a destiny yet unknown that is his and that it has been scripted by the Lord himself. Emboldened so, he grasps the thorn bush. He takes it in both hands, the coarse knotty twist of it, then pulls.

It gives but only a little. Its roots, not deep, are gone wide for water. Papias releases his footholds and scales the cliff face, hangs briefly asway, kicks blood toes off rock, heaves, then rises face-first into the thorn bush till he can get his chest above ground and fall forwards, panting on the upper edge.

He rolls over for breath. The sky is grey and unforgiving.

Papias rises quickly. His face is scratched with thorns. He hurries across the bleak terrain toward the house of Marina.

10

I fail you.

Lord, I am weak. I am old. I forget much.

I fail you.

If a servant fail his master, ought not that master to find a better servant? What I have I hold not. Prochorus is dead. They speak against you even amongst those here. I hear it, though I hear it not. I see it, though I see it not.

I fail you.

It was long ago. I am ancient as dust. I will not see Galilee again.

Give me to drink. The woman of Samaria by Jacob's well. The others gone into the city of Sychar. I stayed with you. You asked her for water, and she was surprised that a Jew ask a Samaritan. You said, 'If thou knewest the gift of God, and who it is saith to thee, give me to drink, thou wouldst have asked of him, and he would have given thee living water.

'Whosoever shall drink of the water I shall give him shall never thirst; but the water that I shall give him shall be in him a well of water springing up into everlasting life.'

Sir, give me this water that I thirst not.

Lord, give me to drink.

I am your poor servant aged as dust.

Weary as ground too often sown. I confess it. What can I yield now?

We are few and weak, and pray that you may come.

Come, Lord, give me to drink.

By the entrance of the cave, Linus sits. He hears a murmuring from the Apostle, endeavours to make out the words. Then there is the silence peculiar to that cave that is not silent but filled always with the sound of water running from invisible source inside the hill above. In the early part of the afternoon, Ioseph comes along the beaten pathway to the cave. He, too, is thin and wiry and sharp-boned; his beard is coarse and white.

'Master?' he says, blinking into the darkness.

'Ioseph, come.'

John extends his hand and the disciple takes it in both of his.

'Master, I come to confess despair,' Ioseph says.

And at once John grasps his arm and rises. 'Come,' he whispers, 'bring me outside.'

Linus stands. 'I will attend you, Master.'

'No. Ioseph will see to me.'

'Matthias has instructed me, Master.'

'To disobey me? Stay. I will return, fear not. Ioseph, come.'

'I will follow in case . . .'

'You will stay!' John's voice is louder, greater than himself. Linus is startled back a step and looks to Ioseph then says: 'You may fall, Master, Ioseph is old and infirm. I can follow at ten paces and . . .'

'A third time: you will stay, Linus. You will not follow. I command it.'

In Linus's chin a pulse of muscle trembles. His pale eyes are a thin metal of disdain. His face is hotly reddened. How dare the old man talk to him so.

The two elders walk past him and go outside. It is after the midday and the sun has not broken the cloud. Disappointed grey light falls. In the sombre sea down the pathway below them short-combed waves are whipped and swallowed. There is a salt tang on the wind. The two men proceed along a route of broad stone to a place where there is natural seating of sun-and-rain-flattened rock.

'He is not behind us?'

'No, Master. He has stayed.'

'Good. Here, then, let us sit.'

John feels with his hand the smooth rock. Always in his touching a tapping, slight, quick, light, as though he affirms the real by his fingertips and knows only then that he is in it. They face the western shore, the Apostle's face tilted to receive what light may be.

'This death has touched me closely,' Ioseph says. 'I sin of despair.'

'You are not alone, Ioseph. It has touched us all.'

'I fear . . .' The elder disciple pauses, presses his palms together.

'Tell me.'

'I fear myself. I fear my weakness. Today I have thought I will die here on Patmos, like Prochorus, waiting for the Lord, when before I had supposed I would live until the day. I know this is vanity. What am I that is different from others? Why should I endure when others perish? For what reason? Because I have believed? Others have believed and been crucified. Because I have lived this long with you, old Master, because we have walked together in lands as far as Phenice and Antioch before banishment here, and because I believe the Lord watches over you and all of us? That you will live until he comes again, I am certain. And so have hoped that I, too, might see the glory. This is my first sin, I confess it: this vanity. Then the death of Prochorus has made me chastise myself. He was my friend. Why should he die? And in the darkness of my thinking a serpent has come: we all will die here, it says. We are forgotten and a plague comes now amongst us. I confess it. I have listened to the serpent, and my flesh has grown cold with the thought. I have clung to myself and wept, touched my face to find plague I dreamt would be coming. My prayers ascend not. They lie about my feet like stone birds. I despair.'

The two men sit. Little wind blows. John's face is tilted, his eyelids closed, his grey-white eyebrows lowered. He says nothing. He is a man for whom time itself seems inconsequent. It is as though, some time past, the turning of one hour into the next became to him of no matter and the numbering of one day to another a thing no longer counted. In his darkness, time is without measure of light. When he speaks of the hour that is at hand, it may be yet an age hence. He will wait. So it is, he sits and says nothing in reply for a long time. The two old men look not unlike statues high on the smooth rock. But the Apostle is troubled. He has known Ioseph more than two score years and never felt in him the despair he hears now. What is he to say? Is he to confess his own fears? To tell his old friend that he prayed for Prochorus to be spared? That he mounted high stacks of petition on the shelf of his mind, and yielded to the death only with a weak acceptance of the mystery of the Lord's way? There would be no consolation in this. He cannot tell his own thoughts. Instead, he holds silence, searches in himself for a voice.

Then, loudly the Apostle says: ' "My sheep hear my voice and I know them and they follow me. And I give unto them eternal life, and they shall never perish, neither shall any man pluck them out of my hand." I heard our Lord Jesus say this with my own ears, Ioseph, in Jerusalem, in the winter, in the time of the feast of the dedication. "And I give unto them eternal life." ' He reaches and finds the other's hands, holds them in his own. 'Old friend, do not despair. Grieve not for Prochorus. He was a loyal servant of our Lord and this day is in the kingdom of heaven. Neither grieve for yourself, Ioseph. For each of us the Lord has his plan. Ours is only to recognise this truth and attend him as servants a master. We wait.'

There are curious seabirds overhead. They watch for fragments of bread, foodstuffs, fish, and cry raucous as though in torment. The sea tumbles. Sky burdened with cloud releases no light. The island seems evermore a prison.

Then John speaks from a psalm. He speaks softly, as if testing that the words like stepping-stones will take him across water.

'When the Lord turned again the captivity of Zion,
We were like them that dream.
Then was our mouth filled with laughter
And our tongue with singing.'

He has found the psalm without looking. The words of it are inside him. It may be that in the lifetime of his preaching he is become a living book. The scriptures entire are scratched on his spirit, written with reed pen, dipped and dug into the soft red pulsing of his inner being. Inside him is a scribed record of testament. The voices of Moses, of Joshua, Ruth, Samuel, the Books of Ezra, Nehemiah, Esther, and Job, the Psalms and Proverbs, all of these are within him, and so, too, all from the twelve chapters of Ecclesiastes to the Book of Isaiah, from the voice of Daniel to Malachi. He is living book and carries their voices and their telling like a wind ever whispering inside him.

'Turn again our captivity, O Lord
As the streams in the south.
They who sow in tears shall reap in joy.
He who goes forth and weeps bearing precious seed
Shall doubtless come again with rejoicing
Bringing his sheaves with him.'

His voice grows stronger as he recites. Ioseph looks at him and is moved. 'We have missed your preaching,' he says simply.

The seabirds circle, as though chained.

'We would benefit greatly, all of us, if you preached to us again.' Ioseph leans forwards, speaks to the blind face in near whisper. 'I fear among us are heresies.'

A gap of sea sigh and gull cry. Light darkens under cloud.

John says, 'I know there are.'

Across the stony ground of the cliff top and through the scrub of thorn bush and weed where tethered is a thin goat, Papias hurries.

He comes down the slope to the place where he buried the children and is relieved to find the rocks unmoved. He prays a short prayer, then continues to the dwelling. He is not sure why he has come. He is afraid of his reasons and leaves them in a corner of his mind. He knocks on the wooden frame. There is no reply. He calls out, but nothing happens. He looks around, behind him, at the desolate waste ground, three crooked sticks where cloths had been hung, a hank of briny rope, a holed bucket. He calls again, then enters.

At first there are only shadows. Papias can make out nothing. There is a stench of rotting, a salt tang of seaweed stewed long ago. He hands the edge of the rough wooden table, holds there briefly, blinks, says, 'It is I, Papias.'

His breath is loud and short. Fear of many kinds is within him. He thinks of the raw red print on Prochorus's face, the rage of the fever, the skin that buckled and bubbled and curled back from the bone blackly as though peeled. Silently he tries to say 'The Lord is my Saviour' over and over even as he breathes the thick grey soup of the air and fears he takes within him the disease. The Lord is my Saviour. He will protect me. I am a fool. I am weak to fear anything. The Lord is my Saviour. He will not let me die. Across the earthen floor a rat scuttles toward him, is apprised by smell or sense, and suddenly turns, darts into the dark. Papias looks down and in the dimness makes out the legs of the woman Marina.

She is not dead. Her mouth lets a slight warm bloom against his cheek as he cradles her head. Her eyes are far away.

'It is I, Papias,' he says. She does not move. He has not held a woman so, and the living weight of her is shocking to him – not the burden in his arms, for she is light, but the living substance of her. Her hair falls on his forearm. Her face is tilted back, and he touches it to bring her eyes towards him, but they are unseeing. Is that a blemish of contagion on her cheek?

The Lord is my Saviour.

Kneeling, Papias brings her head upright on the support of his arm. She is weak, she is collapsed from exhaustion and grieving, he decides. But within him he cannot escape the memory of her telling that she was with demons. He presses the thought away, shoving it deep. But it merely coils and snakes back and slithers now across his chest.

In an instant he sees it rise, actual, large, and loathsome into the dim air of the small room. It flicks back its head, makes hiss, and stretches with deep luxuriance, released from the tight confines of denial. The demon snake is a hundred times a snake. It twists about, rises to the rough mud of the roof, towers above the man and woman, and lets jab at nothing its forked tongue. Papias stares at it and holds Marina, as though aboard a rudderless boat that enters the mouth of a storm.

The Lord is my Saviour.

The demon laughs. Its coils continue to rise, coming from beneath, curling. Its green-gold-patterned snakeskin sliding past Papias and crowding the room. Now it lies along the lower wall, now a second length upon itself, and a third. The demon is unending; it fills the space like sin and thickens the air with a sweet poison. Papias raises his hand and cries out in fear.

The demon laughs. 'How thin is your faith,' it says. 'Look at you!'

Sharply it flicks forward its great head, lets fly its tongue so the thin yellow fork of it lashes like lightning, snaps, quivers not a finger's breadth from Papias's face. He screams, closes his eyes, thrashes at it wildly with one hand, touching nothing. With his other arm he clings to Marina.

The demon retires a small distance. 'You cannot drive me off,' it says, and laughs again as from behind Papias its tail comes and crosses his belly and enwraps him and the woman both. Papias heaves at it, but it is too great a weight.

'Go!' he cries out. 'Go. Be gone!'

But the demon does not. 'Dear friend Papias, where would I go?' it asks.

'My name. How do you know my . . . ?'

'I know all you know.'

'Spare her,' Papias says. 'Spare her.' He is surprised by his own words.

'If I give her to you, what will you give to me?'

Papias looks at the woman Marina, who lies across his arm. He does not remember speaking again. But at once the coils unwrap from about their waist. From above the demon snake descends in silence and crossing coolly backwards across the disciple's chest, with hiss and flicker, diminishes into nothing.

From a joint gap in the planking of the wall, Auster watches. He sees the young disciple hold the figure of a woman in his arms. So this is why Matthias wanted him followed. This is why he had to go up that treacherous cliff after him. Palms flat on the wall, face pressed sideways, he one-eyes the gap. He watches Papias hold the woman close to him. The youth studies her face, moves hair from her mouth, then he lays her down and rises and goes from view. He returns with water but no scoop. He hand-cups it to her mouth, touches water against her lips. And she coughs at last and sputters some and stirs. Her eyes come to, and she partly sits and is in a wild manner beautiful as she turns to look at him who is holding her.

'You?' she says.

11

The day being with little wind, the sea is flat and Matthias decides on a boat. A boat is fitting. He sends word by Cadmus: he has had a revelation and wishes to speak of it. Matthias tells him which disciples to call, which to pass by. So to the shore comes a quiet gathering of twelve. Matthias is pleased; numbers are signs, too. In the shallow water a boat waits.

'Come, follow,' he says and steps ahead of them into the low lapping waves. The under-stones give slightly; his brown robe darkens. He does not look behind him to see if they are following. He walks erect into the sea. Command is in your bearing, and in your mystery, he has discovered, and proceeds in perfect faith.

He is not wrong. The twelve, after a puzzled pause of only moments, step down the stony incline into anklets of surf. Matthias is on board the fishing boat and only then turns to see his flock. He goes toward the prow and stands. He wears the look of revelation upon him, or so he considers. The disciples he has chosen are the younger of those on the island. Their youth gives them a hunger for action, and Matthias knows they are restless in this useless banishment. The hold of the Apostle upon them is weakening every day. How long will they continue to believe? How long before worms of doubt eat them hollow? Will they live into old age on Patmos, confined by the Romans like mad dogs? Matthias has run a speech in his mind, an exhortation, a patina of genuine concern to hide the hooks of intent, but all the time feeding doubt, dropping worms to fish. His skills at rhetoric are considerable; he could argue them into discipleship, but in the end has decided on a different lure.

The boat sails with gentle sway. The island retreats and shows itself for what it is, a barren place of grey rock and scrub. The twelve sit ranked on either side, saying nothing. The water deepens below them, a black-blind murk. Matthias instructs Cadmus to lower the dun-coloured sail, and the boat slows and lingers in slap-water sounds, its mast an inverted cross.

Matthias plants his feet and holds open his arms. The time is now; he will wait no longer.

'Let us pray,' he says. The disciples bow their heads. He has a last moment here, a pause that fills him with power. He enjoys the parallels, this touching of something untouchable.

'O seekers of the Divine, it has come to me,' he begins. 'A vision I saw in ecstasy of mind. And to which I bear witness now. To you. For you are the chosen. I will share with you what has come to me, what light has fallen into my mind, that we may all benefit.'

The eyes of all are upon him. He feels his power grow and lets play a long pause. The sea rocks them softly.

Matthias says, 'Heed this: Jesus was a teacher. A great teacher. This we all understand. His place is great and certain, but heed me now, his place is amongst all the teachers who have come since the time of Moses. This an angel has made clear to me that we might know the truth.' Matthias's eyes catch water light, flicker with fallen scintilla.

'There is, my fellow seekers, an ultimate source of goodness. This is the Divine Mind. It is not of this earth. It is not of water or soil nor of flesh nor bone. It exists outside of the physical world. It is in an elsewhere. This world where we stand was not created by the Divine Mind, but by a lesser god. This world is flawed. What great god would make a flawed creation? What great god would make a world wherein a death such as that visited on good Prochorus would be allowed? What great god would allow the scourging and the torture, the crucifixions? The storms that drown the sailors? The great quakes that shake and open the ground

78

wherein thousands perish? This is not the work of the ultimate Divine. We are flawed, all of us. But' – Matthias raises his right hand – 'within each of us in this world is a spark of the one Divine Power.' He raises his voice to announce it. 'Yes. It is true. I tell you the good news. Jesus knew this. He said so. He knew he carried the divine spark and was a great teacher. This is why his disciples followed him. For he tried to teach us that we are all carrying the Divine. We can all hope to touch the mind of God if we have the right teacher, one who hears the voice of the one God himself.'

Matthias steps down into the centre of the boat. He looks at each of them in turn. He watches on their faces for proof that the hooks of his words have taken hold. Some nod slightly, others are unconvinced yet. Still, it is a beginning. He is not discouraged. He points a finger and lets it roam around them all.

'Our teacher,' he says, 'teaches not.' He shrugs. 'He is an ancient who taught for many years. More years than he can remember. More words than he can remember and in more places. He has now the burdens of his great age. He forgets. Linus heard him say so. And of course he does forget. Why would he not? Is he not human? Is he not flawed? In years gone past I have heard sailors tell they knew stories of another who said his name was John the apostle of Jesus, and that this John was stoned in Iconium, imprisoned, brought to Rome, where he died at the side of Peter. So some have said. I have wondered: how could this our ancient be the same? I have heard some say they have doubted him to be who he says.'

There is a stirring of discomfort; it is a step too far and Matthias turns from his course swiftly.

'But of course this is untrue. He is the Apostle of the teacher Jesus. But he is old. He teaches no longer. He waits. We wait.

'But, beloved disciples, I tell you, we must not. This is the urgency that sent the angel to me. We must be taught to under-stand the Divine that is within each of us. This was the true message of Jesus and of all the teachers before him. We can each be as divine as Jesus if we open ourselves to this understanding.' Matthias pauses. He considers his step and then takes it. 'As have I.'

As he steps further out into his position, exposing what he has kept hidden from them, he feels a surge of power through him. Recklessly it rises from his heart, runs delicious chill along the back of his neck, makes pulse the blood in his very fingertips. Matthias stands as if he is an exhibit. He says, 'This the angel has told me. I, I have been gifted the knowledge. I have understood the message and discovered the Divine inside myself.'

He allows an instant for credence, for the sea sounds and soft noise of the wooden boat. He walks up to the prow of the fishing boat and stands to look back over them.

'If you follow me, I will teach you to do the same,' he says. 'We will become, all of us, the sons of God.'

Marina drinks from Papias's hand. She thinks he may be an angel and this some threshold before another world. She expects the faces of her children. She expects them in winged form in the space above his head. Her husband, she hopes, is in another place, where devils rent his soul asunder.

'Sit,' Papias says, and brings her slight weight against the wall. He does not know clearly why he is come. He tells himself he came to see if she was dying like Prochorus and if he could administer to her and pray for her soul. He tells himself he does not believe he carried the contagion from her to the scribe, but the fear is there none-theless. If so, why has he been spared? On his hands, on his face in the sea pools he has seen no sign. The serpent devil he saw has left him quivering, like a stringed instrument in after-play.

He goes to the small bench to find lamp oil or candle, but sees neither. The rat recrosses the earth floor, and he shouts at it, stamps his sandal, so it darts out beneath the broken end boards of the door. He finds a cloth and dips it in the bucket and brings it to her. With a gentleness he has forgotten is in himself, he washes her face. He has never touched the face of a woman before. Her eyes are open. Water trickles down her neck. Her lips, blistered and swollen, part. She looks above him for spirits winged, then directly at him.

'You,' she says.

'I am Papias,' he says, 'a Christian. You remember?'

'My children are dead.'

'Yes. I have buried them outside. I have prayed for their souls.'

'Am I dead?'

'No. You are living.'

She groans at this, turns her face sideways into the ragged fall of her hair.

Papias feels the fierce hold of temptation then. He is seized by it. His desire does not take the form more easily defeated: it is not her body that draws him. More forcefully it is the idea of saving her soul. He is compelled by the notion that she is one he has come across on his way, one who has fallen into his very path, and that the reason for this must be that he is to save her. It is part of his purpose. The steps to this understanding he leaps three at a time. It is wonderful. Here, the Lord has given him this poor woman to whom he can administer salvation. She will be the first of his congregation, his church of one. The realisation is a sharp thrill. It polishes his eyes with desire.

'Your children are in heaven above,' he tells her.

From sipping at the water, Marina regains herself. 'The devil took them.'

'No.'

'The devil is my hands.'

'No. They are with the Lord.'

'What kind of cruel Lord is he that is same as the devil?' She spits the question at him.

Papias bites his lip. 'The Lord is not cruel,' he says. 'His ways are merciful. But they are mysterious.'

'Bring me a knife, and I will show you. There is no mystery. My children are dead.'

'It is sad, and you grieve. But you have been spared.'

'I do not want to be spared. If there is a Lord, he has forgotten me. He has left me behind like a fish too many for his basket. Bring me the knife.'

'No. You must not say such things. He is merciful. You will be well.'

'My husband is dead! My children are dead!' she screams at him. 'I am with demons; they are in my hands, in my breath!' She blows an air stale and putrid toward him. 'I breathe death.'

Papias draws back. No, it cannot be. If it were so, he himself would be ill already. It was chance. It was the design of the Lord to take the children, and his design is so great, so beyond the understanding of simple man, a purer mathematics than can be conceived, that it is foolishness even to try. It was divine mystery. He will show this woman, Marina, the truth. He will lead her there. Already Papias feels love for her. He feels the kind of love that connects one to another in community; he feels his strength will meet her weakness, and blissfully envisions the entire world so, how it might be saved one soul at a time, how loving and forgiveness can bind each sheaf until there is a harvest so great its golden bounty will stack to the sight of the Almighty. And the Almighty will be pleased.

But even as he is settling things so in his mind, Marina is pressing herself up to stand. She is small and weak but possessed of resolve.

'Wait! Stop. You must rest,' Papias tells her.

She ignores him. In the half-dark she steps past. She knocks a reed basket, a beaked earthen cup that spins and breaks against a table leg. Her head is down and the fall of hair obscures her face. She pats the table. Papias comes behind and hoops his arms over her. He holds her tightly against himself.

'No. No, you must rest,' he says. Her hair smells of salt. But there is something of honey, too. The feel of her in his arms is so slight and yet of substance; she is a marvel, like a creature rescued from overboard, he is thinking. But she pushes out her arms against his hold and cries out. Still he clings on to her. Her head jolts back against him, knocks a sharp rap on his chin.

'Let me. Release me!'

'No.'

She thrashes her torso one way and the other, the hemp of her garment rips. Barefoot she stamps a heel on his foot. Papias yells. Still he will not let her go; he will save her. He tries to tighten his lock about her, his arms pressing across her breasts, her body doubled forward now and her head down. She fights against him. On the table before them is the long knife she uses to cut the fish heads.

'I will not let you,' Papias says. He holds her tight, his fingers dug into the soft tissue of her sides till they feel the bone. Her feet kick at his shins, stamp. Then, realising that she will not escape him so, Marina twists, spins about so she is facing Papias. Their breaths meet. Her eyes hold him, as if she sees further into him than he himself.

Papias lessens his hold. Her hand comes up like a blessing and reaches to the side of his neck, slides inside the robe and down the soft flesh of his shoulder.

Papias lowers his head toward her. She will be rescued. She will be saved. It is a victory. Love is all-powerful.

Her fingers on his skin are cool and delicious. He closes his eyes, letting himself surrender and fall towards her.

Her hand draws him down.

Then she opens her mouth and bites down with full force on his right ear.

The pain is incomprehensible at first. The wild surge of it blows open his eyes, shoots a yell from his open mouth. His hands fly up, releasing her. Still she is attached to him, her teeth fierce and unrelenting, gnawed into the very stuff of him. A pulpy blood stains her. Papias's head is bowed into the grip of her, and he is roaring now, his fingers trying to push her face from him. But still she bites down into him. The sharpness of the hurt lances into his brain, is blinding, makes him slump forward. The curls of his head are in her fists. What fury and grief is in her is set upon him.

Then, as the lance of pain presses on, spearing his mind, the woman Marina bites free the flap of his ear, and Papias falls to his knees. It lies on her lips. She spits it, steps back.

She turns to the table, having conquered the Lord of love and his spurious mysteries. She tears open her torn robe and exposes to him her breasts, her belly. Then she takes up the long-bladed knife that she uses to cut off the fish heads and two-handed plunges it into her chest.

The blood spurts out into the room. Her head jolts backwards. The knife swings, proscribes a range of angles as it protrudes from her. She stands a moment before the kneeling disciple. Upon her face freezes an expression of cruel joy. Then she falls forwards on to the floor.

12

The light I cannot see. The sky. The sun.

What I see is the evil of man. What I see is what grows in the darkness. But how can I cut it away? Lord, what use your gardener if he is blind?

On my lips is the prayer I confess from weakness: Make me to see again. Make me vigorous and whole that I may go about as I please and seek out those who betray you and be again as I once was. Let me show you the love I carry like breath all this ancient lifetime, the love that is yet like a sword that would cut down your enemies.

If I could see.

Let me serve you again with strength of body.

If your hour is not yet at hand, let your servant see again and stand fortified. I would hold what is. I would I were a better servant. Through my fingers now falls the water.

The Apostle sits in the inner cave, Linus by the entrance. He has returned from speaking with Ioseph and his spirit is low. Not because he has learned of the heresy spreading, for he knew this, but because he feels his physical weakness and wishes for the strength of youth, and because in him rage finds no release. The bones of his knees grind together as he moves from the stool and kneels. Suddenly the entire of him is racked with aches. They announce in his bones, in the bending and straightening, in the pulling and flexing of aged ligature. His elbows, from the near infinitude of crooking for prayer, are most comfortable foreshortened, as though his arms are wings folded in front. Each knuckle is swollen with small purses of pain. At the thin joints of his wrists are risen knobs, lumps of discomfort. His back curves, as though some force he resists bends him toward the ground. Here in his neck is a knife pressing; it advances if he tries to lift his head toward the sky. So he stoops forward, holds pressed and cupped the flimsy flesh of his hands, wherein seems a nest of bones. There is the pain of years, time itself a hurt that sings without relent. It is about him, an everywhere. He does not seek the source of it, or a remedy. But instead takes the dolour as a condition of living, the near century of his continuance. It is moments only, as he kneels, the pain orchestrating along the various podia of his body, before the Apostle can pray himself beyond.

He prays the first in words, as if he speaks personally, and knows that he is heard. But soon, to escape the hurt of time, he escapes time and is silent and drifts from the space, and is no longer present to the cave but restored to his own youth and the most meaningful days of his life.

He has scenes of extraordinary clarity. He can feel the sun of a certain day, the dust of the road. A bird he did not know he saw. But these moments are in disarranged order in his mind. He has poor remembrance of their chronology, and this is burdensome on his heart. The record that he is wears away from the inside. But this will not matter if the Lord comes soon. He will have endured; he will have remained behind as witness until the Second Coming.

So, hands held together, as if cupping a small bird of faith, he visits a morning of sunlight.

We were on the road. Coming back into Galilee for the second time. We had been in Samaria and you had met that woman at Jacob's well. The woman with her water pot; the others could not understand why you would speak to her.

'Sir, I perceive thou are a prophet,' she said.

'God is a spirit, and they who worship him must worship him in spirit and in truth.'

'A messiah is coming,' she said.

'I who speak unto thee am he.'

And afterward she went to the city proclaiming, and from there men had come to see. They had asked of you to stay, and two days we had tarried there, all of us strangely welcomed in that un-welcoming city.

Then, a morning of sunlight.

Come.

We left and walked back out of Judea into Galilee.

We were changed then. Already as we walked on that road we were other than ourselves. Andrew had put away his foolishness. Philip was older than himself. Peter. Peter walking as if carrying on his shoulders a burden, a building. Speaking nothing at all. We were returning to our own place, but with gravity, with import now. We knew we would come across others who had known us before. We were aware there would be judgement.

This in the sunlight on the road. Your step, light and long and purposeful. Always.

A prophet hath no honour in his own country.

So why then were we returning?

We did not ask aloud. We followed.

You followed, too. What was written before in scripture. You now like a reed in another's hand going along the letters toward the last word.

A high eagle I saw overhead us. It flew without wing-beat, gliding the blue ridges of the sky. I lost it and found it again. And again. All that day the eagle accompanied us. Watchful. Where we passed caravans and merchants, tent makers, a herdsman with goats, women bearing bundles, baskets of olives, the eagle remained above.

We were watched over thus. In the hot sunlight on the road.

I thought to ask if you saw it. I was young. I was a youth. But knew not to ask.

A wind arose though the sky was blue. It came across the barren land and whirled the sand in circles dancing. A herdsman hurried with his goats. A copper bell rang. We walked on, dust and sand blowing, our garments pressed back against us and fluttering behind as though we were aflame. The windstorm followed us. Blind whirl of sand. James looked to me and offered his hand. I did not take it. I wanted my brother to know I was a man. Our faces burned, skin sanded. You did not stop. You did not say we should take shelter and let it pass over, but walked on, the storm no more than a dream.

It passed as quickly as it came. Above us again, the eagle.

We came into Cana of Galilee once more. The word had gone before us, and it was not as before at the wedding feast. There were rumours of miracle. There were stories of you. There were tellers whose words were wild and far from truth. There were some who told for their own purposes. Who told so that they might watch the eyes of the Sadducees and the anger redden. Some, who had come ahead from Samaria, told of the woman near Jacob's well, and told, too, that you had said, 'Believe me, the hour cometh when ye shall neither in this mountain nor yet at Jerusalem worship the Father.'

So it was reported.

Already there were words spoken against this.

When we walked into Cana, I wondered why we had come back.

But we followed you, and did not ask.

The narrow curve of the street, the low white buildings giving small shade.

We walked past whispers. 'He is the one from the wedding feast. He is the one.'

I looked all in the eye. I would have struck any that spoke aloud against you. I would have drawn a knife and bled them.

So wild is love.

The band of us, the twelve, coming into Cana, into the cool of the shade. Where were we going? What was our purpose there?

The deep faith we had that it would be revealed.

And was.

We sat by steps, a sprawl of men, and drank after the long journey. There gathered a small crowd. They watched to see if a miracle would happen. They whispered among themselves. Bring water. He may make the water wine again. Quick, bring water. Bring water. He is the one. He is a magician.

We were magician's followers.

He is a teller of fortunes.

We were the fortune-teller's followers. We had left our families to follow a fortune-teller. We were no wiser than children, some laughed. No wiser than foolish children.

One brought a stone jar of water. Others water bags.

'Sir, I would have wine for my guest this evening.'

'Sir, wine. Please make this wine. Wine, sir. Wine.'

In this your gentle composure. Like water untroubled in a deep pool. Waiting.

'Master,' Peter said, after the long journey, 'eat.'

But you said, 'I have meat to eat that ye know not of. My meat is to do the will of him that sent me, and to finish his work.'

We sat in the street shade. The Canaanites waited for their miracle. I watched the sunlight retreat on the stone wall of the house of Eli. The blue of sky with nothing in it, the eagle gone.

Patience was short.

'My water, Sir. I cannot stay here all day. I have work.'

'My water, Sir, to wine, please. It is no trouble to you.'

You answered them not, and some grew angry and muttered against you. But left the water jars in case.

They went away, all but a few. It was in the seventh hour when the nobleman came.

'My son is on the point of death, Sir.'

Peter looked to you. There stirred among us a silent anticipation. We had sat a long time by the steps attending such a moment, flies and insects moving in the shade.

'Except ye see signs and wonders, ye will not believe,' you said.

The nobleman fell to his knees. 'Sir, come down to my son ere he die.'

His old face. His love for his son.

None of us spoke, the old man kneeling so.

I watched your eyes. The pity that pooled, this love of the father.

'Go thy way; thy son lives,' you said.

And he raised his face to you, and we could see that he believed. And did not need the proof of his servants coming on the road to meet him when he went back from Cana, and they told him on the seventh hour the fever had left his son.

I believed. I believed already all things were possible to you.

I leaned and touched your robe.

Simon sits with Ioseph. They sip a brown broth of fish and pulses. Simon's face is pale, his eyes running with rheum. He is nearly the age of Ioseph but of a more anxious disposition. He troubles over his health, always certain that he is ill. His pains and aches are legion; he fears clouds and rain and wind, and must temper this against his faith that God watches over them. The death of his friend Prochorus, the sight of the disease blotching his face, has filled him with dread.

'You saw it,' he says to Ioseph.

'I did.'

'He was as a leper.'

'Yes.'

Simon scratches the back of his hands. Itches are intolerable. Heat of blood, he believes, a sign of his ill health. 'But there was no warning.'

'I saw him myself the morning.'

'So it just came. It just came like that, and he was dead.'

'The Lord took him. I am saddened for you, Simon. I know Prochorus was a close companion.'

'Why? Why would the Lord not take him peacefully in his sleep? Why would he not pause his breathing and leave him on his bed mat? I have these itches in my hands since. My breath is shallow; do you think my breath shallow, Ioseph?'

'No, Simon. You are as you always are.'

'What if it is beginning? What if the itches are . . .'

'Simon.' Ioseph lays his hand across his friend's. For him he feels a duty of care, a bond he cannot quite explain; but it as though he is a kind of ointment, or knows the calm of his spirit to be the salve the younger man needs. 'Simon, do not be afraid.'

'I know. I know I should not even think such things. I know I should welcome what the Lord has in store for me. But I want to live to see. I want to live to see the promised day.'

'You will,' Ioseph says. 'God willing.'

Simon scowls at the broth; in the taste is something peculiar. It takes his mind from the itching.

'Matthias went out on a boat,' Ioseph says.

'Yes. I did not go. He did not ask me. But if he did, I would not go. The sea is treacherous this time of year. A storm can come from nowhere.'

'It is late for their returning. Did they return?'

'I did not see. I do not care greatly for our brother Matthias. Do you think something in this broth sour?'

'Only the reflection of your scowl, old friend.'

Simon sips it through tight lips, as if to sieve the sourness. Into the afternoon sky sail dark clouds. There is a wordless gap, the two old men sitting on their various discomforts, then Simon asks: 'Ioseph, do you think we will see Judea again?'

'Judea?'

'Yes. Do you think we will ever walk there freely again? I do not. Only in dreams now will I visit the house of my parents.'

Ioseph does not offer consolation.

'I have this thought, Ioseph; I will confess it to you that you may chastise me and forgive me for it. It is this: what if the Apostle dies?' Simon turns his rheumy eyes toward his old friend. 'I am a fool, and the weakest among us. But I confess I am afraid. What if he dies? What if you go to the cave in the morning and discovered? And the Lord has not come?'

'We believe he will come.'

'But if he doesn't? If this plague takes the Apostle? What will become of us?'

'He has survived many plagues, been imprisoned and stoned, had burning oil poured upon him. Yet he remains. He will not die, Simon. I believe he will not die until the Lord returns.'

Simon scratches at the back of his hands. 'I had a dream. In the dream there was a great storm, and sand blew and a city was lost beneath it. A whole city. No trace of it remained. Not a trace, Ioseph. It was forgotten.' His breath is shallow, his heart is jumping unevenly. 'If he dies, I have thought. If he dies, Jesus dies again. For we will fade away here without our witness, our testament. We will be a city forgotten beneath the sand. And this thought, once come to my mind, will not leave now.'

The light is swiftly fading out of the sky, and before them the sea deepens gray to black and churns like a mind troubled.

'If he dies,' Simon says again. But the words are neither question nor answer, and hang in the darkening. He looks down at the backs of his hands, sees the scratches from which thin blood seeps.

13

Auster presses his eye to the wood chink. Papias howls again and again, hand–patches the black blood and ooze, holds the jagged stump of ear root, touches the unstoppered hole in himself, views aghast the bloodied fingers, and falls unconscious to the ground.

Before him on the floor is the woman Marina, the knife stilled in her chest. Auster waits. He cannot move. He has not believed what has appeared before him. He saw no devil but heard the woman say the devil was there. He believes the devil is as great as God and has looked about him in the sky for signs of rupture, portents of presence. He has heard her say she killed her children. When she took the knife, he thought she would plunge it in the chest of the youth, and he had been transfixed and would not have been able to save him. In the instants after, Auster does not move. He fears evil invisible in the dwelling, thinks to run away, but is held by the terrible conceit that he may see here, now, the face of Lucifer. He presses against the wood wall, eyes downward for a serpent, upward for the fallen angel that might manifest fierce and dark and awesome in the roof space. He bites his lips to blood. He clings to the little dwelling, expectant of a revelation from which he cannot move. In his mind the fiery figure of the fallen, the proud, unvanquished though banished, possesses strange glory. He barely admits it to himself. But here by the fisher's hut it is this that delays him. The life leaks out of the youth. Still there comes no manifestation, no great wing-beat, no descent of fire. The sky is darkening, it is true. Perhaps if he waits longer. Perhaps this is the work of a minion, a lesser devil, and Lucifer himself must come from vast distance, ascend from nether regions, traverse fiery ringed chambers of the damned to arrive with warm flutter and seize the souls for himself? Auster studies the clouds, looks back inside the dwelling, where all is stilled now.

Where is he? Where is the devil?

From the boat, Matthias sees the smoke rise. His words done, they are sailing back to shore. It is a fisher's hut, he realises. It is burning to the ground. The black smoke curls and hangs in heavy pall above that end of the island. Matthias makes no comment. He has asked the disciples to pray with him that all may be enlightened, and their heads are bowed. With grim concern the pilot has indicated to Matthias the darkening of the sky and stirring sea and been given permission to sail them back. The waters slap at the sides, tilt and sway the slim boat with the bowed men, heads like darkened moons.

It has gone well, Matthias thinks. He has taken the step and none have spoken against him. Why should they? Why would his word not be as another's? Why believe one and not he? Belief is not a lamb but a sword. It must be seized and then wielded. We are not shepherds but soldiers. The Romans have already shown what comes of shepherds. The Christians will be wiped out, banished or crucified, until they dwindle away to nothing, confined to the pages of annals where the scribes record the bizarre heresies of the ages. The Children of the Lamb will rank alongside Followers of the Sacred Goat, Disciples of the White Dog. It is the Jews and the Romans who will write the history. In more wise times the truth of the Divine Mind will be understood, and those who have touched it will be honoured as sages. To think of God as a man was a man's creation. Only a man could have the conceit of thinking God was himself, was like a father who sent down his son. No, God was not like a man, nor did he have a son. He is called the Father only so that the simpleminded might understand. And then they took it as the Word. The Father, the son! Childish ignorance. The truth of the Divine Mind was beyond them. God is a spirit, even Jesus had said, and must be worshipped in spirit, but they had not understood. Of course not. Clamour of the blind: What about our temple? What about our high priests and elders? Who will pay the temple taxes? Ignorance of sheep. Yes, sheep, apt.

But here, these are different. These are hungry to see God. They are tired of waiting for the promised return. What is Jesus to them? A story. They never saw him. They have only the word of a blind old man who forgets more every day and soon will not be able to remember his own name. What then of his promise? What credence in a man who will dribble his food and smell of his own waste? No. They were ready to hear. I knew it. When I told them Jesus was only another of many teachers, many who had understood the Divine Mind, I could feel ground fall away in their minds. A whole shelf of faith without foundation falling into nothing. Their love for him is deep, but not so well founded that it is strong. He becomes whatever they want him to become. Now he is fierce, now gentle, now damning the tax collectors, now forgiving all. A convenient god. The kind a man might invent for himself. But I knew to leave him his place in their minds. Continue to pray to him. O, yes. O, a great teacher. A wise teacher. But misunderstood.

The Divine Mind is like the sky that covers the world, I told them. A good picture. A simple one to understand. It is over everything and everyone.

Perhaps Baltsaros doubted most. Perhaps at first Cyrus. But the reverence of the others swayed them. How perfect this boat, too. The setting. Already we were freed from the prison of Patmos and its prisoned thinking. How easily is loyalty won when the disciples believe they have been chosen! The select. Sitting either side of the fishing boat and swelling with their own importance. Realising they are the younger, the stronger, that I have chosen none of the elders. Soldiers, not shepherds. And proud ones.

Flattery moves all things.

'I have chosen you amongst all others. As yet tell none what we alone know and what I have spoken here. Your ministry will follow when the hour is at hand.'

How the words sat like doves in my hands. How else but I am guided by the Divine?

The sea pitches and heaves and Matthias must sit. Still the dark smoke rises above the fisher's hut. The sky is weighted with stones of storm. The pilot takes them to the shallow waters, and those in the prow step gingerly overboard, hold firm the boat. One offers Matthias his hand, and he alights without word or gesture, walks from them across the stony underwater, and stands, looking at the distance as though he hears things told. The disciples come up and attend, their faces pale with soft bliss of meditation.

'I will send word,' Matthias says. 'We will sail again to speak of these things. Go. Go and consider the truth I have told you.'

He turns from them, walks up the pebbled shore with swift purpose. Something has happened. The clouds build on each other still. The air is cooler by the moment. As he ascends the rough stone steps in the cliff-way two at a time, he has a sour twist in his stomach. What is it? What has happened? Wind is turning like a mind; it spikes the scent of burning through all.

When Matthias reaches his dwelling, Auster is slumped before it. The disciple is exhausted and dirtied, the side of his face stained with blood. He does not rise. He does not tell Matthias what he has seen, nor that he was impelled after to set fire to the fisher's hut and leave the bodies to burn. He has not the strength, nor the knowledge even of how. How did he decide? How one moment was Auster outside and Papias awakened, breathing in moans on the floor, then how was Auster entering and seeking the lamp oil and setting the blaze? How? He cannot say. The flames kissed him. He did not run out. He stood in the swift devouring, the whoosh of the fire opening its mouth, its hot tongue taking the woman Marina like a blistered fish skin. Auster had stood too long, mesmerised by what was released there. Too long blinking at the wild smoke, breathing its blackness, until scorch and choking ran him outside. He had flung himself forwards on to the stones, retching. The roof caught. Creak and collapse, snarl, hiss, crackle: the fire ate at all. Then Auster, blur-eyed, throat-burned, coughing at the black gagging that kept him from air, stood, and for reasons he cannot explain, re-entered. To be himself taken by the flames? To allow the fury of the fire to devour him, too? He cannot say. Nor can he yet tell what he saw then. How the fire danced around the walls, how it took all but did not touch the fallen figure of Papias. He cannot tell this yet, nor how he came back to himself in that black place and stooped down to lift the youth up on to his back and brought him from there all the way across the island here to the dwelling of Matthias.

None of this can Auster say yet. He is slumped forwards, like a beast of burden heavily used.

'What is it? What has happened?'

'Papias,' Auster mutters and raises a hand to indicate.

Matthias steps past him into the dwelling. There Papias lies, blackened and blood-faced, but breathing still.

In the small grove of the olive trees is the stranger. Early sunlight plays. From branch to branch birds engage and dart, quickened in the light. The first pale olive leaves stir with emergence, the minor rustle as a bird exits a tree and crosses with swooping flight to another, the morning otherwise still. Tranquil, his back turned, the stranger stands. His feet are unshod, his robe the brown of a gardener. So moveless and silent is he, the birds take no notice and cross the grove singing the new day.

The light is the light of early summer. It cradles the scene, makes of the trees and their undershade a haven.

How he himself comes there, John does not know. He has walked from nowhere but is at the edge of the grove, branches overhead not yet fruited but leaf-heavy and stirring in wind he did not know was there. There is a scent out of old Galilee, a perfume of olives and dust baked in sun. He handles the tough bark of the trees, touching as he passes. The light he sees. How it falls between the trees. How all is balanced, light and dark, as he steps forward. The birdsong is life-full, pulsing. The stranger he knows, even from distance, even though his back is turned. He knows because of how the world is about him. He knows because of this condition of stillness, about him the created-ness of things, how in the stranger's company all seems of one purpose, from the smallest leaf-move in unfelt wind to the traverse of a bird, from the patterned fall of sunlight to the pooled shade beneath. In this company he feels all is intent. Nothing is but what is intended. All has been made. And as John walks forward, he feels the deep solace of this, the knowledge he has almost forgotten that he is loved.

'Brother,' the stranger says, turning to him.

'My Lord.'

'Papias! Papias!'

'What?' Linus answers, startled from sleep. He uncoils his long limbs, moves free an ache in the elbow he slept on.

'Papias?'

'It is Linus. I am coming.'

'Where is Papias? Why is he not returned?'

Linus looks at the old man, his filmed eyes, his white beard, anxiety wrinkling his face. Does he not know it is night? Linus speaks to him as if to a fool, slow and loud. 'I do not know where Papias is,' he says. 'You should sleep now.'

'Go and find him,' the Apostle urges. 'I must speak with him.'

Linus gasps at the arrogance of command, looks away as if to others for corroboration.

'It is night now,' he says, bending his long body down and slowing his words further still. 'Night. There is storm coming. There are no stars.'

'But where is he?'

Linus's lips are thin, his face pinched with scorn from narrow chin to yellow hair. 'I have told you, I do not know where he is.'

'And I have told you, go and find him! Go! Go!' The old man's voice is suddenly fierce, and he waves his arm, gesturing outward toward the cave exit and the night.

Linus steps back. How dare he. How dare he shout at me like that. He has it in his mind to shout back, even to push the old man off his stool, but doesn't. He sneers in disgust and shakes his head, walks out of the cave and stands not a yard from the entrance. The night is doubly dark, clouds gathering all day have not yet fallen, and there is strange cold. He holds his arms wrapped together, broken sleep and the raised voice of the old man making him shiver. The sea is wild. The air smells of salt and burning.

After a short time Linus goes back inside the cave and sits, his head propped against his arm on the wall, his eyes closed, looking in vain for sleep.

'Linus is that you? Are you back, did you find him?'

Linus does not answer. He keeps his eyes closed, allows a thin smile to turn up his lips.

'Linus?' the old man calls out. 'Linus?'

Linus lifts a small stone from the cave floor, pitches it high past the head of the Apostle so it lands with a sharp clack against the far wall. The old man turns toward it.

'Who is there? Who are you? Is that you, Linus?'

Another comes through the air and hits on the near side.

'Who is there? Speak! Who are you?'

Linus holds a hand across his smile.

'I command you, speak.'

The old man gets to his feet and feels in front of him. He is dark against dark, finger-tipping at nothing. A clump of dirt is thrown at the back wall, and a bat falls from hanging, flies, then another.

The blind man spins about. 'Stop! Who is there? Linus! Is that you, Linus?' From the dark there is no answer. The bats circle, swoop, flicker in velvet black. John stops then. And it is as though in three moments he arrests the all of him, makes stop the beating of human fear and anger inside himself and stands perfectly still. Then directly he walks the smoothened floor across the cave to where his attendant sits. But Linus is up quickly and with held breath slides along the wall.

In the dark of the cave John turns his blind face to where Linus stands with in-breath pressed against the wall.

'Why do you act so?' he asks, as though he sees. 'Go I tell you. Go and bring Papias here.'

Linus does not move.

'Papias cannot come,' Matthias announces suddenly, his voice at the entranceway, where he stands watching Linus and the old man.

'Matthias.'

'Papias has been injured. I come to tell you.'

'How injured?'

'He has lost an ear and bled much. He has been inside the fisher's hut with the woman Marina when it burned.'

John feels for the cave wall.

'He is living still, but barely. Auster saved him, brought him to me.' Matthias does not take his eyes from the old man. 'He is in my care. I have prayed over him that the Lord may not take him, and the Lord has spared him to me these past hours.'

'He is living?' John's voice is thin and low.

'He is living.' Matthias shrugs. 'My prayers have thus far been answered. He has woken once and spoken wildly and fallen asleep again. In dreams he cries out, but without import. I speak to him, but he is unhearing.'

John cannot speak. He feels a deep wound of love open.

'Be assured my prayers are with him,' Matthias says. 'He cannot be moved. Linus will attend you these times.'

The Apostle stands. 'Take me to him.'

'The night is wild, the storm coming since nightfall comes still. You must remain. He may not live until sunrise. I come to ask that you pray for me in my ministering for his soul.'

'You must take me to him now. I will be by his side.'

Matthias taps his fingertips together before his mouth.

'For your own good I cannot allow it. You know my dwelling is on the cliff top. The way is treacherous. I near fell several times

myself. I could not answer to the community with good con-
science if anything befell you. Stay here. I will send for you if Papias
lives.'

'You defy me?'

'I act from love, O Master.'

'I would go to him now.'

'Of course. But as it is written, "and the patient in spirit is better
than the proud in spirit. Be not hasty in thy spirit to be angry, for
anger resteth in the bosom of fools."'

'You quote scripture to me.'

'The Lord has placed Papias in my care. So I have come to tell
you. That you might pray for me that I might bring about the
miracle of his living. If it be the Lord's will. Ours is not to
understand the mystery of his ways.' Matthias looks to Linus,
gestures him to move from where he stands by the wall to the cave
entrance. 'The storm will be fierce. You should not leave the cave
until it is passed. Linus, observe what I say. Protect our Ancient.
See he remains here in safety. God be with us all.'

14

He did not burn, though the fire was all around him, Auster has told Matthias. Papias did not burn.

From this, Matthias concluded ignorance and fantasy to be the measures of Auster's mind; the youth had probably been rescued too soon, that was all. Miracles were most often explained by the unreliability of the witnesses. The resurrected were most often the buried too soon, the mere sleeping, who woke bound in chambers and fought to be returned. No, the fire would have eaten the youth soon enough. There was no miracle in that. But now, here – so much black blood leaked out of him, the ear cut away – here there is something worth considering. Papias should be dead. He lies on the very lips of death – a moment and they may open and take him. But still he breathes. Such a one is valuable in these times, Matthias thinks as he returns from the cave. Do not mistake the value of a resurrection. He steps in out of the wild, dark wind that is blowing now. In pulsing candlelight Auster looks up from where he is squatted by the rush mat.

'He lives?' Matthias asks. 'Leave us now, but be nearby. I will implore the Divine to let me save him,' he says.

He chafes his hands, sits in the crooked light. The youth's forehead is cold, his breath as nothing on the back of Matthias's hand. Is he already gone? Matthias presses his head to the chest, hears the thin beat of life.

If Papias dies, I will say it was because God wished it. Or should I tell about the woman? Should I say he confessed to me?

Or better, that he awoke before death and I saw the devil himself in his eyes? Indeed. I saw him and fought against him for the soul of our youth. Verily, I will say. Verily, verily I myself drove the devil off, so that before dying our dear Papias was saved. Alleluia. Alleluia.

If he lives, I saved him.

This is better.

Live, youth.

The night howls. The dark is utter. Whips of rain lash the island. The wind lifts the sea into the sky and lets it fall. In the eastern end the charred shell of the fisher's hut is deluged. Metal flanges, twisted tin spoons, earthen bowls, all are taken by the hands of the storm and carried elsewhere. The ground is cleaned of human living. With dextrous intent the white biscuit bones of the dead are lifted, let fly into salt swirl and then dropped to be washed away into the suck of tide. Seabirds unsheltered try to go beyond the storm but are blown backwards in darkness like the souls of the undeserving from the near bounds of heaven. The stars are undreamt. Pathways in the rocks are awash and tumble water like jagged wounds weeping. It is weather eloquent but in language lost or forgotten. It fizzes the air, whistles, roars, bangs, and in their disparate huts keeps from sleep the disciples. Some are on their knees in prayer, others are curled on bed mats and rocking softly, as though riding from doom. On Patmos in winter they are used to storm. The inclemency of the weather they take as a characteristic of their banishment, as though rain rods are the bars of jail. But this storm comes more fiercely than the last, or the ones that have rumbled off across their memory. There is something happening, it seems to say. Something in the heavens is happening. The disciples cannot keep themselves from taking recourse to the scriptures. They are fluent in the writings of the ancients, the testaments of the prophets, and each has their own favourite. To each there are chapters, episodes of assail and trial that have appealed and found residence in their imaginations. Just so, then, are they unable to keep from thinking of these as the storm howls. One, Eli, huddles and sees his candle blow out and thinks of the verse from Job: 'How oft is the candle of the wicked put out! And how oft cometh their destruction upon them! God distributeth sorrows in his anger. They are as stubble before the wind, and as chaff that the storm carries away.' Another, Lemuel the bell ringer, finding fault in himself, is visited always by the vehement, burly-chested figure of Moses. Here in the fifth book, Deuteronomy, for those who fail to observe the commandments, Moses rages with fierce promise: that the Lord shall send cursing and vexation and rebuke, that he shall make pestilence cleave unto thee until he has consumed thee from off the land, shall smite thee with a consumption, and with a fever, and with an inflammation, and with an extreme burning. Lemuel tosses beneath his blanket, feels his brow hot, his body cold. In the howling of the storm he hears Moses roar: 'Thou shall be oppressed and crushed away! The Lord shall smite thee in the knees and in the legs with a sore botch that cannot be healed from the sole of thy foot on to to the top of thy head!'

The disciple scratches wildly, prays contrition, screws tight his eyes.

The storm rages.

Something is happening.

Indeed, the heavens are wild, Matthias thinks. He sits forwards, elbows on knees, fingertips a tent below his lips. Perhaps Prochorus hammers on heaven's gate. Perhaps the Divine makes clear his displeasure with him, blows him thither to a furnace beneath.

It is a thought.

Papias breathes still, but thinly. The candlelight is canted, the small room umber and dark, shadows long and twisted. To the howling there is no end.

I have my twelve. But no miracle. This one, the servant of the old man, is most apt. What better disciple. I save him and he follows me. It follows as numbers, one upon the next.

But live, youth. Live.

Outside wind and rain contend. The dark is beaten with fury. The skies crash and bang and no dawn approaches.

But beneath all, prone on the bed mat, from the lips of death Papias returns. His chest expands more profoundly. Matthias draws the candle closer to examine if indeed the colour comes in his cheek. When he is convinced, he blows out the candle and shuts the narrow room into darkness complete. Then he goes dimly to the door and cries out into the storm.

'O heaven! O Divine!'

He has to shout again before Auster comes from beneath a covering, stands in the gale.

'What? What, Master?' he shouts.

'It is Papias. He is dead. Look.' Matthias draws open the door into the dark. Auster sees what he has been told is there, the motionless body of the dead, and is turned back by the hand of the other. 'Go, go and tell the others,' Matthias says into the wind. 'Go and tell the old man.'

Auster nods, blinks, shouts against the storm: 'But the fire did not burn him.'

'Go! He is dead. Tell them to come at sunrise. Go now! Hasten.'

Fool. Belief is easily created in a fool.

Matthias waits a moment, admits surprise himself at the push of the wind against the chest; a man cannot stand upright in the world tonight. His dark head he tilts upwards to the starless vault, flesh of his cheeks pressed flat to the bone, eyes watering with salt. He turns to re-enter the shelter but catches sight of a blanched lump not far off. What is it? He cranes toward it, this whiteness, then goes seven steps in the dark to see lying there what seems a fallen swan. He sees the one, and then another, then all about the dwelling, in a vast littering he can make out the bodies of white seabirds slain. There are a hundred, maybe two. He cannot count. The image of them, a mass of white feathering pitched out of the sky and slung there about his dwelling, makes Matthias gasp. There is a sky army fallen. He holds an arm above his head, as if a rain of birds may descend still. He looks up into the deep dark, the swarth of night, sees the nothing there is. He foots a seabird next to him to be certain it is dead, toe-feels the cold, wet plumage; with heavy looseness the neck slides further into the stones. For moments Matthias cannot move, the appalling sight of so many arrests him. It is as though the world is turned upside down and the earth-sky studded with birds. They are legion, and may continue beyond the dark edge of vision. Matthias holds a hand to his mouth. The night blows at him. He thinks of plague and contagion, all manner of canker and pestilence that may be broadcast in such upheaval.

He regains himself, turns to hurry back to his dwelling, but cannot keep from another gaze. He looks back at the swan sea, considers, nods.

A portent. Useful. Mythological. The Night of Resurrection it happened that.

Stepping inside, Matthias relights the candle, stoops to see Papias is breathing well.

They will come at daybreak for prayers. There is an hour, maybe less, beforehand. He readies himself. In the earth of the floor next to the bed mat he scrabbles two depressions, rubs at his knees with a small stone till they redden raw, then kneels into the holes. In fools appearance is the foundation for faith. A soul cannot easily be resurrected. There must be effort, and of this there must be evidence. He considers his posture when they come to the door. He will bend down so, he will have prayed himself into the very ground so – nay, look at the imprints. He will have his two hands lain upon the youth's forehead and be praying and not even look up or notice they are arrived.

But I will need another sign. Something of the cost of inter-cession. That it is not the business of mortals, but only those who can touch the Divine.

A wound. I should have a wound.

From where he kneels, Matthias looks into the shadowed room. Upon the table is a short metal spike, holed one end as a needle. It is within his reach. How the Divine provides for his own.

Matthias waits. He listens into the whirl of the wind for the bell ring and for those who will be coming. He is perfectly poised. Papias breathes easily now and soon will wake. He may hear or not, it is of no import. The others will let him know Matthias wrestled him back from death.

Then, faintly, like a distant bird lost, the bell sounds. There is no light. No daybreak is apparent to Matthias, but must be. He takes the metal spike, touches its tip to the candle flame, then he brings it to the corner of his eye.

I will weep blood.

With one hand holding the spike to the outer corner of his eye and the other raised behind it, he begins to press. The needle burns minutely. With a sudden blow, he smacks hard the hand that holds it, and it pops with blood spurt in past the corner of his eye socket. He shrieks out, pulls and lets fall the spike, then must fumble in the dirt to find it quickly and throw it out of view. The pain is wild. Blood blurs his seeing, but he finds the needle and flings it away. Roughly he pokes at the wound, the pulpy blood and watery leakage of himself, draws a weep line on to his cheek. His teeth chatter and he has to bite hard to keep from weakness. Their footsteps approach. He throws himself forward, lays both hands on the youth's forehead, and says aloud the prayers in a voice not his own.

Then John and the disciples step inside. They see the shocking figure of the kneeling mourner, the blood flowing freely from his eye. Then Linus sees the chest of Papias rise.

'He lives!' he cries out. 'Papias lives! Look. Behold, he is brought back!'

15

The younger disciples fall to their knees. The Apostle stands.

'Papias lives?' he asks.

'He does,' Auster says. 'Praise the Divine.'

There is the murmuring of prayer. The door being ajar and the gathering both inside and out, the storm blows amongst them. The framing of the hut creaks, the cloth tenting slaps and snaps angrily. A beaker rolls on the floor.

'Bring me to him,' John says.

Ioseph leads him. Auster and Linus offer their arms to lift Matthias from his kneeling, his bloodied eye-weep making the others look away.

'God has answered my prayers,' Matthias says aloud. 'Praise him.'

'Look how he has prayed himself into the ground,' Linus whispers, pointing to the imprints.

John reaches his hand, pats the dark until his outstretched fingers descend to find the face of the youth. He kneels then. His fingers lie flat against the cheek of Papias and he bows his head. He says nothing. He touches the ravaged ear and a shudder passes through him. His blind eyes he shuts tightly.

O Lord. O Lord Jesus.

I am a poor shepherd who loses his sheep.

Forgive me.

*   *   *

His lips do not move; his prayers are unheard. Some leave to accompany Matthias and to dress his wound. Others kneel on their uncertainty. John stays, and in his staying suffers the pain of self-knowledge. He sees his weakness, his withdrawal, his waiting. He sees how ineffectual he has become, how the community itself falls away to nothing. How day by day time erodes what had been built with blood and suffering. It is his fault, vanity that made him believe his work was over and the Lord Jesus would respond by coming now. He has been blind in all ways, not merely in sight. But above all, he has forgotten the essence that returns so powerfully to him now. He has forgotten love.

On his knees by the side of Papias it suffuses him. He feels it like a course of water coming, sluicing from gates unlocked. It roars into the very blood of him, his ancient arteries quickened, laved. Love. Love. His eyes weep. He draws his hands together. The knuckles whiten in fierce clasp. Love. What comes pouring, flowing to every end of him is the awareness of love. And within it sorrow. Here flows and intermingles the sorrows of failed love, of untold love, of love afraid and perishing, of love twisted by pride, made silent, destroyed. He loves Papias, as he loves Ioseph, as he did Prochorus, but feels he has failed all. He weeps, his shoulders shudder. Ioseph kneels down at the Apostle's side, as do others of the elder disciples. The wind whirls in the little dwelling, the day breaking with little light. Still John is bowed, his heart inundated. We are nothing lest we love. We are of God, who is love. Therefore let us.

The thoughts course, swollen with feeling, carrying in bright effluvium flotsam of phrases, things he might say. Antique channels of him open, wildly irrigated and overflowing. Comes the vivid recall of the love he felt for Jesus, the absolute, the unconditional. This is light and water both. Flowing, flowing, and he a vessel. Love. How a man might be filled and overfilled and feel the radiance of all creation to be the radiance of love, the daylight itself awash, dazed, deluged. How he might be humbled so to feel himself connected to the everlasting, the infinite flood of love, the bounty therein. And feel himself taken, carried, helpless but hopeful, full, filled. A man filled, light-filled, touched like the wick of a candle with flame so he trembles. Love. And knows a bliss of gratitude, an ecstasy of soul to witness himself so capable of such light, such water. Water of life itself. We are nothing lest we love. We are of God, who is love. Therefore let us.

John's frame is bent over, his brows knitted, his white hair a gleam waterfall over the prone figure of the youth. He is other than himself. Not yet is he thinking of what happened to Papias, of the fire or the woman or what Matthias claims. Not yet is he considering the straying of the community, the meaning of what happened, or what must follow. For he is breathed into with spirit, in-spired and at one with what was from the beginning.

At the fifth hour Papias opens his eyes. He lies still. He sees the host of elders gathered around and wonders if he attends his own funeral. Does his spirit float free? The faces are grave, heavy-featured, the room dimly shadowed. There is a noise like the sea that is not the sea. Has he drowned? Has his body drowned and he been thrown up on the shore to be laid out before burial? The waves whisper.

The elders move their mouths. Papias falls back beneath the sea.

The pain in the eye is exquisite. It shoots in from the corner, needling deeper than the needle with the slightest movement of the head. Matthias's vision is smeared as with ointment. The pain pierces. He would shriek if it were not for the others. Baltsaros dabs at it, then lays a poultice he has prepared. It stings fiercely. Matthias feels holed into the back of his mind.

But it was worth it. How they look upon me now. Pain is proof. How the ignorant love suffering in another.

He lies with his back rested against a goatskin cushion of lambswool. (Who of them harbours such a thing?) Linus points Phineas to the reddened knees, but Matthias waves him away, a movement that causes a wince, as though a hook embeds in the jelly of his eye. He sips the thinned winter-berry wine, its sourness recalling him from the hurt. There are figs; there is a bowl of raisins swollen in honey. There are dried pieces of goat meat.

Such dreary offerings. My disciples.

'Master, you saw the devil?' Auster asks, kneeling, his plump face pale and his eyes watering like one fevered.

'The devil had taken the youth; I had to pursue him,' Matthias says.

'He was a serpent?'

'He was serpent in form, but greater than a serpent. He twisted in the youth's eyes, two-headed.' Matthias pauses. They want more. They hunger for detail. Struggling against weariness and the pain, he continues. 'He had taken possession of the spirit, and he rose out and up above me, in size enormous, as to sink his venom in me.'

There is a hush. His twelve, and Auster and Linus attend. He sips the sour wine.

'I called to him to be gone. I opened my arms wide like so, and in my hands were swords of silver. Light shone from them and lit the room and dazzled the devil, but he twisted upon himself and spat and became then a creature breathing fire. "Be gone," I cried out. "Be gone. You know not who I am." The fire he breathed burned me not. I was as one bathed in light divine and he cowered back. One head sucked at the youth for the last of his spirit, the other spat skyward, and a flock of birds it seemed fell from the sky slain. I raised my sword and plunged it to him. It sunk into the hardened scale as though in hide. Black blood of him, hot, flowed. Verily it did. He was wounded, and my sword plunged again and again till he twisted back from me and the youth and departed into darkness.'

Matthias allows a pause. None speaks. The pain in the eye pulses from the telling. He touches the poultice, tries to mask the shudder that passes through him.

'Papias?' Baltsaros asks. 'He was dead?'

'The youth was dead. Auster saw. But his spirit was not taken. It hovered still between this world and the next.'

111

There is nodding. There is a murmur. There is reverence.

'I knelt then,' Matthias tells them. 'I knelt then to pray that I might be able to intercede on the youth's behalf, that he not leave this world yet. That he be spared to me and returned from death. I summoned the Divine, and found it within me, and touched Papias's forehead, and behold! he lived again.'

There is a gasp. Matthias bows his head. The others do the same.

Wonderful. The power of a story to the credulous.

When Papias wakes a second time, he sees the face of the Apostle. John is bent low over him and must feel the moment, for he turns his head at once.

'Papias?'

'Master.'

'Praise God.' The Apostle reaches his two hands to lay them on the forehead of the youth. The fever is gone.

'Can you hear, Papias?' Ioseph asks.

Tenderly the youth touches his ruined ear, as if his fingers recollect, he nods. 'Yes.'

'Come, we will bear you to the cave,' John says.

'Master, I can walk.'

'You will be weak, Papias,' Ioseph counsels, 'let them bring a litter.'

'No. I will walk. And guide my master. Please.'

And so Papias stands and seems at once to the elder disciples as though he has aged greatly. There is in his bearing the prudent air of one who has come through peril, as if a traveller from lands of plague and famine. He is slow and deliberate where once sudden. He offers his arm to the Apostle. 'Master?'

They go out into the day. Though the storm has moved to the west, the sky is overhung with clouds and the light poor. The disciples progress silently from the dwelling across the smooth rock face polished with wind. The slain seabirds lie where they fell, but none make comment. The dark sea throws itself about, unsettled yet. On the stone steps Papias takes care to attend the Apostle, offering both hands. Wind whirls the white hair and beard. The elders stop and wait. They do not voice opinion on what Matthias seems to have brought to pass; they will wait to hear the word from the Apostle. They have the reverence of ones aware they are in a presence, and though each feels turn inside him the tireless wheel of human questioning, they keep silence. Something is happening, and has happened, but it is not for them to know yet, they believe. All will be revealed. Their faith now is founded as before on the telling of the acts of Jesus the Christ, the Son of God, and the Apostle is as a roadway leading back to that reality and onwards to the Second Coming. He will tell them when he has considered it. He will tell them if Matthias has worked a miracle.

At the cave entrance they stop.

'You must rest now, Papias,' Ioseph says. 'We thank God that you have come back to us.'

'Back? I have not been gone.'

The elders exchange looks, some lower their eyes to the stone path.

'Before the dawn bell you were announced dead,' John says.

Papias looks at him. 'Master, I was not dead.'

None speak. John holds on to the youth's hands, a frail bridge-way, windblown. The illumination of the night is about the Apostle still. We are nothing lest we love. He finds himself welling like a spring struck. His chin trembles with emotion. He fears he may weep with gratitude, may seem the oldest of old men to the elders and buckle with love. It keeps coursing through him. The poor daylight, the sealight, the sounds and smells carried on the wind, these, the disciples who have followed him in banishment all these years, the loyal youth: all are touched with the same blessing. He cannot think of one without feeling love. It is as if he has been rescued and returned to himself, to a time long ago when he felt so. This is his understanding of it now. It is love that informs all. Nor is this love a thing soft or immature like a new bud, but rather that which comes coursing through the vine itself and makes it strong, durable, pliable, makes it spread to encompass more and more ground, cling to the wall, bear fruit. He has been weak, and foolish, and forgotten love, but no more.

'Come. Come all of you. Come inside,' the Apostle says. His blind head at an upward tilt, he releases Papias and waves both hands. 'Come. All. Be with me.'

When they are entered and sit around on rush mats and stools, and Papias has been given a lambswool blanket for his shoulders, the Apostle speaks to them. He speaks as he has not in a long time, and from his first words all of the elders feel a shiver of knowledge, understanding the words he speaks will outlive time.

'Beloved,' he says, 'we must believe not every spirit, but try all spirits whether they are of God, because many false prophets are gone out into the world.' He touches his tongue to his lips, raises his voice louder and stronger still.

'Hereby know ye the spirit of God: every spirit that confesses that Jesus Christ is come in the flesh is of God, and every spirit that confesses not that Jesus Christ is come in the flesh is not of God; and this is that spirit of Antichrist, whereof ye have heard that it should come; and even now already is it in the world.'

None speak. The elders and the youth look at the blind apostle as though at a column of light.

'But ye,' John says, 'ye are of God, my children, and have overcome them, because greater is he that is in you than he that is the world.

'They are of the world; therefore speak they of the world, and the world heareth them.

'We are of God: he that knoweth God heareth us; he that is not of God heareth not us.

'Hereby know we the spirit of truth, and the spirit of error.'

He pauses. The phrases are like platforms in his mind, the construction building one upon the next, rising as steps he discovers just as he arrives at each one. It proceeds with perfect logic, as if out of a natural pre-existent order. The words are there just before he needs to find them. He raises his head, his whitened eyes, his arms he holds outwards.

'Beloved, let us love one another: for love is of God; and everyone that loveth is born of God, and knoweth God.

'He that loveth not, knoweth not God.' Again he pauses, as if he is in flight and discovers a higher plane of purer air, then flies up into it. He says aloud the four words that seem carved on the invisible: 'For God *is* love.'

His speech has the quality of truth, beyond dispute, and the disciples need no persuasion. Some nod silently, others stare as if at a marvel. The Apostle draws to him his arms, presses together his hands. None have heard him speak so before, for this is not the telling of the acts of Jesus, there is no narrative. This is not the preaching Ioseph heard from the Apostle many times when they wandered in the dusted lands of Bithynia or Troas or the stony fields of Thessalonica. This is other. This seems a pure distillation.

'Beloved,' John repeats, 'he that loveth not, knoweth not God: for God *is* love.

'In this was manifested the love of God towards us, because that God sent his only begotten son into the world, that we might live through him.

'Herein is love, not that we loved God, *but that he loved us*, and sent his son to be the propitiation for our sins.'

The cave catches the wind; the air sings like the sea. Light and cloud-shadow cross. The old apostle raises his hands a last time.

'Beloved,' he says, 'if God so loved us, we ought also to love one another.

'No man had seen God at any time. But if we love one another, God dwells in us and his love is perfected in us.

'Let us pray that it will be so.'

John bows his head, the others likewise. In the cave on Patmos they kneel in the darkness, flooded with light.

16

Now is the moment.

Matthias stands on the seashore, before him a great mound of the dead seabirds that Auster and Linus have gathered and now set alight. Lamp oil takes flame, sea faggots, flotsam of storm wrack, timbering. Black smoke in a banner unfurls.

Now is the moment. I will win to me no more but Papias. He alone of the others would be of value. Testament. Eyewitness. My own Lazarus. How quickly they carried him away! It will matter not. I will confront him: You were dead; I went after and brought you back. How deny that? Arise and follow.

The bird fire burns poorly. Smoke smudge thickens against the daylight. The grey sea twists as though in chains. In the near distance some few fishers are about, starting late because of the storm, hoping to bring home a heavy catch of fish foolish to seek sanctuary in the shallow waters. The boats cut across the waves on quick wind till the nets grow heavy. Auster and Linus stand by the pyre. They are in open-eyed amazement still at the discovery of the seabirds after Matthias had told of them in his struggle with the devil. When Linus saw them, he vomited, Auster wanted to clap his hands. The birds were a brilliant display, all the more awesome for the substantial weight of each as Linus and Auster dragged them over the sand. What power it took to strike them from the sky! What flash of mind forked into the night to plunge them headlong! The two disciples watch the smoke rise and curve in upon itself and uncoil, caught by the wind. Matthias walks away down the stony shore, stands.

The storm will have passed by this evening. At daybreak we will leave.

Lemuel comes with the news. The Apostle has announced the community will take supper together. There will be a communion before sunset. Matthias returns to his dwelling, his eye pulsing with pain. He removes the poultice, palms water on to his face from a bowl. The hour is near. His heart is quickened at the thought. He palms the water a second time, touches gingerly the throbbing, winces. Still, the wound has its worth. He sits to consider how things must proceed. After a time he sends Auster and Linus to tell the others to come to his dwelling before the supper.

The Apostle is renewed. He has a vigour and resolve unfamiliar but to Ioseph, who has known him the longest. He sits by Papias, who tells him, 'You need not care for me, Master. I recover quickly.'

'Call me not "Master", call me Brother, or call my name, John.'

'I cannot, Master.'

'My name is John.'

Papias lowers his brow, his complexion waxy and pale, his eyes glossed. 'I must call you "Master",' he says, then adds, 'and Master, I must confess.'

'And you will be forgiven.' John bows his head and Papias tells him in whisper the story of the woman Marina and her children and the vanity of thinking he could bring them back from the dead. He confesses to temptation and concealment, to the potent seduction of power. His face reddens as before a fire. His voice drops further so the words are smallest sounds. John listens, holds out his right hand and prays. 'Walk in the light,' he says.

After, he tells Papias, 'I, too, must confess. I have forgotten myself. I have forgotten love. I have been harsh and have tired of the burden I carry within me, which burden now is made light as air. Papias, from this day forth the sun shall not set but I will have told you and all our brothers the word of our Lord Jesus. The sun shall not set but I will have related what was, that it will be still. My telling will continue while does my breath till he come again. I confess to you, I have forgotten myself. I have fallen down, but now stand up, my burden light.' John's face smiles, deep furrows paired, cheekbones prominent. He is both the Gallilean fisher, Zebedee's son, John, brother of James, mender of nets a lifetime ago, fleet barefoot boy who ran one end of his father's boat to the other, untoppling, gifted with balance, and also this other, this man who seems footed in two worlds, this and the next. He is the boy and the old man both.

Now he rises. 'We must make ready,' he says.

Ioseph brings him a white stole he lays over the Apostle's shoulders. With Papias he draws two tables together, and for them benches.

The sun retreating, the elders approach. They bring some of the flat fire-baked bread the islanders make, two skins of winter-berry wine. The events of the night past are still in their minds but age and experience and faith quiet the questions. They come none-theless with the awareness of heightened moment; the storm, the death and return of Papias, the fall of seabirds, are as currents that converge. The call to communion is another such. So as they enter the cave the disciples bear themselves as if to counsel and revelation both. Something is happening, and they are its witnesses.

They stand. John goes to each and takes their hands. None speak of Matthias and the younger disciples, though all notice they are not there. Ioseph goes outside to look. Behind clouds the sun nears the sea. He returns, tells nothing. There opens a long pause.

'My brothers, sit,' the Apostle says at last.

And they do, gathered in the yellow lamplight about the tables, Papias at the right hand of John.

'Brothers, whom I love in the truth, the darkness is past and the true light now shines. Let us give thanks and break bread and take of wine in memory of our Lord Jesus Christ, the Son of the Father.'

'Amen.'

The bread is broken and passed. The elder men watch the Apostle for signs. They can see in his demeanour renewed vigour and purpose. The communion is not yet properly begun when Matthias comes.

'O Beloved. Why do you begin without us? Are we not also chosen children of the Father?' About and behind him Linus, Auster, and the other disciples bear torches and stand in fire glow.

'Indeed you are welcome, brothers,' John says. 'All are welcome to give thanks to our Lord Jesus Christ. There is room at the table. Sit.'

'We do not come to sit,' Matthias says and comes forwards. 'We come to announce the true light. The Divine.'

There is a murmur. Some of the disciples look down. John says nothing, his face held upward, as though to take a blow. Matthias walks to the top of the table.

'I come to speak the truth. For it has been given to me. "I am come a light into the world that whosoever believeth in me should not abide in darkness."'

'You cite the words of our Lord Jesus?' John's anger flares.

But Matthias turns from him, throws open his arms, booms his voice. He glares down at the assembly. 'Why do you speak of Jesus as a messiah? Any of you? Because this ancient says so? Because this Jesus was his friend, because he was the beloved disciple, of this carpenter's son, a Galillean like himself? The Christ? How convenient! His own relation, his neighbour!'

'"I am the resurrection and the life," said the Lord, "he that believeth in me though he were dead shall he live",' John calls.

'How, old man, how shall he live being dead? You are a fool. And all of you who follow him fools, too, who cannot see how he has led you. That he might have caretakers in his ancient years, attendants who serve him in his dotage.'

'Matthias! Be silent,' Ioseph calls.

'I will be silent hereafter. I come this time and this time only to announce to those who will follow. Hear me: there is a light divine. It is the One. It was from the beginning and ever shall be. It is as the prophets tried to tell us. Even as the prophet Jesus. Its illumination I have felt, have touched. I myself.' His right hand he slaps on his chest twice.

John stands. 'Jesus said: "Verily, verily I say unto you, I am the door of the sheep. All that ever came before me are thieves and robbers, but the sheep did not hear them. I am the door: by me if any man enter in, he shall be saved."'

'The sheep! The door of the sheep! Is that what you think? What you believe, all of you? Are you sheep? Is that what you were born for, to be sheep? Is that a man? A sheep? Is that why you remain here on this rock? O apt indeed! Sheep going through a door?'

Ioseph stands up beside John. 'Blasphemer!'

'Ioseph,' John extends his hand, holds back the other by the shoulder. 'Leave him. Let him to speak.'

'He takes the name of our Lord in vain, Master. Though I am old, I would strike him down.'

John shakes his head. 'Leave be, Ioseph.'

Emboldened, Matthias moves down along the table. 'Listen, listen now this time that ye might know the truth and choose for yourselves. I, Matthias, son of Ignatius of Amphipolis, have been chosen by the One that I might bear his light as witness into the world. The light that was from the beginning and is and ever will be. Which light makes other lights a darkness. Though others preach their own words of God, these are but poor versions of the truth, as candles to the sun. Listen now, I am come to tell you what is. We must be soldiers, not sheep. We must leave here and go out into the world. I fear not. I fear no Roman, nor any man. Nor should any who follows me.'

He comes along the line of disciples, passes Lemuel and Simon and Meletios until he stands behind Papias. Both hands Matthias places on the youth's shoulders.

'I have faced death. I have faced him and fought him myself for this youth who was taken from us. The divine light shone upon me. I was as one lifted from myself. Not in this world nor the next. But in the Presence. The Presence who made me all-powerful against death.' He leans down, his face next to Papias, and speaks loudly. 'This youth was given back to me. As proof. That you might know, that you might believe. Stand, Papias.'

Under the scrutiny of all, uncertain, puzzled, full of torn pieces, hearing for the first time the extraordinary account of his resurrection, Papias stands.

'Look upon him. See. Believe. Behold the miracle.' Matthias allows his witness a moment; he takes a half step back, opens wide his arms as if the youth is a thing conjured out of the dark. He smiles, his head inclined away to better view the marvellous, then he says, 'Papias, go and stand by the others.'

But Papias does not move. His face reddens. All are looking at him.

'Papias,' Matthias raises his voice.

When still the youth does not move, Matthias taps him on the shoulder, then leans in to whisper: 'Papias, you will be the wonder of the world as we walk in it. You will be marvelled at and praised. In time you will recall the truth of what happened and tell to gathered multitudes how death came for you and be living witness of that other darkness. You will spread fear and wonder. You will tell what was and is on the other side of this mortal domain. You shall be by my side as an angel to the Divine, testament to the Omnipotent. Men and women shall fall before your feet. The sick and infirm shall seek the hem of your cloth. Consider. You have been chosen and cannot deny it. It is your destiny I bring you, good Papias. Go, take your place at the forefront of the others.'

Along the table the disciples' faces are turned towards him; in firelight by the cave entrance Linus, Auster, Cyrus, Baltsaros, and the others watch. Papias is still weak; his ear wound pulses. All seems stopped. In the mute delay comes the vision of himself as another, as this Lazarean disciple, this thin figure of return still printed by the fingers of death. Lands far and strange whose names he does not yet know, places of dust and sand, blue rivers, villages where they might arrive like ones traversed down from another world: these he sees. He would walk at the front beside Matthias.

He would wear a white robe. Perhaps the Divine might touch him, too, and give him the power to resurrect. Why not? It was likely. Had not Matthias just said as much? And it would all be in the name of goodness. There would be no gain sought. It would be for the glory of the Creator. If he could do that, would that be wrong?

'Good Papias.' Matthias's face moves close to him again, his voice low. '*Beloved* Papias, be not afraid, go.'

Pain beats at his temples. Papias must close his eyes. His head he inclines slightly.

'Auster, Linus, come, help our disciple, he is yet weak.'

'Leave him!' the Apostle cries out. 'Lay not your hands upon him!' He comes forwards so he stands facing Matthias, his white head back. 'Papias, be not seduced, but abide with us here. This is the very voice of the Antichrist amongst us. Listen not.'

'Old man, old fool!' Matthias shouts, 'Jesus-lover! You dwindle to nothing.'

'Brother Matthias!' Lemuel shouts, standing stoutly, and Matthias flares back at him. 'Brother? I am not your brother,' he says, his eyes narrow and dark, his lips spitting the words. 'Why call each other brothers, ye are not so. Some of you mistrust the others, some envy and despise. Brothers! This is a mockery, a mask ye hide beneath. I know you all. Brothers! Call me not Brother. I am Matthias, son of Ignatius of Amphipolis, who has known the Divine, the One. Stand back, old man. Your time is past.' Matthias turns to the youth. 'Papias, come with us to your glory.'

There is a moment, the cave like one breath held.

In whisper, dream voice and eyes as if upon a distant truth, Papias says, 'I will not.'

Matthias leans nearer. 'Be not a fool! Do not let the old man sway you. You have no need of loyalty to him. Do not be afraid. You are of us, and know it.'

Papias says nothing. His lips quiver and he presses them together as if they might utter betrayal.

'He has spoken, leave him!' The Apostle touches Matthias's shoulder, who shakes the hand roughly away.

'I could break you like a stick. I could make you fall to the ground with vomiting and wailing, old man, if it were my will. Touch me not. You know not with whom you deal.'

'I have no fear!' John replies sternly. 'We come gathered here for communion, for our community of believers, brothers in our Lord Jesus Christ. If you are not of us, then be gone.'

'We will be gone. By sunrise we will have left this hell.' Matthias paces down the table length. 'And you, you all, old men, what will you do? Stay here till death, like Prochorus, lie beneath mounds of stones and be forgotten? Yes, forgotten. Old man, old teller of a tale, your tale is threadbare and runs to nothing. This carpenter's son messiah. Do you wait, all of you, do you wait yet? That the carpenter will come again? Ha! Because the hour is at hand?'

'Matthias stop!' Papias cries.

'You will be bones and dust. Dust and bones. All of you. And your Jesus not even dust on the pages of the books of history. Remembered a few more years, then forgotten. You are fools, credulous fools, to follow an old fool.'

Papias comes forwards as though he will strike the other. Matthias stops and looks into his face.

'And you, the greatest fool if you do not come to your destiny.'

'Be gone.'

There is a moment, the face of Matthias an implacable mask inches from the youth, his lips pressed tightly, his dark eyes burning. Then, as if he releases in disgust what he himself has caught, he wheels away.

'So be it.' He walks swiftly to the cave entrance, stops. 'Hear ye. We, the chosen, the believers in the Divine, will leave this island at sunrise. Those who will follow are welcome. Consider well, Papias. Those who remain on Patmos will die on Patmos. Your Jesus does not come. Your Jesus does not care. Because your Jesus was a man, and is dead. Behold, the truth. Fools of Jesus, farewell.'

Matthias raises his two hands and brings them together in a loud clap. Then he turns on his heel and leads the others from the cave into the night.

17

When the bell rings at sunrise, the Christians do not know their number. In their separate huts they do not know who will have left and who remained. In the aftermath of Matthias's departure from the cave, the Apostle called them to sit again for the supper communion, Papias at his right hand. There was a pause first for prayer and contemplation. Then John broke the bread and gave thanks. He spoke the words of blessing they had heard many times, but there was a hardened edge to his voice, as though now there was an imperative. 'Jesus said: "I am the bread of life: he that cometh to me shall never hunger, he that believeth in me shall never thirst."' The Apostle held aloft the cup of wine and said, 'Who is he that overcometh the world, but he that believeth that Jesus is the Son of God.' After, he had turned his head to each as though he could see and spoken loudly: 'My brothers, truly our fellowship is with the Father, and with his Son Jesus Christ. God is light, and in him is no darkness at all.'

He spoke on and the disciples listened, marvelling at urgency of voice, the vigour and conviction that seemed of old. He spoke of the light as if the darkness was nearer now. Papias and the elders attended as though the words were newly necessary, and in their telling remade the world, as if therein were retraced maps for the lost.

The old Apostle had taken the hands of each as they left the cave and went out across the dark. The night was blown about, unruly winds and heavy starless sky. Papias and Ioseph had remained. In the course of the night they woke and slept both, but neither could say they saw the Apostle rest.

Now, at the rising of a timid sun, the bell rings, its leaden clapper hand-beat to make a dull sound as the disciple Lemuel crosses the first thin light on the island and comes along the upper ridge to sound the call for prayer. In the chill gloom are shadow figures, silent, stepping the stone path to assembly. Birds are not yet astir; nothing sounds but the sea turning the key of its tide. In grey, like shades crossed from another world, the Christians. First there is only Lemuel, the bell ringer, then the woken form of Danil, then Meletios, and others, each uncertain as they come outside if they alone are left, if all will have followed Matthias. They take comfort from one another's company, but say nothing. They cross as always up the beaten way to the promontory where the flat table rock stands.

The sun rises.

The Apostle and Ioseph and Papias come – they, too, feeling the human consolation of community, and more, the enduring witnessing of their belief. The disciples have each prepared themselves in the night to be the only remaining in the dawn, and thinking so – having ventured into the wild dark of their own spirits, to seek the truth of what they believe and then live by it – they have accepted it. Each has thought to abide with the old apostle in a community of two or three, if so be it, to wait in prayer for the coming of Jesus the Christ. But now they see, there remains all who sat to the supper communion, nine in number. And though they are less than half the community of before, from this each takes strength.

By the table rock they stand. The daylight reveals them where they pray to the Father.

Below, the sea unveiled, a boat waits. To it, in form like a snake, Matthias and his followers come. Behind them they leave their huts afire that nothing be left but darkened prints upon the ground.

I think of the multitude.

I think of the great multitude who followed you because they had seen your miracles on those who were diseased. The crowd whose number Simon Peter could not count but said were more than five thousand. Up the stony ground of the mountain following, the time of Passover near. The multitude in the heat of day. I looked back upon them, marvelling. How many there were. Philip saying to me, 'We become a nation.'

As we believed and were witness thereof.

The great company murmuring, whispering, expecting, climbing the mountain behind you to the place you led, where was a grassy expanse.

'Whence shall we buy bread that these may eat?'

The boy who carried five loaves and two small fishes. The sun shining upon the multitude.

I saw the loaves and fishes carried to you in the one basket. Your prayer of thanks over them, your eyes to the heavens. And breaking the loaves and fishes that they might be distributed among many and sending forth: 'Gather up the fragments that remain that nothing be lost.'

The twelve baskets that were filled. And again, and again, so a clamour arose among the multitude. They stood and cried out. 'O Prophet! O Most Mighty! Hail Holy King! Hail Holy King!'

For, in fervour then, they were for coming and taking you by force to be their king. The great multitude of your believers.

But you departed hence alone into the mountain.

We stood before the great assembly. Philip said, 'What number in the world there will be of us will outnumber stars.'

For so it seemed.

The multitude.

O Lord, if it be thy will, send us your mercy that we may abide. If it be thy will, send us a sign.

'Papias?'

'Yes, Master?' Papias still cannot call the Apostle by his name. It does not seem fitting. For the truth is he wishes him to be other than mere human, not merely an old man called John.

They sit outside the cave in the afternoon. It is some days since Matthias and his followers have left.

'You are well?'

'I am.'

'What I ask you will obey, Papias?'

'You have no need to ask me.'

'Nonetheless. Answer me.'

'I will obey you.'

'God be with you.'

The weather is broken, the island in bleak light. What was empty before is now more so. Where before the younger disciples carried out many of the chores of the community, catching the fish, drawing the water, such tasks are now fallen to the elders. In the aftermath of the departure there is renewed vigour in belief, but hardship, too. The Apostle is aware of this. More than ever now he wishes their faith might be rewarded. He wishes there might be something to avouch for their staying on, for their refusal to surrender though their number is diminished. Long since, he has accepted for himself that there be no obvious exchange, between heaven and earth no simple traffic of plea and response, whereby all that is sought is granted. But nonetheless he feels there exists always the listening presence. He feels love. Always the prayer is heard; the judgement of its merits is the Lord's. But now, in the bleak aftermath, John feels the urgency of the time. There is a turning. He can sense it in the air, in the fall of the sea. It must be now. Now nears the hour. So he says to Papias, 'I am to ask the community of our brothers to fast with me. We will fast that our spirits be made pure and our prayers ascend. I will ask this of our brothers, but not you, Papias.'

'Not me? But I am the youngest. I am the most able. I . . .'

'No. Not you, Papias. I command it.' John extends his hand, takes hold of the youth's shoulder. 'You have suffered and serve the Lord as he wishes. I am grateful for your love. But you should not fast. Bear with us. For forty days and nights we shall take only water. The time is near for our Lord.'

★   ★   ★

The disciples are told at communion. All consent. They eat the last bread and taste the last wine. Then quiet falls on them. Their faces are old and lined. The flesh of Ioseph's cheeks is white and sags from prominent bone. The bald head of Lemuel is wrinkle-creased, his brown eyes deep; Danil is in his sixth decade, narrow-jawed; Melitios, with the long face and blue eyes of Iconium, has forgotten his age; in his narrow chest Simon breathes wheeze. They are all in various manner infirm. In ordinary time they suffer the multitude of ailments visited on the aged – rheums and aches of joint, poorness of breath, wheeze and gasp and cough, vision blurry or marred with floating fish-hook nothings, dryness, deafness, flakiness, dolour of source unknown – and are poorly suited to the rigours of fasting. Nonetheless, each agrees without discourse. By nightfall they are begun.

The first days hunger comes for them. It comes like an unwelcome companion at mealtimes. Its teeth are sharp, its breath foul. It licks its lips with wet red tongue, spits aside the dust of the day and impatiently waits. It says the names of foods. Warm soup of lentils and beans. Pepper spices. Dipping bread. Pottage of sweet lamb with crushed herb of rosemary. Fat onions fried. Baked fish filleted with lemons sliced inside, drizzled over with honey. Touch it. Suck your finger burn. Taste the juices. Sip from the wineskin, pour and watch the beading bubbles, purple mouth swallow. Swallow in the gullet, for the good of it. Taste the sweetness of a honeyed cake, warm from the fire. Break its crust, go on, let free the scent, breathe it deep. Finger the soft food. Eat. Eat. Eat, the cruel companion urges. But the elders endure and do not relent. They sit with bowed head. Some pray the same prayer over and over so it curls about them and is cast like a cocoon. Others find a place, at first in the real, in the mid-distance, a rock, a minor landmark, and stare at this. They focus intently and do not move. They watch an hour, two; they watch while the stiffness comes in their necks and locks tight the vertebrae, they watch themselves into perfect stillness and on until through the place they see they see another, and this

128

takes all their sight. To this other place they go, escape the unwelcome companion who cannot follow.

By the end of the first seven days they are already noticeably weaker, thinner, as Papias brings them water. How can they continue for another thirty-three?

The spring is coming to meet winter. Winds blow down off bright skies of swift white cloud. Seabirds in the twist of season fly low across the broken surface, search the first fish of season. The light changes by the moment. The heavens throw down fists of hail, darken the island then make brilliant with the sun. Light and shade compete across the stony shore, outpacing the flight of gulls. Suddenly the air warms. Up the coast of Greece come mild drafts, gusts carrying the scent of the lemon trees leafing. While the disciples fast, the sea turns blue before them. White sails cross. All is renewal. The plate of the earth itself seems borne upward toward the sun.

Whether the disciples note this or not, Papias cannot say. He comes and goes from each without word. They are both present and absent, their silence deep. The Apostle lies by night on the bed mat of dried rush, sits by day outside the cave, his face to the sun. What prayers he says, or whether he prays at all, remains a mystery. Does he sleep? Does he rest truly? The fasting is a purge of spirit, a paring back to the root. It is painful before it is purifying. In perfect stillness, their faces composed, some of the elders' eyes weep. Twin tears thinly gloss their cheeks, as though they mine a source. Then the water stops. They sit or kneel on, travelling further to another place in their soul, where some history of their weakness or failure awaits.

But the weather is clement, and clemency seems the coming mood of season. Papias himself prays thanks for his rescue; he does not know or understand yet the reason and prays to know his purpose. But for now that purpose is the care of these disciples. The words of the Apostle concerning love are with him like a white stole. God is love, he says to himself many times, and feels in this a vast illumination as though a rock has been pushed back and a bright revelation beheld. If he can hold on to this, if he cannot forget for one moment, then the world is easily lived, he thinks. Within the white aura of this radiance he can put aside any thought of Matthias and the others. He can banish the disturbing thought of the rupture in the community, the versions of his death and resurrection, and the evidence that evil exists.

The sun shines.

By the twentieth day the spring is truly come, but the disciples weaken visibly. Papias thinks to squeeze berry juice in their water, anything that may give strength. But then chastises himself for not trusting the Lord. He himself tries to eat little, but the hunger is fierce and he fears he grows weak and risks illness, so he takes a little more. As he brings the water from one silent old man to the next, he watches for signs they need more. But rarely do their eyes rise to meet his or is there the slightest indication they know he is there. They are as ones gone away, their bodies like cloaks cast off. Nonetheless, Papias can see the wastage. He can see the bones emerge, the skeletal features of Meletios, the sharp jawbone of Danil, and worries compete with his faith. How can there be twenty days more?

At sunrise each day he goes to the table rock alone. He has been asked to ring the bell for Lemuel, though none are to gather. And so he does, hand-beating the dull notes to the pale sky, where the birds turn over in surprise having forgotten men exist. After the prayer bell he rings again, one chime for each day of the fasting past, then he kneels alone and prays. Sometime across his prayer there comes to him the image of the greater world. He has a glimpse of places far away, the villages and towns where the ordinary business of markets and merchants continues, where the day is begun not with a bell but stalls and salutes and the cry of prices. He sees the world gone ahead without him and for moments feels the melancholy of that loss. Out there is the life he might have lived, might be living now, with a family and neighbours, the joys and complaints of every day. On his knees by the table rock he must pray himself back to concentration. No, he has chosen this other life. Because he has a purpose. Because the Lord has a purpose for him, though it may be no more than to attend the Apostle. So be it. If that is his will. Amen.

By the thirtieth day, speech and food, company and discourse seem things of a lifetime ago. Never was so much loneliness. Here is the lone moving figure of Papias crossing the near shore, where the seabirds rise lazily before his approach and land not six paces further on, as though he will not come there. They alight and land, cawing, scuffing the sand, wing-brushing where sandflies stand. He goes with heavy heart to the path across the island, and hurries then to the place of his private grief and guilt. In this season of purge he returns to the burnt ground where stood the house of the fisher's wife Marina. His stomach turns as he approaches. He feels he might fall down, but doesn't, but in him breaks the cords in which are tied up his emotions, and his shoulders shudder. He sees the blackened stone mound of the grave of the children, and a wail is torn out from inside him like a line with jagged hook.

O Lord, hear thy servant.
   O Lord, if it be thy will, send us your mercy that we might abide.
   Forgive us our trespasses.
   If it be thy will, send us a sign.

Forty days and nights of fasting. Forty days and nights of prayer ascending. John remains as he was in the beginning. The Apostle is as ever, some part distant, as though a portion of him is perpetually engaged elsewhere. He suffers the fast without evidence of decline. It is as if for him food and sleep have already been abandoned and the necessities of life for others are for him idle. He remains. His great age matters not. He may live for ever, or until the Lord Jesus comes for him. So it seems. In his blind silence he sits, a rock of faith. He touches the water to his lips only; they flake and scab, but he pays them no attention. His praying is like the instrument of the gifted. He knows its form and features so well that it is become his second nature. He is more than comfortable within it. He sees the words in his mind without saying them. He sees the distance between heaven and earth in terms of height and tilts his head slightly backwards as if in his darkness he will see the light coming. The prayers flow from him. Sometime he finds in himself the words of the psalms, and twenty, thirty of them flow past his mind; other times a single one recurs and repeats until it becomes like the noise of a wind blowing upwards. He prays. The forty days and nights pass over him.

18

The springtime comes all about the island as the disciples fast. It announces itself in light and air. Warm breezes play at the cave entrance. The sea sings lightly. What sign is expected, what the community seeks, has not been said. The fasting was for each not for reward, and God is not to be bargained with.

But as he rings the bell for the fortieth day, Papias feels there will be something. Something will happen. He knows it. He has food prepared for the supper after midnight. All day he feels the strange exhilaration of imminence. The disciples have come through. Though they have weakened, their faces gaunt, their flesh a yellowish hue, and the eyes of many shot red with blood, they have endured. He rings the bell as loud as possible. Let the sound peal out! Let the heavens hear! It is the final day.

He walks the shore with quickened step. The sky is perfectly blue, the light thrilling. Papias's belief in miracle is such that anything could happen. It might come from the sea or the air, he thinks. The waves themselves could stop in mid-fall and then curl back as they did for Moses, or the blue canopy overhead open, amber-fringed, and golden chariots with angel charioteers appear. Winged horses could thunder down the sky, trumpets herald the Almighty. It could be so. It could be. At any moment the Lord might come for his beloved disciple. So the day has been made lovely, so the sea glistens like polished glass.

Papias walks the full length of the curved sand to the rocks and then back again. He prays to be worthy to witness. He prays that our Lord of Infinite Mercy forgive him his sins. The tender skin of his ear wound burns with the sun. He holds a palm against it as he walks, as though to keep in something he hears. His footprints parallel those of earlier days. Birds are in the sky. He watches these, too, for the possibility of signs. Anything can be used as the language of the Lord, for he created all. Just so, even flies. The world is thus to the youth as he comes along the shore, it is charged, loaded with meaning; just beneath the surface of all is this pulsing sense of advent. It is the fortieth day.

He returns the full length of the eastern shore to where he left the handbell in the sand. He goes along the stone-way and looks back over the island edge. Not yet, he thinks. He does not come yet. But it will be soon. With light, swift stride he goes back the dry scarp to the dwelling of Danil, where rainwater brims a trough, and he dips two buckets and brings these back to the cave. He empties the water into a large earthen pot and returns to the trough with the buckets to fill again. All the time he keeps his eyes on the sky. Is the blue made thinner? Is the sky in some manner *stretched*? The color seems less, as though a white albumin has been pressed on to a palette and worked into the blue. Does all now not seem *whiter*? Is there not a milky opalescence? Look, how the distant rocks are softened in light! How pearled is the very air!

Several times, as he comes and goes with chores readying for the end of the fast, Papias thinks the moment is at hand. He stops. One time he drops to his knees so certain is he that he hears trumpets clarion. But the noon passes without event. The day remains strangely bright, but nothing more transpires.

'It will be hereafter,' he counsels himself. 'The fast will end at midnight when I ring the bell, and then, then . . .' He does not finish. Although there are none listening, he does not want to say aloud the words lest he be guilty of presumption and upset the order of things.

The afternoon is long, the evening longer.

The disciples continue as before. As Papias brings to each a beaker of water, none show sign of even knowing it is the last day.

They sit or kneel in silence. He wants to tell them. His mind flutters with a hundred thoughts, caged birds. It is nearly done, he wants to say, and the day shines brilliant with thanksgiving and God's glory. The hour is near. It is near at last. But Papias can do nothing but pour the water and bow and leave and visit the next.

The sun weakens. He comes inside the final hours and kneels by the Apostle. On the face of John, too, there is no sign of the nearness of the end. He is away in himself and has passed beyond the suffering of time.

Across the darkness, at last, Papias goes. Sky is million-starred, moon-lovely. He goes first to the furthest dwelling, that of Lemuel, and rings the bell. Then he hurries back along the ledge walk, where are Meletios and Simon, and beats the clapper there, then – his excitement making slip his sandals on the rocks – to Danil, Ioseph, and Eli. He cannot move quickly enough. It is as if an instant after the bell sounds the heavens may open, the stars fall away down the sky. His heart races. It will be now. They have done it; they have fasted forty days and nights and are as pure as any of God's creatures walking on the surface of the earth. They are as lights lit. From the highest point in the heavens our Lord could see them shining, and at their centre his beloved disciple.

Come. Come now.

Without word – absence from speech making the muscles of their mouths tight – without the slightest show of victory, through the glittering dark the disciples move. They gather into the cool air of the cave. John reaches out a hand for Papias.

'Help me to stand, Brother.'

Papias takes the thin fingers. The Apostle is bent down, his head low, and at first can raise only his arm above him. It is as if he has prayed himself into the earth, and his knees and torso are as a tree grown into a stone.

He makes a small groan as Papias crouches down to place his left arm around him and ease him into standing.

'Thank you, my brother.'

'I have water here readied.'

'Good. Bring me to it.'

Into the tall water pot Ioseph dips the scoop and empties it into the cupped hands of the Apostle. John washes his face, his hands, and then his feet. The others do likewise. Cleansed so, they come and sit in a circle.

'Let us give thanks,' John says, and when they have, he says the psalm, ' "Behold how good and how pleasant it is for brethren to dwell together in unity." '

The disciples pray together for an hour before coming to share the supper Papias has prepared. They can eat only little, but take of the communion bread and wine. They say almost nothing. None refers to the fast or utters any hope of what may transpire. They have about them a quiet, radiant contentment, but Papias wants more. Twice he leaves the table to go outside and watch the sky.

Now. Surely it will be now.

But moon and stars retain their places in the firmament. The face of night is unchanged. After the communion supper the disciples take the hands of one another in love and thanksgiving and return to their dwellings.

No angels come. No trumpets sound.

But soon after sunrise the following morn the thin figure of Eli comes. He hurries up from the fishers' huts, where he has gone to bargain for salted fish.

'Come. Come, there is news!' he cries out, waving the other disciples to follow him to the cave. 'Good news! Come!'

He is in his sixth decade, but with the short, wiry strength of the Bereans. Papias comes out to meet him.

'What is it? What is it, Eli?'

'Good news. Good news.' He stops, waits for his breath to catch up with him. The others are approaching across the stone-way. John comes out into the full of the sunlight.

'Tell, good brother Eli,' he says calmly.

'I went to bargain for salt fish, and there was a boatman come from the mainland. "O Christian," he said, for he had been told of us. "Good news for Christians." "What news?" I asked him. "You have not heard?" said he. "We hear nothing of the outside world," I told him. "The emperor is dead," he said. "But before his death he did decree that all persecution of Christians should be ceased, and banishment lifted herewith." '

Eli stops, his breath heaves in his thin chest. There is a stunned silence, in the mind of each disciple a great throng of questions pressing forwards. They look to John. A moment. Another. His white hair gleams in the light.

'Praise God,' he says at last.

'Praise God,' they all rejoin.

Then he holds wide his arms, as if he takes to him light or love.

'My brothers,' he says, 'the Lord has spoken. Our work is not over. It is not even begun. Prepare. We leave this island in three days. We sail for Ephesus.'

II

19

They have three days to prepare. In spring light the community is quickened. Age falls off the elders, Papias thinks, and the weakness of after-fast vanishes as if their bodies are things of no consequence. Beneath blue skies the island is no longer a place of banishment, but where they have been steadily preparing their spirits for this, the return. With light step he crosses to the dwelling of Simon, who is caretaker now of the papyri of Prochorus. He brings the message that nothing must be left or forgotten, and is to offer his help. They must bring with them the testaments of their long enduring and belief. Now persecution is at an end. In Papias's mind he understands it as though the world has been cured of an illness. It was not ready before for the Christian message. But time makes all things come to pass, and now, now the glory is near. He moves nimbly up the stones. Perhaps more than the others he feels triumphant joy. He wants to shout out, sing praise into the wide sky. He, after all, has known nothing of true persecution; he has no experience of being despised, spat at, jeered, locked out of the synagogue. He knows the history, but it is not scarred into him as in the elders. He imagines their arrival in Ephesus, the word spreading from the dock as the boat pulls in, the excited crowds that will gather as they walk into the great public square of the State Agora. At last, at last the world will see. Now will commence a time of brotherhood, of charity, hope, of faith. This is what the Apostle meant when he said their work was not even begun. He knew, Papias thinks. He knew with the wisdom of ages that if he waited long enough on this island, eventually the world would turn, the world would at last be ready. And now it is. A time of love is born.

With such rapturous vision, Papias comes inside the dwelling of Simon. He stoops inside the open doorway to see the elder disciple seated on a low stool, his face in his hands.

'Brother Simon.'

The elder raises his head from the mask of his fingers.

'Do not approach!' he calls out.

Papias is startled. 'I am come to help you collect the scriptures of Prochorus,' he says.

'Do not approach further! I command it.' Within the brown umbra the disciple's pale face stares.

'Brother, are you ill?'

'Stay out, Papias.'

'You will feel better if you come into the air. When we come to Ephesus, all will be better. We will have proper dwelling. Real walls,' Papias says, smiling, touching his hand to the mud and stick overhead.

'Stay out!'

'I am only come to help you collect the papyri.'

'It is done. They are all collected. I will leave them by the entrance. You can take them when you sail. I am not coming to Ephesus.'

'We are all going.'

'Not I.'

Simon's eyes are fixed on the faraway. He does not incline his head toward the youth, but considers instead the truth that is before him said aloud in words for the first time.

'But why? Brother Simon, the persecution is lifted, the banishment over. The time of glory for our Lord is here. We go to glory. To Ephesus. To begin the great work. You cannot stay on Patmos.'

'Nonetheless, I shall. I shall remain here and die like Prochorus.' He raises a hand. The sleeve of his robe falls back, and in the half-light Papias can see his hand and arm are bedded with sores. His neck, too, where one side turns, reveals a raised canker black and bubbled.

Involuntarily, Papias brings his hand to his mouth.

Simon nods. 'It is true. I have the plague that killed Prochorus. Though I kept myself from my good friend in all manner when he fell ill. Though I did not allow myself to touch his hand or pray by his side at his deathbed. Though I have lived in poor faith, always fearful for my own health. Nonetheless, I have it. I must remain here. Go and tell the Master.'

Papias does not move.

'Go and tell him.' Simon waves a hand, and now Papias can make out its gnarled form, long incisions where itching has grown intolerable and wounds opened with dark, lumpish gristle. The youth cannot breathe. Fear and guilt stop him.

'Go, Papias. Go with God.'

'We will not let you stay, Simon,' he blurts out. 'In Ephesus there will be healing, there will be cures, food, shelter. You will recover.'

'I will not risk you all by coming with you. It is decided. Go.'

Papias is bewildered. He looks at the bald-headed figure as though he is part of a puzzling dream, a design that does not fit. How can this be? How does this have meaning?

'Go. Be not troubled, young Papias. I am at peace.'

But Papias is troubled. 'We go to Ephesus to begin our great mission,' he says. 'You must be with us.'

'I will remain here. Truly. Only my blessing will go with you.'

'But . . .'

'Good Papias. Go lest you take this plague from me. My prayers are only that those who sat to my sides at communion, Ioseph and Danil, are spared.'

'I will go and tell the Master,' Papias says at last. 'But you will be coming with us. We will not leave you.' He turns out into the day and draws a deep breath. His forehead is beaded. He blinks at the light. Below, the sea glistens. On the foreshore are Ioseph and the Apostle, and at once he takes off to race down toward them, spinning stones from underfoot, hurrying down the curved pathway until he meets the sand soft then hard and calls out into the wind.

Ioseph and John stand, and when Papias arrives to them, he breathlessly gasps, 'Simon is ill. He will not come. He says it is the disease of Prochorus. I saw his sores.'

The sea sighs. The waves collapse and come to their feet.

'Say again,' Ioseph says, 'and slowly.'

And Papias does and Ioseph bows his head and holds it so in silence some moments, as though his spirit absorbs a blow.

'He fears for you and Danil,' Papias says to Ioseph, looking at where John's hand lies on the old disciple's arm for guidance. 'He fears a contagion that would kill us all if he came to Ephesus.'

The three stand on the shore. John does not remove his hand from the elder's arm.

'I will go and reason with him,' Ioseph says at last.

Papias is flush-faced and agitated. 'He will not allow it. He is resolved. And . . .' He presses his lips tightly together. As if to hear the unspoken, John turns his face toward him.

'And?' Ioseph asks.

Papias shakes his head. He will not say before the Apostle. But John says simply, 'Tell.'

'What if it is true? What if he carries the disease? What if it is on his flesh, in his very breath? What if we bring him with us and we come to Ephesus plagued? Though I love Brother Simon and all who are our community . . .'

'Yes, Papias?'

He knows he has spoken rashly. The sign of it is in his cheeks, in the wideness of his eyes. He lowers his head.

'Papias is right,' Ioseph says, 'Simon must stay.' A tall wave unfurls, slowly falling, then he adds, 'And I with him.' His voice is calm. 'I will remain and attend him until the disease passes or takes us both.'

Once Ioseph has said it, all three know it will be so. It falls out as if by natural decree, as if such bonds of love and selflessness are written in air and await only discovery. Ioseph turns to the blind apostle, whom he has known and followed a lifetime. By the sleeve hem of his robe he begins to lift the arm that lays on his and to place it instead on Papias. But John raises both of his hands and leans forwards, reaching till he finds the face of his old friend.

He says nothing. He holds the face in his hands. The wind lifts and lets fall the thin strands of his white hair. Ioseph bows his head. The sea breaks in foam.

When at last Ioseph steps back from the embrace, he bends forward and kisses the sleeve of the Apostle's robe, and, leaving him with Papias, he goes along the shoreline to the stone-way that leads to Simon.

Later, John sits by the cave entrance. Papias attends him. Meletios and Danil have been instructed to gather what things they will not need and bring these to the fisher families on the far shore. They come and go from the cave. What will they need after all? What lies ahead is for each differently imagined. They have lived so long on the island, the greater world has fallen away, first into memory, and then into the shifting domain of dreams. The world they keep with them is the one of childhood. The dust of summer in Judea. The streets of Jerusalem, the shadowed cool by the synagogue, running fleet and barefoot past the merchants' stalls. It is a world from before hearing the Word, before each of their lives were stopped and turned about. In silence and exile on Patmos, almost all had to let go the grief of their days before banishment, the spitting, the name calling, the stones. Each, through dream and prayer and will, had to come to a place of understanding whereby suffering and persecution were part of the Lord's plan, where the ignorance and scorn of the world made it easier to leave it. And leave they had. On the island the world was elsewhere. In the first years of Danil's dreams his narrow jaws ground together until he had a vision of wings sprouting at his ankles and moving him three feet above the ground. He woke and understood they were to live now between heaven and earth, and he lost all resentment of banishment. To Meletios the island took on the form of a great ship pulling away from the shore and sailing on through day and night toward a New Jerusalem always just beyond the horizon. Lemuel, bald-headed and genial, smiled at this. 'The world is light and dark, is day and night rising and falling over us. What need have we of any other world? This place is all places,' he had told Papias. 'Why need we ever leave?'

And so, variously, they had each come to acceptance, and even gratitude. Their prison had become a sanctuary. And now that John has spoken, not all feel, as young Papias, the glory of the return.

Meletios takes a wooden table and Danil stools from the cave across the upper plane of rock. They do not voice dissent, nor even consider it. But yet there is a shadow. What will it be like to leave? The island, bare and harsh in winter, has become a part of them, and the world at Ephesus that now awaits is unknown. Is it perhaps better to remain like Ioseph, even to die there? The Roman lifting of banishment does not mean hatred of them will be gone. Hearts will not have changed, only laws.

They carry the furniture across the island and come down the shale to a crooked hut of stone and boat planking. An old fisherman sits there. They greet him.

'We are, all but two, leaving this island,' Danil says. 'We will leave with you what goods we have in thanks and blessing.'

The old man looks impassively at the gifts.

'There is more. We will bring more,' Meletios tells him, but in the tangled nets of wrinkles the fisherman's eyes do not brighten.

'You can tell all. There will be things of use to be shared,' Meletios continues. Then, uncertain the old man hears them, he raises his voice to call, 'WE GO TO EPHESUS. THE CHRISTIANS GO TO EPHESUS.'

Slightly the fisherman nods, but shows no emotion.

'To Ephesus. We go to Ephesus,' Danil says. He is a short, sturdy figure and his voice is strong.

The old man narrows further his eyes. His mouth is drawn tightly, a downward curve of dismay at all the world. The sunlight silhouettes the disciples before him. He says nothing. What is the price of this bounty? What is asked for all this Christian love? He and other of the fisher families on the island are considered converted, but the old fisherman knows the conversion is a convenience merely, a present tide. Once the Christians leave, their teachings will ebb away, the islanders will remain with only the concern of fish and fire. Who knows what believers may come next? In his mouth the old man turns salt spittle of seaweed. Of his face the sun makes a wrinkled map. He makes no gesture or response to the gift, but studies the two disciples who stand puzzled before him.

Danil looks to Meletios.

'Peace of our Lord Jesus Christ be with you,' Meletios says. He raises a hand in blessing to the fisherman. But the old man remains unmoved. The blessing passes over him. The sun moves behind cloud. He considers a last time these two, sees the torrid future that awaits them in Ephesus, and the very texture of their skin paling with immanent ghosthood.

The disciples turn and walk away. When they are gone, the old fisherman rises and takes the table.

Gather up the fragments that remain, that nothing be lost.

You said.

Gather up the fragments that remain.

The Apostle keeps his word to teach to Papias. When Ioseph leaves, he walks first with the young disciple down the sand in silence. The bright wind blows, the sea tumbles near. This news of Simon must cause him suffering, but Papias sees it not. There is only this calm, this exterior of serene acceptance. He is the manifest of faith, Papias thinks. This *is* faith, this quiet in grief, this coming of knowledge, understanding of divine ordinance. He can learn this from the Master. He can learn to shorten the bridge between suffering and acceptance, to surrender himself, to understand. In the Apostle there must be sorrow. He must have thought to return one day, if not with Matthias and the others, then at least with Prochorus, with Simon, with Ioseph. But now there will be only the few. It must wound him, but he bears it so.

They step into the prints of themselves moving, where an apron of surf melts into sand. Above, seabirds hang like banners on the wind.

'Great work is ahead for us, Papias,' John says at last. His voice is almost without tone. There is no excitement or anticipation, but an even sounding as if the words are stones placed carefully to step a stream. 'In Ephesus we will begin a new time of the Lord. We will bring the Word of the truth.'

'The glory is at hand, Master,' Papias says.

Still they walk. The tide touches their ankles.

'Yes, Papias. But such will not be simple. We will meet with opposition. The world may not be ready.'

The blind apostle stops. He turns towards the youngest of them, in whom lies his greatest hope. He touches the air with his hand. Papias thinks to take it, but thinks better of it. He offers only the sleeved arm. For some moments there is this wordless bridge-way between them, frail transport of love and hope and faith.

'There are others gone before us. You know this, Papias.'

'Yes, Master.'

'There will be many Antichrists who will deny that Jesus is *the* Christ, is *the* Son of the Father.'

'I know.'

'But now, Papias, now it is the last time. And though we will sojourn in a place of mistrust, of jealousy, though we will be despised and by some hated, we will know one another.' His voice has a sudden quiver in it. In his lost eyes there moves perhaps the future. Perhaps in an inner white domain he can witness their coming, see them, the Christians, and how they will be received. His hand holds tightly the other's arm.

'Papias, we will know one another. We will know one another by love. For this is his Word. We will abide in him, that when he shall appear we will have confidence. Remember this. Behold what manner of love the Father hath bestowed on us that we should be called the sons of God: therefore the world knows us not, because it knew him not, Papias.'

The phrase is as a thorn at his eye. The Apostle winces. *Because it knew him not.* Through the deep layering of acceptance sings this oldest of wounds: that the world did not see. It is in him yet, this piercing. The world *knew him not.* And if it had? What history then there might have unfolded? What time of love and forgiveness? What if all had embraced him, allowed that the Father had sent his Son? What world might have been? In his mind John cannot white away the images of the thousands crucified, the roads marked with them, the thin, head-hung figures crying out from crosses in the darkening sky. *Because it knew him not.*

It is the grief of love: that in finding your heart blown open, in seeing the wonder and miracle of another, that this is not perceived by all. The love was not shared. The multitude that followed the signs was turned aside. They spat on him John loved. The wound leaks an old bitterness. The blind man tastes it rise and is quiet.

The seabirds come close to the two still figures, reclaiming their shore.

'We will abide in him,' Papias says. In his voice is a tremor, seeing a first glimpse of what lies ahead.

20

You are coming.
  We go to meet you.
  To prepare the time, for it is near now.
  Truly, you are coming.

What turned before will turn back again. The multitude that was by the shores of the Sea of Galilee. The great number calling out your name that would have taken you and made you their king. When you left them and crossed the sea, they came after by shipping to the temple at Capernaum. They came, though already for healing on the Sabbath the Pharisees had spoken against you.

They came, their number great, their voices loud. We twelve about you in a circle. I, full of pride and love, not knowing they would turn.

I thought: your time is come. I thought: your glory has already begun.

Then said some from Jerusalem: 'Is not this he whom they seek to kill?'

And another: 'Do the rulers know that this is the very Christ?'

And above the murmuring you cried out: 'Ye both know me, and ye know whence I am; and I am not come of myself, but he that sent me is true, whom ye know not. But I know him, for I am from him, and he has sent me.'

And some pushed in the crowd to lay hands upon you, and I and

James and Philip raised our hands to ward them back. But already they had sent officers to take you.

Already there was a turning.

Yet a little while am I with you, and then I go on to him that sent me.

And some said: 'This is the Christ.' But others, 'Can Christ come out of Galilee? Is not this man Jesus son of Joseph the carpenter?'

And the turning was as the sea and we upon it.

In the fall of even we went, the twelve, with you on to the Mount of Olives. But you withdrew further and we sat below and spoke of the unrest. Though the night was still and cool, I did not sleep. I watched where you sat further up on the mount, the stars about.

The early morning we followed you again to the temple, each of us knowing what talk and judgement awaited, what already was said against you. The scribes and the Pharisees brought you the woman taken in adultery, asking if you would break the Law of Moses and not have her stoned. Seeing if they might accuse you.

For now there was hatred and some who sought to kill you.

You judge after the flesh, I judge no man. I am the one who bears witness of myself and the father who sent me.

And they said, 'Where is thy father?'

You neither know me nor my father. Whither I go you cannot come. You are from beneath; I am from above. You are of this world; I am not of this world.

If you continue in my word, then are you my disciples. You shall know the truth, and the truth shall make you free.

And they cried: 'We are Abraham's seed and were never in bondage to any. How shall we be made free?'

The crowd pressing forward, James and I stepping in front of you lest they try to seize you.

Your voice crying out above the clamour. Those who shouted against you, who pushed against us. One who stepped to the pillar and called, 'See, say we not well that this is a Samaritan and hast a devil?'

The jeering. The mockery. The ones who raised their fists, sought in the ground for stones. One standing on the pillar shouting, pointing. And the first stone coming, and the great surge of the people to seize you. Philip striking out against the head of one; James with both hands outstretched pressing back a number. I pulling down one by the pillar, dragging him by his garment to the ground, falling down upon him amidst the sandalled throng, the sea of anger.

The turning.

That now will turn again.

For you are coming. Your time is at hand.

Facing the sea, John sits against the rock wall, his head back. As light into a cave, memories. Detail, words, voice. They come without summons, vivid, startling. The decades since fall away and he is returned to himself as a youth. He can see each place as if standing there again. In a grove of olive trees. On a road not far from the pool of Siloam. Whole days, sights, weathers, things he did not know he knew, or were ever in his mind. So it comes to him that such were not lost in his memory but are *gifts*. Out of the great length of time he has lived, out of the constancy of his enduring, his body has weakened, his mind been betimes unclear. But now he is lit. All is strangely clarified. He hears the words of Jesus spoken a lifetime since and knows that change is here. He hears them as if in his company again. There is a sense of nearness, and of imminence; he sits by the rock wall and suffers illumination with a pulsing joy. His blind eyes flicker as if at sights.

Papias thinks to visit Simon and Ioseph before leaving. He thinks of the contagion that killed Prochorus and now stops the two eldest from joining them. Is it my fault? Is it of the air or the flesh? Is it me? Should I have told Ioseph I would stay in his place? I should. It was cowardly not to. Why did I not speak up?

In the cave he gathers and wraps in cloth a few precious things they are taking: two chalices, scrolls, three oil lamps.

What stopped my tongue? Why am I so weak?

Is it simply that I fear death?

Is my faith that small?

Or is it just that I want fiercely to go to Ephesus? To be there when he comes? To witness?

Is my vanity that great?

Papias sickens his spirit with questioning. He has so anchored inside him the elemental prime desire – to be good – that his failure twists in his stomach like a rag rope, leaking loathing, sour, fetid. Goodness – not the act of it, not an incidence considered and carried out, but a constant way of being – is his goal. Papias considers this an answer to heaven, a cry of gratitude for his creation; we should live in the image. We should be as near angels. Imperfection is in each of us, but this we can strive against until our flaw is so near to healed as to show the glory of living, what we can become. Goodness, to be good. Can a man not be good all the time? If not, then we are greater flawed and thus the Creator lessened.

In Papias imperfection is a grievous failing. It rises from his spirit on to his skin. He finds an itch behind his left shoulder blade; at a site he cannot see he scratches roughly. In the cool of the cave he feels hot. He needs water. He hurries the readying of the things so he can go outside.

The Apostle sits in reverie. The day is bright and blown stiffly.

'If you do not need me to attend you, I will go to the well and fill water bottles for the journey,' Papias blurts.

The old man turns his sky-tilted head, his pale eyes. Perhaps he already knows the other's inner condition. 'Go, Papias,' he says. 'Go with peace to get the water.'

The sea is high, the waves white. There is the rolling turbulence of spring, the restless energy of the world returned. He hastens along the wind-way, the water bottles on their cords knocking. The furious itch does not quiet. He walks, chin-in-elbow, with his right hand over his shoulder scratching, so it seems from behind he is drawn forward one-handed by an otherwise invisible other. He shortens the route by cutting upwards across the rock slope, needs both hands to clamber forwards over a steep incline, then again scratches as he stands upright on the high point. The island is all below him. And for the first time since the Apostle's announcement, Papias realises he may not see it again. He has been here and nowhere else as a Christian. It has become even a place of comfort, because here the community dwelled as one without significant interference from others. For all its harshness Patmos has been home. He knows its contours, its goat paths and water holes. Ahead there is only the unknown. He might have taken more time to consider this, but his face is hot and flushed, a cold tide of sickness in his stomach. He needs water. Even the wind blowing against him as he crosses the high rock cools him not. What if I, too, have the contagion? What if it is in me and I gave it to the others and now bring it with us to Ephesus? What if I pass disease to the Apostle, bring about the death of all of us, the end of Christians?

Thrice he strikes his hand hard against the itch in his back and shouts out against its persistence and intensity. He flails at the itch with his nails. What heats so in my blood? Is there a bite? Vividly he sees a night serpent cross the cave floor to his bed mat, stealth and slither, the head finding access in the low back of his robe.

'There was no snake. This is not a snake. Don't be a fool, Papias,' Papias says aloud. He licks at his dry lips, palms a pasty sweat from his forehead, and suddenly feels pulsing pain where his ear has been bitten. He touches it tenderly, as if its healing is turned backward and the ear grows raw and bloody again. As if what goodness was in him is now overcome. He begins to run.

He runs across the top of the island like one who would take flight if not for the absence of wings. He runs against the wind, his long legs clapping his sandals against the rock. He comes breathless and wild to the water hole. It is a dark cleft. A bucket is left. He throws down the water bottles and falls to his knees. He scratches furiously over his shoulder, then takes the bucket and dips it. He draws it back quickly; it cannot come quickly enough. His eyes are blurred. The thing that eats at his left shoulder ravages away, and his head is so hot he thinks in a moment it will flame. He moans with defeat, clasps the bucket, and brings it full to his face. He pours the water into his mouth so it fills and overflows and washes past him down his throat and chest as he gulps. He empties the bucket on to and into himself, drops it and draws it again. His hands are trembling, his arms; the whole of him pitches in shakes. Papias takes the next and again drinks furiously. He is awash in water, his knees in pool. He opens his mouth a wide chalice and fills it, letting overrun before drinking. He cannot drink enough. The water hole itself he will empty. He wants to be inundated, to have all that is within him sluiced, laved. Again and again he drops the bucket to the water. Again and again, from his position on his knees he pours it into and over him. His face and hair, his chest and torso drip. He pulls back the opening of his robe and then roughly draws it off him. He is naked in the wind. The bucket he fills once more. Once more he gulps, his throat aches under the deluge, but he cares not. He tilts the bucket into him. Is there end to what man can take of water? Papias thinks not. His eyes weep it, his body bucks with the assault, but still his thirst. It will not be slaked.

He is crouched there, dousing, land-drowning, with no relief, drinking near an hour later when a fisher's boy comes and stands watching the strange Christian, the left side of whose back is bloodied with raw wounds, as though seized from above by a claw.

21

A new time begins, Matthias thinks. He steps on to the shore. His eye wound stings, but he displays nothing of the pain. He wears a tight smile of tolerance moving amongst the crowds. I have forgotten the common ignorance of the world. So many without so much as a drop of purity. Bodies only, brute as beasts.

The holy are different as fish from dogs.

A grizzled trader with stink breath approaches. He stops Matthias with a hand, rough-coaxes toward his wares. At once Auster comes forward. 'Do not hand him! Leave off!' he cries. There is brief jostle and commotion. The trader unsnaps dogs of curses, but Matthias stands unmoved, unassailable, smiling his one-eyed smile.

A new time indeed.

At first light on the third day Ioseph hears Lemuel ring the bell. He opens his eyes, pauses before stirring from the bed mat, into his heart a seep of sorrow. They will pray before leaving, he knows. They will pray for safe voyage, and for he and Simon, and that all may be cradled in the hands of God. In the moment before he moves, the loss of the community flows darkly into him. In an hour they will be gone. The greater part of his life he has lived in the company of many like-minded disciples. He has the idea of a shared soul, as though each grows to become part of the whole, and is both one and many. Now there is to be only him and poor Simon. He feels the sundering. What happens when the community is so broken? First the death of Prochorus, the going out of

Matthias and the others, and now this last, each a blow. Ioseph cannot deny the course of grief, the aloneness he feels. The Apostle would have had them stay to attend Simon, but Simon would not have allowed it. He would have drowned himself in the sea rather than risk them. And so now, now there are to remain on the island only two.

Ioseph moves his thin legs stiffly, rises from the rush mat. Simon lies in a shuddering sleep by the wall.

He sees the spreading light of dawn. The sea is calm. He draws slow, full breath, then kneels down on the stones to pray for Simon's health and for the community's safe passage to Ephesus.

After, he comes back inside and prepares a new poultice for Simon's arm. There is a mortar and pestle, herbs and oils. He works in the half-light. When the remedy is prepared, he draws the stool to the other and sits. Simon's eyes startle wide.

'I am sorry to have woke you.'

'In my dreams I heard a bell ringing, Ioseph. Calling me. Is it calling me to death? Am I at death now?'

'Calm yourself, Simon. You are not at death. It was Lemuel ringing the dawn bell. Be at ease, Simon. I have a fresh poultice made.'

'They are going now?'

'Soon.'

Simon sits upright. He is thinning by the hour. Lengths of white hair lie on the sacking of the pillow. His brow, fretted with a lifetime's worry, he palms tenderly like an egg.

'It was ringing in my dream, too,' he says. 'Or I lose my wits, Ioseph. Do I? Did Prochorus go mad? He didn't, did he?'

'Calm, Simon. It is all right. You are fighting the illness. You will defeat it. I will be here with you.'

Simon lowers his eyes. 'You should go,' he says unconvincingly.

'I am not going until you are well.'

'What if I give you the, the, this?' He holds out his arm. The sores worsen. What was red is blackened now and smells putrid.

'Then I will have it with you, and we will cure together.'

'Agh!' Simon turns toward the wall. 'You are losing your wits already,' he says.

'Perhaps.'

'You have a last chance. You should go now. Take the boat.'

'I am staying.'

Simon's eyes burn as he turns back. 'What if this is my punishment? What if I am meant to be left alone here, to die alone? Have you considered? What if it is the Lord's plan? It will not be so easy to care for me. I am not . . . I won't be . . . accepting.'

'I know.'

'I will say things I shouldn't. I may cry out against the Lord, against you. I know myself, I am weak. You must think of the days ahead, Ioseph. When the illness ravages not only my body, but my mind. Ioseph, kind Ioseph, go. Go with my blessing. Take the boat.'

Ioseph's chin rests on the bridge of his hands. He considers the urgent face of his old friend, the prominence of the cheekbones now, the pallor of flesh, the eyes aswim. The first signs of rash are progressing faceward from the left ear. Simon seems to have grown smaller in sleep, frailty making him a thin, ancient boy.

'I am staying,' Ioseph says. 'It is decided. Now be still and I will apply the dressing.'

Simon's chin trembles; he presses his lips tightly. His arm he extends, his head he turns away.

After, wordless, in the dull tranquillity that follows acceptance, they go together outside. Though he needs it not yet, Simon uses a stick of olive wood slightly curved. His head is lowered near his hand-grasp. They come some fifty paces, no further, to a little platform of the rock. Light is risen. Gulls and other birds cross the wind. Side by side the disciples stand and watch below the small remnant of their community progress across the shore to a fishing boat with cream-coloured sail. They watch, unspeaking. Lemuel helps the Apostle to step from the water onboard. Then Papias, Danil, Eli, and Meletios, are by turns hand-pulled up. It is done in moments. Then the fisherman turns the sail and swiftly the boat slaps away into the shallow waves.

They watch it go like a candle flame, bright above the darker water, but with each instant diminishing further into the distance, until at last they can see it no more. Neither man moves. For a long time they watch the nothing that remains of it on the horizon. Then Ioseph sees that Simon's hand shakes badly where it holds the stick, and for support he places his arm under the other disciple and leads him across the silent island to a rock where the sun warms.

The fishing boat cuts quickly into the water. The disciples do not speak. Each carries jumbled burdens of anxiety, uncertainty, caution, of regret as well as hope, but these remain unvoiced. They look to the Apostle, who sits in the prow, his blind head aslant to the sky. Then, each to their fashion, they try and lighten their spirits. Sand-haired Meletios looks back at the island, as if it is part of himself that retreats now. He sees its contour and dimension for the first time and is astonished that it seems so small. How can this have been where such faith was? How can this mound of grey rock have been home to the entire community? It looks no more than a dark fragment, fallen off, adrift from the greater mainland, rocky anchorage of a lesser God. The years they have spent there grow small even as the island does. All that time, the day after day of waking to the dawn bell, the rituals of their faith, the silent enduring through harsh winters, blazing summers, seems in some manner diminished as the boat pulls away. Will none of it matter if in Ephesus they are not received? Will the world be ready for the Word? Meletios holds his hands tightly. The island gone, he lowers his head, and is like Danil and Eli across from him, bowed over a stomach tangle of questions.

Lemuel the bell ringer is not so. He stands by the mast, his face turned upwards in a smile. His eyes shine. In the slap and roll of the sea beneath him he delights. He is remade a boy and opens his mouth with surprise at the strength of the wind, the crack it sounds in the sail. He bounces six steps down the boat following a high wave, and though the others wish he would sit, they don't say. The voyage to him is a wonder. He leans to the side to see the Aegean depth, what fish silver the under-boat, what brown-and-white gleams flash past and sink into sea ink. A wave crashes the old salt timber of the bow, and the splash rises to his face. He cries out and the others look up, but for a moment only. Lemuel laughs. He laughs full-mouthed with head back and hands by his side. Great whoops of joy escape him. His eyes are blue of lapis; he is in his fifth decade but in dripping seaspray is giddied back to an earlier self, awe-filled, juvenate. He cannot sit down. The fisher captain shakes his head. This is the sea-madness of the Aegean, the sometime elation that takes hold of a soul skimming over such blue. Sky and sea alike are *ultra*, are blue beyond blue. The whitecaps of the waves arise like rapture. Lemuel bends across the side, his heels out of his sandals, his head and shoulders out of sight where he reaches to put his hand in the moving tide. He five-fingers the flow, watches the eddy about his white hand. There is such pull, such energy of motion, such elemental force. Lemuel lets his hand get pulled away from him through the water, then tugs back through the wake. What it would be to slip over into the current now, what easeful peace to be carried swiftly away in the blue.

'Lemuel.' Papias places his hand on the bell ringer's back. 'Be careful.'

The other moves back from where he hangs overboard. He looks at the younger disciple and beams.

'It is dangerous, Lemuel.'

'I am filled with joy.'

'God is with us. He brings us out of exile.'

Lemuel smiles. He cannot keep a smile from his round features.

'We might best to sit,' Papias suggests, but Lemuel shakes his head. 'This flowing of the sea, it moves me, Papias. I have forgotten.' He smiles again and turns back to the slap and splash of the side, the fishing boat tilting now in meeting currents, angling over deep into a seam in the sea, then righting as it seals up beneath them. Lemuel stands and rocks, in the slow rhythm of the Aegean not imagining water sprites, sea serpents, or other of the vast population of mer-creatures mythic and storied, but only as it comes to him a memory he does not know he has remembered: in his mother's womb, the sea, and he a sail.

What we are.
    What little we are, we are for you.
    We who have remained and come now as witness.
    In fellowship.

John prays. His prayers take mixed form, both the ancient texts of the psalms, scripture he has known since a child, and short simple phrases addressed to Jesus. He converses as though certain he is heard, though he hears no reply. He says all silently. He sits hunched down in the front of the boat, a small white form with blanket about him. Strands of his hair fly about. Spray saddles his shoulders darkly. The fisher captain offers him sea grass to suck, but he declines. In the blind dark where he is, John is far in contemplation. The physical world is gone. What is prayer and what is thought are not delineated. He has lived so long distant from the measure of time, the reality of the body, that he is as might be imagined a spirit, a portion of light in the corner of a fishing boat.

The sea moves past. Adjudging the spring currents treacherous, the fisher captain sails them northwesterly. They leave behind them the Dodekanisos, the twelve, heading in the direction of the island of Ikaria, where they will pass the first night out of exile. The fisherman has a cousin in Agios Kirykos. The small boat is borne swiftly, a ragged banner of the gulls of Patmos overhead. Other boats cross before them, fisherboys and men eyeing the strange crew of Christians who cast no nets. Lemuel waves to them. Wind flaps and cracks in the sewn sail.

'Are you well, Master?' Papias asks. 'I have water if you thirst.'

The pale face turns upward to the voice. 'Thank you, good Papias; no, I thirst not.'

'We are away from Patmos.'

'Yes.'

'I had forgotten what it feels to move freely.'

Though he has not indicated fear, the Apostle says to him, 'Be not afraid, Papias.'

The youngest disciple sits by John. He drinks the water himself. In the sea he feels still an unslaked thirst.

They sail on in silence, the disciples burdened each by fear and hope alike. Do they come in triumph now? Is this at last the time for salvation, the age of Jesus Christ the Lord and Saviour come now, and they its harbingers? It is long since they have walked in a busy street, had casual converse before a trader's stall, laughed at wit or anecdote, dwelled in the flux of everyday that the ordinary is to be extraordinary for them, and as such holds a fascinating terror. *How shall it be?*

As the boat puts Patmos behind them, with every moment the world draws nearer. Danil looks up at the sail, tight with wind, and wishes the breeze might lessen for a time. Might not the breath of the sky be stilled awhile? Sudden change in sea condition is not unheard of; wind as easily goes as comes. Why not now? Why not a brief respite, and they to be left adrift mid-sea, meandering the blue waters for a time until their hearts were ready? It has been too quick, Danil thinks. Three days to change a lifetime. To turn around to face the world. Would it have been so terrible to have waited a week? Even a month? What is a month to the Lord, who has all time unto eternity?

The wind does not lessen. It sits in the sail like a chest-proud athlete pressing forwards. Hunched against the creaking, salty timber, shut-eyed, Meletios rocks softly to the rise and fall of the southern Aegean. Next to him, Eli knots his fingers, knuckle-bones a rough bridge beneath his chin, and stares at nothing. Lemuel alone looks at the world approach.

In the proximate noon of the day, the bell ringer at last sits and then kneels in the bow, and the others do likewise. As has been their way for years, they pray the twelfth hour, and, bent in the boat travelling the sea waves, are as in the side gallery to an invisible altar.

The blue is unbroken above them.

Seeing them so the fisher captain is moved and steadies the sail. Abashed by the reverence and being witness to the peculiar intimacy, he looks away into the wake. In the trailing white water he sees a silver school of fish. It glitters just below surface, a great wide V, following, fleet, as if pulled in undertow. In all his years of throwing nets he has never seen so great a number. He studies the waters about them, what might betoken this uncaught catch, what manner of thing is happening. But the sea on all sides is as ever and reveals nothing. He takes a step on to some wooden crating for a better view outwards and down. In the full scope of his vision, as far as the furthest ripple they have left in the sea, is this gleaming arrow of fish. It comes in their after-waters catching light, then shadow, then light again. Though the boat moves cross-current toward Ikaria, the fish follow, a silent suite, opaque as souls, profound as mystery. Such might last a moment, might in ordinary fish life be the happenstance of tide and timing, a brief meeting of man and creature in the sea hectic, but this is something other. The fish follow. While the disciples pray, bowed in the boat, the multitudinous school swims after and grows greater until it seems a portion of light itself fallen from above and by means unknown attached to this strange cargo of Christians.

22

They come ashore at Agios Kyrikos. The island of Ikaria is verdant and fertile, and it does not escape the disciples how barren and unforgiving was Patmos by comparison. Here are green arbours, olive groves, many freshwater wells to the single shallow, poor one in Patmos. The disciples step from the boat like innocents, heartened by the loveliness, by the ordinary that seems to them tender and full of marvel, even by the noisy movement of traders by the boat docking.

'What have you got?' a short, sour-faced trader calls to the fisher pilot.

'Travellers from Patmos,' he says, and looks behind to where the fish are no longer to be seen.

'From Patmos? What do they bring? What do you bring?' the trader asks, his head pressed forwards on his neck and his eyes narrowed, as if to scrutinise this puzzle.

'We bring the word of the Lord Jesus Christ,' says Papias with blunt innocence.

The puzzle revealed, the trader pulls back. 'Christians,' he scowls, 'you have nothing so.'

'We have . . .'

'Papias, come,' John interrupts, lifting a hand toward the trader. 'God be with you.'

They move away, staying close together. They wait while the fisher captain visits his wife's cousin, brings the news that she is with child. They walk the unfamiliar way into a street of dwellings that seems to crowd toward the water. Outside dark open doors, men stand conversing in the shade. They stop to watch the strangers.

'God be with all,' John says quietly as he walks on, leaning to Papias's arm, progressing up the street and leaving behind them murmurs and whispers. Word of their arrival slips away into the open doorways of the village like a cat making rounds. When they are passing near the top of the street, a large man of heavy jowls salutes.

'Greetings, strangers. Be most welcome to Ikaria.'

The disciples stop.

'God be with you,' says Lemuel, his blue eyes smiling.

'And with you, strangers,' the man says, and makes a shallow bow, laying forwards his arm in the air and drawing it back as though he rolls out before them an invisible carpet. 'I am Cenon. This is my dwelling. You have travelled from Patmos?'

'We have,' Lemuel answers. 'We are Christians come from exile to bring the word of our Lord Jesus Christ.'

'You must be hungry, Christians? I have food,' Cenon says. He places his hands on the amplitude of his hips and rocks gently in his sandals. 'Come in and eat.'

They are hungry, it is true. Momentarily they stand in the street shadow before the large figure, given pause by the surprise of generosity. Is this how the world is to be? Is this the sign of the coming times when the hungry shall be fed and the weary given rest?

'Come, come inside. The old man looks weary. Come sit in the cool shade and rest yourselves,' Cenon offers, and turns sidelong as though he obscures the attraction of the entrance. He takes two steps towards it, holds out his hand, smiles back at them. His eyes are small as dark beads.

When the Apostle does not speak, Lemuel answers for them. 'We will, with thanks,' he says.

They enter a stone house for the first time in many years. The straightness of the walls, the carpets, the cushions of lambswool, carpentry of table and stools, all such are as marvels. So, too, the sudden quiet. For, inside, they no longer hear the sea.

'Sit, sit, Christians,' Cenon says, and indicates the best places, the scented water bowl where they may wash. The room is dim and smells sweetly. 'I have figs from Thessalia,' he tells them.

When they are seated, there falls a hush in which the disciples feel lost. It is so long since they have sat in the company of others, they have forgotten.

Roundly Cenon chews a fig, offers the bowl. Fat-fingered, he scratches at the brown curls above his ear.

'So tell,' he says. 'You have been in exile on Patmos?'

'We have,' Lemuel answers and beams, as though in telling it now there is only humour.

Cenon nods. 'There is no cruelty like Roman cruelty.' When this brings no response, he says, 'Drink, drink your fill. You must thirst after the voyage. I have berry wine. Old sage, will you drink wine? Here, give this beaker to him.'

'I would drink water,' John says, 'with thanks for your kindness.'

'Water, here, water first. Drink your fill.' He pours it. He stares at the blind apostle. 'You are a great age, O wise one.'

'This is John, the beloved apostle of our Lord Jesus Christ,' Papias says. He has said it before he realises he shouldn't. He has said it before he sees Eli and Danil shake their heads.

'Indeed?' says the large host. 'I am honoured.' He rolls a hand over thrice in front of his chest, as though spreading a fragrance. 'My house is honoured.'

Papias looks down, his face burning.

Cenon presses his great weight forward. 'You were with him in Jerusalem? What wonder! What miracle your own enduring! I have heard from travellers' tales of this great prophet, this Jesus. They say he could make water wine, turn rocks to bread. O mighty prophet indeed!'

'The message of our Lord is love,' Papias says, thinking to recover himself.

'Love, indeed love. Noble message, young traveller. Love, O that we love one another. I am myself a servant of love. Have loved long and wide, am known for love. Ask any. Indeed a noble

166

message. Drink, more berry wine; these olives are without parallel. I offer them in love.' Cenon bows slightly, chin pressing fat folds forward. 'So you were exiled to Patmos?'

'We were.'

'Bare nothing. Verily a rock, nothing more.'

'It was where we held our community,' Meletios says. His soft-spoken manner is suited to kindness, to the sympathy of this stranger.

'Of so few? Did you suffer plague? They say there is pestilence on Patmos? You are all . . .' He does not say 'clean'; he says '. . . well?'

'We are,' Danil replies quickly, the berry wine strong. 'We bring nothing but the good news.'

'A wonder. A marvel. Verily I thank my good fortune in encountering you. Blessings upon us all.' Cenon draws a fig, pulls back its flesh with his top teeth, turns it in his cheek. 'But you, O sage,' he says, swallows, 'you in truth are the marvel. You have been at the right hand of Jesus of Nazareth?'

John does not answer directly. There opens a brief unease, but Cenon is quick to dispel it. 'O a mighty prophet,' he says, 'a most excellent prophet. Here, I have roasted goat meat crusted with herbs. Christians, help yourselves. Be welcome. Be welcome.'

Unfamiliar with charity, the disciples are unsure. They look to one another for consent, for guidance. Hunger turns in the empty bowls of their stomachs.

'We thank you,' Danil says, and goes to where the meat is laid. Eli and Meletios and Lemuel join him. Papias stays by John's side. They hear the commencement of a prayer of thanks.

'Shall I bring you some meat?' Cenon asks. His breath is sweet. 'There is plenty for all.'

'Water is food enough for me, my thanks,' John answers.

'You are a wonder, Ancient one.' The large host considers the others eating his food behind them, then he leans closer still to the old disciple. '*I know*,' he whispers. He looks back; the others have not heard. Papias, although present, is ignored. Cenon brings his mouth to the Apostle's ear, hotly whispers again: 'I know. I have heard of you. I have heard tell there was one, an ageless sage who remained. I have heard he, too, did miracles and wonders. Cured the sick, made whole the infirm.' Cenon turns his tight eyes back to the others. 'There is sweetbread with honey,' he calls. Then he whispers again: 'I know your Jesus made more than water into wine or rocks to bread. What use of wonder are these? I know he made stones to gold and silver, too, and why would he not, being able to? And is this what he taught you, O sage? To Patmos did you bring a wealth, or did the Romans take it from you? It matters not. You have the power still. You come back to make the golden temples to your Lord, and praise be to him. Praise indeed! But for my kindness, for my welcome, something small.' Cenon draws the bowl of olives and places it in the blind apostle's hand. 'Make these to gold, it will suffice.'

The disciples have noticed the intensity of the exchange and have come forwards. They stand close.

John holds the olive bowl a moment only, passes it to the side. The anger in his voice is apparent at once. 'Our Lord Jesus Christ is the Son of God,' he says.

'O indeed, I doubt it not,' Cenon answers quickly. 'The Son, the greatest of the prophets, a spirit of almighty powers! Hail to him! I am a believer like you, like all of you. And ask only a little reward.'

John stands, Papias with him. 'Blessed are they who give and seek nothing.'

Cenon blocks their way. 'A bowlful of olives. No more. Just this,' he asks. 'So that I might spread the word of your master,' he says to the disciples.

But already they are moving to the entranceway.

'Stop, stop, reward a believer!' Cenon calls, and when it is clear they will not, he puts down the olives and cries out, 'You have eaten my food! You have taken my generosity! And given nothing!'

The disciples come out into the sunlight with the fat host hurrying behind them. At the rear, Meletios stops. 'We have no coins,' he says. 'We give you our thanks, we have some seeds.' He offers a handful. Cenon slaps them into the air.

'Seeds for wine! Seeds for meat! You are robbers all of you! Christians are thieves and beggars as they say of you!'

The disciples move away. They do not look back. Behind them Cenon roars and curses. He picks from the ground stones of hand size and throws these after them; his aim poor, they land short and thud into the hardened dust of the street. But a boy, watching, serious and intelligent, lifts a smaller stone and offers it. 'Fire it! Go on! Fire it! Thieves and beggars!' Cenon cries. Briefly the boy stands, perplexed with the licence to wound, then he flings the stone overarm. It whizzes through the air and catches Danil in the back of his head.

'Good boy. Good boy, another. Another for a sweet fig!' the fat trader calls. But the boy, studying the ground for another stone of just such weight and size, allows the disciples to escape down the street.

They hasten down the shaded side of the crooked line of dwellings. Some have come outside to see the commotion and watch without comment this elderly caravan of men pass. A woman cradles a basket in her arm, considers Papias, whose bitten ear sings redly. With the old apostle on his arm, he looks away from her. They cannot move quickly enough. Danil leads, then comes Papias guiding John, with Eli, Meletios, and Lemuel behind.

The Apostle's gait is uneven and uncertain. The stones of the street catch his toes; he stumbles and sways and is borne upright on the strong arm of the youth. This is a new dark. In the years John spent on Patmos – first seeing, then blind – the geography of the island he took inside himself. He knew how each path ascended from the sea, which rock-way crossed to the altar stone and which to the well. Each crag and slope, each fissure, terrace, and fall of ground, he knew as one might come to know as an intimate the features of a prison. The island became to him an inner as well as outer place, in time first familiar and then even – though it went unsaid – in some manner, comfortable. To leave it was a considerable challenge to all, but to him whose blindness had become lessened with acquaintance it was an arduous decision.

So he finds the way troublesome. John has never set foot before on Ikaria. He has no sense of the street, its upwards slope, its crooked turnings. He does not know where they take him, nor what figures watch from doorways. Dimmest blurrings of light he catches if he turns his face full to the heavens, as though the blue above is thickly veiled. He knows the earth and the sky, but little more. He is made breathless with their flight out of the village.

'None are behind us,' Danil says. 'We can stop.'

'Here, rest here, these rocks.'

John's right hand reaches down, Papias guides it to the rock.

When they are sat there none speak. They are like ones that bear the pieces of a broken vase.

It is the afternoon of the day. Behind them the land greens with April. Olive trees are in bud. The sea air is softer than on Patmos, and the springtime of the year is everywhere. But the disciples are spirit-wounded and sit slumped in recovery. In each is the need to reassemble the idea of the world they go to meet. It is an old story, the misunderstanding, then the hatred and the persecution. And though their experience thus far is of only one, this fat trader Cenon, it has echoes in a hundred memories. Silently they chastise themselves for the simplicity of their hope, and then must rebuild it stronger. They must believe in a new world. They must believe in it strongly so to accept that the last vestiges of the old one, the age of intolerance and hatred, are still present, but that it is also about to end, and that they return not only as heralds, but as architects of the time of love and forgiveness.

It is an onerous and intricate spirit-labour. They sit in silence. Some pray. An hour falls past them, another.

In the changing light, a thin figure approaches. Papias gets quickly to his feet. The others stir. The figure comes the dry dusty road very slowly. He is in the sunset and they see only the silhouette. Soonest to defend them, Danil rises and stands before the Apostle. They are old men for fighting now but if needs be will give their lives for John. The figure stops. Only now has he seen them by the side of the road. There is a moment of delay, a brief interlude in which the figure must consider their number and strength, and then he comes forwards.

Where the road turns him out of line of the sun, he is shown as himself. Papias knows him at once.

'It is the boy from the village,' he says, 'the boy who threw the stones.'

He is sallow-faced, a thin, wide-browed youth with intense eyes. He comes to within ten feet of them and stops. He looks with cool regard, as if they are species beyond catalogue in his experience.

'For what have you come, boy?' asks Danil.

The boy turns. Only then does Danil see the stone in his right fist held loosely down by his side. The boy does not answer directly. It may be he is himself trying to answer, *For what have I come?* What reason underlies the reason?

'For what have you come?' Danil asks him again.

The boy studies his questioner closely. He seems so intent on the disciple's face that it is as if he expects understanding to be found there. There is further delay, time fragmented, the boy still and profoundly serious. For what has he come? He holds the stone tightly. They are near about him. Is he the emissary of hate? Does he come to win praise by wounding them, these old men and one youth? Is this his reason?

Papias steps forward, puts his hand on the boy's shoulder, who turns to face him.

'You are forgiven,' he says. 'We bear you no ill.'

'Truly,' says the short, stout figure of Danil.

The stone slips to the ground. The boy opens his mouth and makes a guttural noise from below his broken tongue. It is expression in no language, a low choke sound the mute boy

171

can make. He stands amongst them, reading their lips, and coming to a first understanding of the question Danil asked.

'Go, go with our blessing,' Meletios says to him.

'Go with the blessing of our Lord and Saviour,' Papias urges, and pats the boy's shoulder.

He turns away from them and walks back a small distance. He stops and sits by the roadside.

He remains as the evening comes. He is there as the disciples realise they will not sail from Ikaria that day and must make bedding beneath the spring stars. He is there as they pray together before nightfall.

The Apostle tells them, 'Jesus said, "Verily, verily, I am the door of the sheep. I am the door, by me if any man enter in he shall be saved, and shall go in and out, and shall find pasture."'

He pauses, tracing back through a vast terrain to find the place and time again. Then he says, 'Jesus said, "I am the good shepherd; the good shepherd giveth his life for the sheep. But he that is a hireling, and not the shepherd, whose own the sheep are not, seeth the wolf coming and leaveth the sheep and fleeth, and the wolf catcheth them and scattereth the sheep. The hireling fleeth because he is a hireling, and careth not for the sheep. I am the good shepherd and know my sheep, and am known of mine."'

Again he pauses. The disciples wait, uncertain if he will continue. Darkness is fallen.

Sorrow rises in John's throat. He touches his lips together where a tremble moves in them. He swallows loss and the suffering of love. It would be easier not to recall. Knowing the outcome, knowing the end of Jesus's days with him, it would be easier if afterwards his mind had been taken, if in his great age he had forgotten all. But he remembers. A light shines inside him. He raises again his voice:

'"And other sheep I have which are not of this fold," Jesus said. "Them also I must bring, and they shall hear my voice, and there shall be one fold and one shepherd."'

The disciples nod. They think of what lies ahead in Ephesus, of the other sheep that are not of this fold. By the words, by the enduring presence of the old apostle, they are consoled. They barely hear the whisper on which he finishes: ' "Therefore doth my Father love me, because I lay down my life, that I might take it again." '

He lowers his head. He hears the words as if spoken for the first time. Rising around them is the memory of after and those turning against Jesus, of fierce debate and anger and accusation from the Pharisees.

John remembers. He remembers Jesus slipping away before they would stone him, and he a youth following, protective, moving to the street and hastening from there by the side of Jesus until they were again beyond Jordan and into the place where John the Baptist had begun. A return to the beginning, he remembers. And the time that they abode there when peace was, and when John wished they might have stayed living in tranquillity with the disciples, out of Judea, in the simplicity of love. The time they were by the river is in memory sunlit and golden. A time out of time. Though he knew then it could not continue, nonetheless he wished it so with all the fervency of his young heart. And they did stay on, and Jesus stayed among them there, until a man came walking with the news from Martha that Lazarus was sick.

Cold night of glittering stars spreads overhead. The disciples untie blankets. From his place nearby, hunkered, holding his knees, the boy watches. Meletios brings him a bedcloth.

In the first wafer of dawn light, when Lemuel rings the bell, the boy is discovered to have come nearer in the night.

When the Apostle gives the day blessing, the boy's head is bowed like the others.

23

The fisher captain finds them in the morning. His eyes swim in the night's drinking. His footing on the ground is uneven, as if the earth is not flat. The tide turns, they must hurry.

They follow him through the village, the mute behind. Papias tells him he must return to his parents, but the boy simply follows a few paces after. Villagers with looks quizzical or mistrustful arrest and stare. A dog yelps, dances in frenzied tailspin barking. At his doorway Cenon scowls, tips a bowl of yellow foulness at their passing.

'May God curse and strike you down for thieves and beggars!' he cries. He looks to the blue sky. 'O God hear my prayer!' Then he sees the stone thrower. 'Boy. Boy, come here! Throw fresh stones. Boy. Idiot boy, come!'

But the boy doesn't. They board the fishing boat as before, the captain making ready the ragged sail. Wind awaits. The mute watches them. Then, as they are leaving, he holds out a hand and Danil pulls him aboard.

Their route takes them north-east. They pass the islands of Thymaina and Fourni to the south, sail the steady waters between Ikaria and Samos. All are silent. Even Lemuel sits and clasps his hands together in thought.

John turns his face to the oncoming wind, as though he sees.
It is coming now. Now we return.
Ephesus. To Ephesus.

He knows where he goes. For he has been there before. In a lifetime since, it was to Ephesus he came with Mary after the crucifixion. To a small, low house with a vaulted doorway, where she might be kept safe. It was as he was instructed, but it was not what he had wished. He was young. In the aftermath he wished he might die. In the shadow of the cross he wanted a sword. He wanted to run against all, flailing a blade, to kill as many as he could. He wanted to be crucified. Nothing other could appease the loss. It did not matter to him then that his discipleship would end at once, that there would be no continuance, no preaching or conversions. He had seen the nails being driven and turned away, biting away his lips to keep from crying out. How could he stand idly by? What was to be gained by living? He had stood at the foot of the cross in the wild lamentations. He could not look up at the body with the downfallen head, the glisten of sweat and blood in the thunderous dark. The cries were all about him. Murmurings and jeers, whispers, pointing. He wanted to shout to them all, to say, *Look, look what you have done*, that here was love itself nailed and dying before them. How could he not cry out?

Then, knowing his grief, Mary had turned her head towards him. She did not speak. In her was a calm like a white robe folded. From the cross Jesus said, 'Woman, behold thy son.' And to John, 'Behold thy mother.' And the youth he was knew his last instruction was to care for her, and he did not think yet there was another meaning coming after and into his care would be an entire community, a Church.

It was a lifetime ago. It was the day he most wanted to be dead. To be with the Lord, not to live and care for his mother. But he obeyed and remained.

They had stolen away from Jerusalem weeks later, after the third time the risen Jesus had shown himself, leaving the city by night with a single ass and going northwards as if following a star, though in the sky none shone. They moved like lepers under darkness, wore coverings of thick blanket over their heads, spoke to no other, their route at first not direct nor expedient but the staggered meander of a small creature stunned under a blow.

Ephesus. They had come to Ephesus to seek asylum, to be unknown in the crowded city, where believers were varied and many. When they entered the low stone building at the end of their journey, they sat in the darkness without words. Neither peace nor rest was there, only an exhausted quiescence. In the stillness of after-travel, grief caught up to them and came with its paring knife. They suffered it without complaint, each in the unimaginable torment of having lost the company of Jesus.

Ephesus. John remembers. He was there before the beginning of his great travels. He knows it is there he must return.

Bent forwards in the boat, Papias's back stings. The mainland of Asia Minor is before them. The disciples watch the coastline with volatile mix of hope and apprehension. Glory awaits, Papias thinks. We are almost here. The scabs in his back sting, but he does not itch them. Tremors of excitement move in his blood. It will be now. Now the work will be done. The way will be prepared for the Lord once more. And though I am unworthy.

He stops. He sees the shoal of fish in their wake. He takes from it instant meaning, and his spirit is further stretched and in joy flaps like a sheet held at each end. He dips a hand in the swift sea. Then he notices that the mute boy is looking directly at him and has seen the fish following, too. Papias smiles. The smiles keep rising like bubbles off the floor of his belief. He cannot keep them from his lips. He lowers his head when he fears he might burst one in laughter, then smiles at the boat bottom at his feet, the small slop of saltwater in which sit his sandals. Sunlight plays upon their heads, makes liquid dazzle, and their arrival is accordingly imbued. All will be well, Papias thinks. We are in his hands now. Eyes shut, he raises his head to let light flood his face. His smile goes heavenward. Noise of the near shore is within hearing, traders, boys, labouring carts, those in converse whose eyes turn to consider the cargo arriving.

The fishing boat slows, bumps, sounds a rough drag, and sways back and over twice.

Though I am unworthy.

Papias opens his eyes to the great joy that is to begin. He stands as do the others in the tilt and knock of the boat. He holds out to the Apostle his arm and touches it against him so as to ascertain its support.

'We are arrived.'

As the old man reaches out his thin hand, Papias takes the briefest look behind him. But in the murk waters the fish are no longer to be seen.

24

Be with us.
   Be with us even as we come to meet you.

They are on the outskirts of the city only, but already in the commotion and press of commerce. Traders, dealers in fish and fruits, merchant's boys, eye all arrivals for bargains. Sun falls on the Christians as they leave the fisher captain and come on to the mainland in a tight cluster. Even in the flux of travellers who frequent that place, coming from the four-cornered world, it is apparent at once that these are other. They wear a frail hesitancy and cannot keep from looking at all that surrounds them. The ordinary is rendered miraculous, all the loud and untidy activity of human engagement. Cries, calls, laughter; there is such noise, Meletios thinks, turning his head this way and that at each voice. It is truly now that the long silence in which they have lived is apparent. The island has transformed them, among its actions the ablution of the memory of this, the rough animation of man. They have forgotten what it is to move in a crowded street. Some push against them, going elsewhere. Others call overhead the price of a catch, are haggled down, cajoled. A crate of fish is carried past; stacked silver and mouth agape, the fish appear in astonished pose no different to Meletios, Danil, Eli, Lemuel, and Papias.

   The disciples move up away from the sea unsure of exact destination other than to enter the city proper. Danil leads. Behind him the thin, remarkable figure of the Apostle on Papias's arm, the others behind, the mute at the last. They are a ragged parade in clothing and manner, and all but vanish in the throngs.

Nonetheless they are seen. The one who sees them is himself unnoticed. He stands in against a white wall in his white garments. He watches some moments to be certain. He counts their number, then hurries away with the news.

Ephesus, great and ancient, lies at the mouth of the Cayster River. Its coinage as old as any, it has already been a city for twelve hundred years. To here come the merchants from up and down the coast of Asia, from Miletus, Pergamum, Smyrna, and beyond. Here was born Heraclitus, who said from water the soul wins life, then proclaimed that fire was the central element of all the world. Here, too, were born the philosopher Hermodorus, the poet Hipponax, the painter Parrhasius, and these among a full galaxy of artists and artisans, geographers, astrologers, goldsmiths. The city has a history of the gifted, but the arts alone do not account for its greatness. Almost two hundred years ago it was in Ephesus that Mithradates signed the decree ordering all the Romans in Asia to be put to death. One hundred thousand are said to have perished. But in four years Sulla again took control and slaughtered in Ephesus the leaders of the rebellion, returning it to Roman rule. It is territory soaked in blood, but traversed by pilgrims, too. It is here, on the marshy banks of the River Selinus, that Chersiphron built the wonder of the world that is the Temple of Artemis, that which was burnt down and then rebuilt for a hundred and twenty years to the plans of the architect Dinocrates. The route to it is packed hard with the feet of petitioners. It is to the glory of the female, and brings to the goddess bountiful offerings from all parts. It is a city so, suited to the supernatural, its citizens acknowledging the higher world. To many it is considered almost a portal, a place where the gods might hear more easily the myriad of entreaties and respond with favour. Here, too, now decades since, a first Christian community had been established under Apollo, a disciple of John the Baptist, and Paul had come there and for a time worked to establish a new church in Ephesus. He had taught in the schola of the rhetorician Tyrannus before being forced to leave because a goldsmith, Demetrius, preached against him and rose a public outcry. 'Great is Artemis of Ephesus!' the goldsmith cried, because he feared Paul weakened his business in the selling of golden statues and tokens of the goddess. Paul's disciple, Timothy, had remained, and been in time martyred.

John has not been there in fifty years. When he left Ephesus, it was to go to the first council in Jerusalem in the time before his travels. When he left, it was in the belief that the Word was about to be spread in the world entire, that churches would be formed everywhere, that they, the apostles of the Lord, would form them. When he left, he could see.

Now, returned, such history is in his mind. The world is not as he thought it would be. Time and again he must accept the mystery of what is. He must press on, though time seems soft sand beneath his feet. Papias leans to tell him where they are.

'There is a terrace of streets with high frescoes, three stories high,' he says.

'Yes.' John nods.

'A mosaic of Hercules and Acheloos.'

Two small boys run up to them; in chasing each other bump against the old man, who staggers in surprise, turned about in his blindness.

Papias calls out to them. 'Get off, go!'

But John's hand stills him. 'Leave be, Papias,' he says. Then, as if it has come to him only now that he has lived so long in their absence, he says, 'They are children.'

There is in his manner some import, and Papias looks at the blind face. The old apostle's head is half turned to where the boys have run in the street, as if his thought follows them.

'Children,' he says again, as if the word is a key he discovers in his hand.

They continue past the temple to the emperor, where a statue four times his size in life gazes down. Below it is inscribed 'Ruler and God.' The Christians go in the crowds following the natural progression of streets toward the State Agora, a vast public square that opens into the sunlight. Lemuel stops at the edge of it in the busy thoroughfare. Before them are all manner of stalls, tenting, barrels, tables, coloured awnings beneath which sellers ply for trade. Dogs sniff. Cats curious idle and rub against the ankles. There in a line are goldsmiths with coins of various size that bear the image of Artemis. She is everywhere. She can be found on copper, too, for those less able to afford or for minor offerings. There are draperies of spun cloth, wool traders, weavers, a loom being worked and orange and purple threads crossing the air to become a handsome waistband. There are fruit sellers, fortune-tellers, traders in all that might be imagined. No need is unmet.

And to the disciples it is both wonderful and terrifying. For Ephesus seems a place of great significance, it is fit theatre for the new beginning, its excitements, its *life*, pulsing all about them, and yet in it they realise they are as nothing. None pays them attention. If they stand out in the square and call out for followers of our Lord Jesus Christ, who will pause to listen?

How, here, are they to begin?

Standing in the middle of the narrow passageway with stalls on either side, they are jostled, knocked, passed brief quizzical looks. A trader in skins calls out.

'Come, come closer. Good prices, good bargains! Come! Feel the skins, soft.'

His call alerts his neighbour, a fat seller of figs, who extends a palm. 'Here, travellers, good figs. Figs sweet as honey!'

Sensing easy prey, the other traders thereabouts join the clamour. Fish, olives, bread, brooches, votive tokens of gold, the disciples cannot hear one offer for the other. Two hands draw Meletios forward, his kind, long face puzzled; there are three men about the short figure of Danil urging to him the merits of various merchandises. Another holds a slab of herbed cheese to Eli and Lemuel. 'Taste, good flavour.' In the bustle Papias keeps the Apostle close. They are caught in the stream and can go neither

181

forwards nor back. Stench of sweat and oil and endeavour are about them. It is a sensual assault, the world, volume, smells, sights, the pressing of the physical. The disciples are not prepared. Nothing in the life they have led on the island can have readied them. Their heads spin. Bewildered, meek Meletios is across the way at a stall of stuffed olives. Danil has embroidered cloth in his hands. He turns to look back for the others and cannot see them.

'No,' he says. 'No, I do not want it,' and puts the cloth aside, only for the trader to lift another at a lesser price, press it into his hands.

'Feel. Feel it.'

'No!' Danil drops the cloth, and in hot agitation says loudly, 'We are Christians. We have nothing. We do not want your wares.'

'Christians?'

'We are followers of our Lord Jesus Christ, come to bring the Word.'

The trader pulls the cloth back.

'You have nothing?'

'We have the good news of our Lord Almighty.'

The trader spits a yellow-veined globule that lands on Danil's cheek an olive stain. He calls to his rival neighbour, who is urging on Meletios the merits of garlic stuffing. Then he, too, as if stung, pulls the merchandise away, calls something down the stall-way.

Danil and Meletios step backwards, an air of menace descending. Lemuel and Eli are next to them. Of them, Danil is most likely to go forwards and strike, but Lemuel presses his shoulder. They turn quickly to find Papias and the Apostle and the mute boy, still in the middle of the passageway pressed about with sellers and buyers. 'We must go,' Lemuel says, 'we must go, quickly.'

And they do, the tight band of them, turning into a side street where lesser sellers have their stalls, where traders in charms and fortunes sit in doorways and await the misfortunate and the doomed. They bundle past, the pace too quick for John, so he stumbles and is borne on Papias's arm and brought forwards again. Down a street of entire shade they go, until they are beyond all

182

dealers and their merchandise and in the cooler air of that empty place at last make pause.

They have no words. They help the Apostle to take rest on a stone step by a closed doorway then arrange themselves thereabouts in rumpled disquiet.

It is not to be as they had imagined.

They sit without speaking, a broken urn of expectation between them.

25

So they are come.

They are come even as the soothsayer that Auster met foretold. The troubled moon she saw is they very same darkness they bring. Here to our beginning, to the glory of the One, they bring their clouded ignorance. Credulous fools, lamb followers of an old man who follows a younger one who is dead. The doctrine of a ghost. Preachings of vagueness and confusion. Doors, sheep, bread. How do they imagine to have followers? They know nothing of this new world. They are themselves without clarity or understanding. All is mystery, O indeed. Indeed to them it is. They who drink the blood and eat the body of their ghost.

Savage their practice, outlandish their creed, will be the cry.

I know. None knows better than I.

I who before was blind and now see.

They will be despised and jeered and then in their tediousness ignored.

But still.

But still, with the imperfect knowledge of the plebeian, they will darken us. By existing they besmirch the true Divine. In the dim mind of the commonality there will be confusion. There will. In the muddied perception, the Christians, with their preaching of the Light of the World, will seem little different to our truth.

This is the very word of the fortune-teller. The portent: the moon fighting to be free of cloud.

For true light to shine, she must vanquish them.

Verily.

So, they are come.

I will pray. I will pray for strength, that through me the light of the One may blind them into darkness and oblivion.

I will tell Auster to warn Diotrephes they are come. They will seek him out, thinking he a follower.

Let them.

The Apostle and the disciples sit in the shaded street. In silence they compose themselves.

The day well past the noon, Papias asks, 'Whither should we go, Master?' His voice is quiet. In the interim since they left the marketplace he has had to remake his hope. The repaired fracture is frail. 'Should I go and seek for lodging?' he asks.

'We will all go, Papias,' John says.

'But we draw attention to ourselves, perhaps it is better if Papias alone goes,' Danil offers.

'Or I will go with him,' Lemuel says. 'We will find some place and come back for you.'

'It may be safer,' Danil agrees.

Though these two are as old soldiers in the face of unknown opposition, their anxiety is sharp and clear. It is not for themselves they fear, but for the treasure beyond calculation that is the Apostle. Though they do not word it so, all are aware of how vulnerable he is, and so, too, how their community takes its meaning from him. The world is a threat. It is not something any have considered, that in the quotidian will be peril and from it they must shield him.

They exchange looks across him.

'We will all go,' John says, and presses his hands upon his knees to rise. 'The Holy Spirit guides us. Be not afraid.'

He stands amongst them, his demeanour serene, his face upheld as is become his way.

'But in which direction do we go, Master?' Papias asks the blind man.

'We go towards the quarter of the city where I once lived,' John says. 'It is to the south of here not far.'

He takes the first steps as Papias gives him his arm, and they go once more.

It is not long later, walking into the warm sun that fills a broad thoroughfare, that the Apostle tells them they are there or there-abouts.

'Tell me,' he says to Papias, who describes for him then the stone dwellings, their porticoes and groves beyond.

'There is one a little withdrawn?' John asks.

'Yes, Master.'

'A low building facing the rising sun?'

'Yes, Master, I see it.'

'Lead me there.'

Papias does. The others pause at the entranceway while the Apostle is led on. He holds a hand out just before him. His thin fingers waver slightly as though in air he finds traces of himself years before. Here is where he lived once. Here is where Timothy lived after him. Here, too, where he heard Philip had once sojourned before travelling further into Asia. His lips press against each other as he approaches the doorway. There is a minor tremble in his chin.

He has no idea what he will meet, Papias thinks.

John's left hand is light upon his arm, his right extended.

Behind them, waiting, are the others. They watch intently, as if for revelation.

'Here, the door?'

'Yes, Master.'

And the right hand of the old blind man rises, fingers extended flatly, as if for an instant it calls halt to what fear or doubt traffics there or is raised upright to draw down the attention of one looking from above.

It rises and holds, and then thrice the old apostle bangs it on the door.

He stands without display of emotion. Papias looks to him and then at the door itself, bracing himself for rejection.

There is nothing. For a moment they are islanded so, awaiting the arrival of the Holy Spirit.

Then the door opens and one of the dark-haired daughters of Philip is standing there. She is a woman of more than two score years, her father already dead a long time. As she opens the door, around her come running her three children.

Her name is Martha. She knows John, having never met him. She knows him for the resemblance to her father, though Philip was more broad and full-haired. The resemblance is in the expression, in the eyes a light familiar.

'I am John, son of Zebedee, brother of James,' he says.

She brings her hands to her mouth. She has thought them all to be dead. She has thought hatred vanquished them all. At the sight of the Apostle she cannot speak. Her children hold to her robe. She allows for the miracle that is this old man before her to assemble. Then she says, 'Forgive me, come, welcome, welcome all.' She waves a hand to beckon forward the others standing by the entranceway. She tells the children to step back to allow the visitors. Papias bows his head to her. But she cannot yet fully comprehend what is happening and forgets her manner. Truly to her they are like ones from another kingdom, and their reality is at first no other than figures from a dream.

They come inside, a shy, quiet cluster in poor clothing. They appear nervous in the company of a woman.

With an urgent hospitality she tells them to sit. She tells them her name. When the disciples hear that she is the daughter of Philip, there is as a wave of light breaking in each.

'Philip,' John says.

'He is buried in Hierapolis in the province of Euphrates,' Martha tells him. 'My sisters also.'

'But you remained here?' Papias asks.

'With my husband, who died twelvemonth ago.'

She rises and brings them jugs of water. Her children follow her. 'Forgive me my poor welcome. You have had a long journey?'

'From Patmos. We have been living there in banishment and

exile,' Meletios says softly, 'but come now for the glory of the Lord.'

She sits by the Apostle.

'You cannot see,' she says.

'I see all that is,' he replies. 'You have kept the faith of your father.' His hand reaches out. She bows her head and his fingers alight upon her.

The small children watch with large eyes.

Though the house is small, they are welcomed to stay. They eat a supper of salted fish and bread. Martha names her children for them, Philip the eldest, and Mary and Ruth, and to them the mute boy makes faces until they laugh.

'If it please you, tell me of my father,' Martha asks.

And John does. His brow wrinkles momentarily. Whether the act of recall is painful or it is the substance of the memory, briefly his face is knotted. Then he touches his tongue to his pale lips and says, 'When Jesus was passing, he stopped and saw Philip and said, "Follow me."'

He pauses on that cusp of action, in his mind the entire drama brought to this essence, this absolute. Jesus gives no explanation. There is no precursor, no expansion nor reasoning, no rhetoric. The dynamic is in the mystery. Why should Philip follow? Why should he walk out of his life on just those words?

John blinks his blind eyes, as if the sun-bright scene is again before him.

' "Follow me," Jesus said. And Philip did,' he tells.

And Philip did. It is the simplest of tales, the two words themselves potent and revelatory, in gentleness and command both. *Follow me.* John does not have to paint the scene for them to picture it. He does not have to relate the shy and sober character of Philip or tell what forces might have struggled in him on that instant of beckoning. Nor does he need to narrate for Martha the lifetime of consequence that followed, the sacrifice and hardship, first the witnessing and then the wandering, the endless road of bringing the Word that was still, even to his death, a continuing obedience to that first bidding. Of Philip, John tells her, 'He was my brother and I did love him in the truth, and not I only, but all who have known the truth.' He says, 'Little children, listen.' He tells of a day when Philip said to Jesus, 'Lord, show us the Father and it is enough for us.' And that Jesus replied to him, 'He that sees me, sees also the Father.' John leans forward and holds the hands of Martha. 'Philip saw,' he says. 'Philip saw and knew the truth. And knew it thereafter always.'

From Martha's eyes tears flow. Her children are about her. Her son, Philip, touches the tears, streaks them on his own cheeks.

After, the disciples are shown a square room where, under the watch of the children, they lay the thin mats of their bedding close together. For the Apostle they pile the blankets that Martha gives them. Though the sun is gone down, the room is warm from the day's heat. They sit in quiet with their thoughts, humbled by welcome. They are arrived on the threshold of triumph, of themselves as proof of enduring belief, but in the dark hours of night questions worm up to each from the clay floor.

What lies ahead? Danil wonders, turning his thorny knuckles over and back in the cup of his hand. What is it that is to be done? And how?

How in this city do we begin, is the question of Meletios, when everywhere there are believers in a pagan god? What will they say of us? Will they listen? How will I have strength? I am not strong.

Will there be followers? Lemuel asks. If I ring the bell will they come? Will they throw stones?

I miss the island, Eli thinks. Why do I miss the cool air and the sea whispering? How are Simon and Ioseph tonight?

In the summer dark Papias sits holding his knees, his head lowered. The mute boy is already asleep by his side.

In the morning we will go about in the city. But the Master is frail and should not risk the crowds. Do we say who he is that is among us? Do we proclaim him? What then if some turn against us? What if they seek to harm him?

Papias must divert himself from fear. Wounds in his back suddenly itch furiously. Sitting, he rocks slightly, then pats both feet against the floor as if beating a rhythm to make the questions retreat.

We are come out of exile for the glory of the Lord.

We are come out of exile for the glory of the Lord.

We are come out of exile for the glory of the Lord.

The hour is at hand.

26

'They are in the house of Martha,' Auster tells.

'Indeed. How many?'

'Five I saw with the Ancient.'

'Five only?'

'Yes.'

'Papias?'

'He led him on his arm.'

Matthias's dark eye pulses; he presses a palm against it. 'Leave me,' he says.

The footsteps retreat.

So it is, he thinks. In silence the world awaits a battle for souls.

Before daybreak the disciples are all awake. Their sleep, curdled with dream, leaves them uneasy. In separate dark the disciples lie and think of the city they have awoken in. Within it they have no presence as yet; there is no sense of belonging as there was on the island. Rather, there is a feeling of displacement, of being not only in the wrong place but in the wrong time. They feel *alien*. Other. Motionless, awake on their bed mats, they wrestle demons. What they must believe is twofold: first that their actions are designed, that the Apostle is guided by the Lord and that Ephesus is where they are to be, that it is so ordained, and what awaits is what is intended. This belief is not difficult. It is the bedrock, the tried and proven constant in their spirits, made to shine crystalline in the years of exile. The second is what taxes them most, for they must believe in humanity. They must believe in others, that when they go about the city they will find first an audience and then followers. They must put aside the ingrained hurt of previous experience of man, dismiss the jeers, the mockery, the insults, the beatings, stone throwings, all style of assault. It is not that they must wipe free the entire chronicle of grievances, being driven from the synagogue, the bitterness and hatred, but harder still, they must remember and yet still believe. Theirs was a history of contempt and rejection, so now how difficult to wake and believe the world transformed, to believe the very heart of humanity turned around and ready for the message of love. How difficult to forgive absolutely.

They are not fools. They know what they go to meet may not at first be welcoming. If it were, belief would be unnecessary. Instead, as they lie on their bed mats before the sun rises, they must anticipate rough beginnings and be not dismayed. Their faith must be stronger than the evidence, and they must be armed with this, their very souls like shields of tempered metal.

Lemuel rises first, and the others stir at once.

The Apostle, too, has not been sleeping. His head is propped upright against the wall, his face becalmed.

Does he know what is to come? In the boundless dark of his blindness, does he see? Or is his faith such that he abides without seeing or knowing and draws breath after breath in the certitude of love, of being loved, and that moment by moment the divine source draws closer?

In the crowded room they pray.

Then John tells them they will stay in this house a few days only. Danil is to go to seek quarters for them elsewhere in the city. Martha has told that there are others who have kept the faith, but they are not many. Lemuel is sent to bring the news of their return to one such, the house of Gaius. Meletios will go to one Demetrios, Eli to Josiah, and Papias to Diotrophes. They are to go as heralds to the coming time, to announce that they are come out of exile in Patmos and to begin to gather to them the new community of Christians here in Ephesus. They are to prepare the way and bring the news that the time is turned, the Lord comes.

The mute boy watches their discourse. He cannot tell his name and by John is given 'Kester' and made by Papias to understand. The Apostle is moved by his presence among them. He tells Papias to care for him, to teach as best he can the character of their faith.

Papias looks in puzzlement.

'He must know we are Christians by our acts,' John says.

Brilliance of sunlight, untrammelled trust of morning, birds and men crossing the early daytime. Dust of street is unrisen. Leaden bell-tolls; smells of bread. The city partly sleeps. What doorways open reveal but shadows within, figures silent at domestic matters. Streetways near antique as time give one to another, a crooked route. Narrow and damp some, for small light falls. A man pushes a cart of wares, wheel creak continuing in his aftermath. A sullen boy follows.

Above, the sky absolute, a blue more blue by moments. A windless day. A corner and from a stone doorway a white robe is shaken out. A happenstance, its immaculacy seems yet to the disciples an augury. Flag of hope, emblem of spirit at this their beginning. They pass. Soft slip-slap of sandals.

Where four streets meet in a cross they stop; Lemuel indicates their various directions as he has been told. They are to one another more than company. They are part of one another's belonging and purpose and have not been separate. In the street-cross bright daylight beholds them, their wordless pause, their look from one to another, then embrace, then departure.

Emissaries, urgent and grave, they go into the shadows.

The day rises overhead. Man is announced in noise, from inside dwellings a discord of pots, jugs, clanging of metal, movement of wooden stools, tables, voices. Questions called, curses shouted. Into the streets come hastening traders, merchants minor, figures in varied dress, elbowing, inquisitive of all that might betoken business. Some with jewelled fingers, others in robes fringed with dust. They have their places to be; they know the best junctures, in what corners accumulate the most likely buyers. The city is theirs. A stranger is a purse yet unopened. The passageways are soon crowded. Ordinary clamour of humanity sounds, news of cousins, of sickness, of deals struck, fortune found. In the jostle of men, dogs moving. Men of generous proportion and slender spirit kick at them. With olive breath, spice breath, lemon fingers, honey-water wash, they exchange tales of outrageous boastfulness, how their acumen won riches, how the goddess shone down upon them, sent fools with deep pockets, how a mere two golden tokens in offering brought untold recompense. Ephesus is their city, a place blessed, where in return for sacrifice, the gods repay tenfold. In the traders there is this confidence, a practice of commerce they understand, that in the exchange between heavens and earth a tabulated costing exists. It is so: such an action brings such a response. For them, it is only to recognise the beneficence, to see what Artemis has sent them up the river or unloaded on the dock. So the early morning is beaten with haste and anticipation.

The sun burns. It seems to near, to descend, and make rise from below scents warm. Flies find the day come and take to the air. All species of gnat, spider, biting insect, traverse shadow and light in first quest of flesh.

Where Papias and Kester go some such hang in the air, a gauze drapery that falls across their faces. They are swiftly stung, the tiny black creatures virulent. Papias cries out, swats, slaps his forehead, his cheeks. He shuts his eyes where they swarm upon them. He fists into them; when at last the creatures are gone, he blinks into the light and realises that Kester is gone. The street pushes past him. He goes quickly back some way, then returns, hurries into another. He looks in doorways, scans the morning crowds. Panic races his heart, makes sing the bites in his cheeks, the wounded ear. Where is he? Where is he gone? Has he been *taken*? You were to watch over him; he was placed in your care. How can you have lost him? Accusation bubbles in his blood. His back itches wildly. He stands against a wall of rough stone. Beneath his robe the scabbed rash that runs from his left shoulder toward his spine is blossomed purple and craves his nails. Anything sharp will do. The ruined skin is inflamed and must be scratched to bleed. Papias could rub his back then against the wall. He could find relief so. But he doesn't. What pestilence is in him, what makes his skin rupture and blisters to weep, he fears, but he cannot drive it away. His itching is more furious than any; upon his skin, within his skin something crawls. But he will not scratch. Instead, he stands in near the wall, shaking. The craving worsens. Tightly he screws his hands to fists. He will outwait it; it will lessen. He shuts his eyes to make his mind see only the Lord. To see the face and the suffering. His lips move in prayer.

Let it pass, let it pass. If it be thy will, O Lord.

He prays not for healing, only a salve. The healing will come from the soul outwards and is not yet. He knows.

Across his back crawls the creature of his own unworthiness. Strike at me, it seems to say. Strike, scratch, draw nails across me. It is a wild torment. Papias knows he cannot defeat it, that if it scratches it will worsen.

Near the wall, he stands.

Traffic of traders passes, but not Kester. The boy is gone.

An old woman, kerchiefed, with hollow eyes and shadow moustache, watches. This man may be in the throes of bliss, may be an interlocutor, may against the wall be in receipt of an ecstasy divine. In Ephesus she has heard of such. The city draws them. The sacred and its mysteries are the local speciality. She gums sour spittle, watches. The man is white-faced, young, thin as all that have forgotten the body. Will he fall down in writhing as she has heard some do? Will he cry out in tongues? In Ephesus it would be no surprise. She has heard of such displays to bring followers. The outlandish, the extravagant, are the mark of theists now, such practice and manner as the Romans despise. The man barely moves. Sunlight comes down the wall to meet his head. His eyes are shut and his head tilted upward. Might it catch fire now? Might the gods let it burst in flame?

The woman watches. A cat comes to her feet. She loses the man a moment in the laboured passage of a laden cart. When she looks

195

again, he is looking at her. He is righted. Has something happened? What is different? Has she missed the God moment? She kicks at the cat and to escape the man's eyes turns quickly inside.

The fury gone, Papias breathes. But where is Kester? Why has he run off? Did he not understand that they welcomed him? Did he not feel Christian love? Papias can find no comfortable answer. He steps out of the sunlight and continues to the end of the street. A figure of youth and curious intensity, he crosses the city and comes to visit the house of Diotrophes.

There are several buildings, all proportioned in style of wealth. The principal is a large dwelling with white portico, even placement of cypress trees on either side. The sun is hot; Papias will be glad of shade. At the entranceway he is readying what he will say when the door is opened. Before him is a man his own age with flaxen hair and eyes of palest blue.

'I am Papias, disciple of John, come to greet Diotrophes in the name of our Lord Jesus the Christ.'

The man says nothing. He looks at the stranger then turns and leads down a corridor to an anteroom. He raises a hand to indicate Papias should wait, and then is gone.

Here is the beginning, Papias thinks. Here is the first true beginning, the commencement of the gathering of the community. Diotrophes will have followers, he will know of others who have kept the faith and bring them the good news of our coming. They will join with us. How many? Maybe as many as three score. Maybe a hundred. And with those whom the others go to tell, by nightfall we may be a community of . . .

He has not time to calculate the number, for the attendant is returned and gestures him to follow. The room he enters is long and clouded with the burning of frankincense. In its centre standing is a large circle of silver, an empty O. At the top of the room is a raised dais upon which sits a chair of ornate carving. Here sits Diotrophes, a man of sixty years with grey beard and deep eyes pursed in wrinkles. He wears a robe of dark blue and a chain of gold.

Papias goes forward and greets him.

'I am Papias, disciple of John, who is come out of exile on the island of Patmos to bring the good news.'

Diotrophes sits impassive.

'John, son of Zebedee,' Papias says a little louder. The frankincense is stifling. 'John who was the beloved disciple of our Lord Jesus the Christ, who was from the beginning and at the end, who sat at the right hand of our Lord, who . . .' He has to pause for better breath. The air is so thick and sweet.

'We are come to bring the good news. I am to tell you that we rejoice in that you have kept the true faith and the time is now upon us for the coming of the glory.' His lips are dry. Is he not being clear? Is he failing to show the miracle of what is happening? 'It is a great time,' he says. 'We are full of joy.'

'What do you ask of me?'

The voice is cold, drops the words from the raised seat like lesser coins.

'I am sent with the good news,' Papias says falteringly. 'Though we are small in number now, we will soon . . .'

'Again, what do you ask of me?'

The frankincense stings in the nostrils.

'We ask that you will receive us. We seek dwelling that we may go about the city to gather to us the community of faith. You have many buildings.'

'Wherefore should I receive you?'

'Because we are come in the company of the Apostle to bring the good news.'

'The apostle John?'

'Yes, the Beloved.'

'The one called the apostle John is dead.'

'No.'

'He is dead. Another pretends to be him; he you follow.'

Papias blinks. The world shifts out of its focus. Do the walls slide slightly? Does the light buckle? 'It is not true!' he says loudly. 'He lives. It is he. I have lived by his side these years past on Patmos.'

'John is dead. He was killed in Rome, stoned and crucified, years since. This man is another,' Diotrophes replies, his voice unchanged, his manner cool, as though he but tells the hour. 'I have it on good account. You are fools. It is widely reported. Your numbers have diminished as the truth has enfolded. This man tells outrageous falsehood and some believe him. It is the way of the world. Ignorance is everywhere.'

Papias does not know what to say. The man sits before him, his hands upon his knees, his deep eyes slow and spiritless, as though he studies dull wares.

'This John,' Diotrophes says. 'He speaks of Jesus the Galillean?'

'Our Lord Jesus the Christ.'

Diotrophes shakes his head slowly. 'The Christ?'

'The Son of God.'

The phrase makes the elder man respond; he blows a half sneer to the ceiling. 'I have not heard it said outright until now,' he says. 'I had heard it reported but not spoken in my own presence. Jesus the Galillean, the Son of God! I should drive you from my house for blasphemy. You are a fool who has been taken for a fool.' Diotrophes's face warms with anger. His eyes now dark, he points a finger at the other. 'I should spit upon you for speaking such, have you beaten by my servants.' He sighs, looks above him, his nostrils wide as he draws to him the frankincense. 'But Diotrophes must be great of spirit,' he says. 'And is great of spirit. Your hope lies only in your ignorance. That you may be instructed. You are ignorant. John son of Zebedee was a fisherman who followed Jesus a prophet. Nothing more. Jesus was a wise teacher. Nothing more. John claimed for him this. Nothing more. John was killed in Rome by Romans. The rest is lies.'

'Jesus was the Son of God,' Papias says. His voice is quieter than he wants, as if he tells himself.

'Again, the Son of God?' Diotrophes raises his voice. Spittle flecks whitely his beard.

'It is what John believed,' the disciple says, then corrects himself, 'what John *believes*.'

'There is no John, you fool. You know nothing of God. Do not you speak to me of God! Do not utter it! Do not defile my house with your blasphemy. What gives you right to say this man was the Son of God, or that one? Why not my servant Galen? Why not Absalom, why not Ezra, why not my fatted goat, why not my horse? Any one of them no further from the truth. God the One forgive you, for you are ignorant. You are not fit to say his name. Be gone. Go before Diotrophes is removed from Diotrophes and is ruled by anger. Go, tell this John he is false. Tell him to go back to his island. To die with the fools who follow him. Tell him Diotrophes knows God the One, the True. Tell him a new age is come, that his Gallilean Jesus is forgotten and his John with him. The holy are not ignorant fishermen now, not carpenter's sons, but wealthy and important people. Look at my house. Do you see my house? Is this the house of an ignorant follower of your Jesus? Is this not the house of one whom God loves? If God loves me not, why do I prosper? Diotrophes is pre-eminent in God's eye. You tell this. Go. Go tell him this. Be gone from my house.'

Papias does not move. What is happening cannot be happening. It is a dream. It is the infection in his blood speaking. His mind is disordered. He stares up at the bearded man, whose head shakes in scorn. What is he to say? What reply can be make?

Beside him appears the flaxen-haired servant. His audience is over. He is touched on the elbow to be led away. But Diotrophes cannot let go yet of the outrage, and before Papias has reached the doorway, he calls after him, 'Tell him he is discovered a liar and a blasphemer! Tell him if he comes to my door I will have him beaten away! Diotrophes will punish him for God. I will bring the wrath of God upon him. Tell him that!'

Diotrophes puts hand in fist behind his back, walks from the dais and out into a side chamber.

Papias's head spins. His cheeks are aflame. He is like a bird stunned from flight, falling. He cannot see what he passes.

Then he is outside in the street once more, and past the cypress trees and the avenue.

He cannot think what to think. Is he blind or seeing? There is such sudden dark. He leans to a wall to steady himself.

He does not see Auster watching, nor Matthias pass on his way into the house.

27

In the evening they are gathered again. Lemuel has good report of Gaius, who received him well, as did Demetrios, Meletios. Josiah was ill, Eli tells.

'What of Diotrophes?' asks Danil.

Papias looks at the serene face next to him. He is the apostle John, Papias knows he is. But he cannot unhear what Diotrophes said, nor can he break to John the news of hatred.

'Diotrophes, Papias?' Lemuel prompts. 'Did he receive you?'

'No. No, he was elsewhere; his servant told he was away,' he lies. He looks at his hands, sees tiny specks of dead gnats. He has not told John yet that Kester is not returned.

Their host, Martha, brings them wine and bread, her children about her. The disciples, unused to the presence of a woman and of children, sit quiet in humility. But John most easily demonstrates gratitude. He finds in Martha virtues forgotten. Or perhaps it is that in her he traces back to others of the women in his life. Perhaps in her modest manner, in her voice, in the soft sounds of her movements, he is carried back into the century past where was his mother, and Mary and the Magdalen and another Martha, and others, too, such women. Perhaps it is only now, after years on Patmos, that he recognises how greatly he has missed the virtue of woman. He is deeply moved, it is clear.

So, too, by her children. In the day the disciples have been absent, he has become familiar to them, and sometime in their presence reaches his hand out into the air and one or another takes it briefly, and the Apostle's face breaks in smile.

No other dwelling has yet been found. They must burden their host a little longer. Martha tells them they are welcome, though the space is small. At sunrise they pray together, the first frail day of their return over.

The darkness is past. The light is again.

We are in fellowship with you.

We walk in the light now, and have no occasion for stumbling.

In the morning John tells that he will go about in the city. The disciples, having witnessed the crush and noise of crowd, rough traffic of human commerce, are concerned for his safety.

'He will be knocked aside,' Meletios says. 'The numbers are too great. You all saw how the streets are thronged. He should remain here. You must tell him, Papias.'

'I?'

'Yes, you can tell him it is unsafe.'

'He is resolved. I have never known him to turn.'

'Then we must bear him on a litter,' Danil says. 'Or a chair, that he be out of the crowd. Ephesus is not Patmos. And if a number rushed forwards to touch him, even that they might touch one who had touched the Christ, what then might befall? Calamity and grief.'

'You should tell him, Papias, that if he must come, we will bear him above us.'

The Apostle is seated outside the doorway, his face to the morning light. The habits of his life on the island remain with him. His robe has been washed by Martha and all but shines whitely.

'Master?'

'What troubles you, Papias?'

'It is thought the city is too dangerous.'

'I am come not to stay hidden. I go into Ephesus to begin to prepare the way.'

'I have told that you would not remain here. Danil says that we bear you on a litter, or a chair shouldered between us.'

John smiles. 'Go, tell that they must not fear. I will walk. And I will come to no harm.'

Papias has known this would be the answer. He turns to bring the news inside when John says, 'Papias, the boy Kester did not return with you?'

The disciple pauses on the precipice of truth. 'He went away from me in the street,' he says. 'I could not find him after. I thought he would be returned here. But he is not come back.'

The old man nods slightly, says nothing.

They leave the house soon after in small phalanx, Papias and the Apostle at the rear. The day is already hot, the merchants and traders already installed. They come the narrow streets slowly.

Some standing in conversation, or idling in shadow, take notice of the thin figure robed in white, his long wisp hair, his blind eyes. What new sage is this? What soothsayer? Where will he set up? Perhaps he can read fortunes. Look, already he has followers.

The disciples head toward the open square of the State Agora and the basilica. Short, tense, Danil squares his chest, leads at the front. Noise of voices, cries of exchange and barter, of prices, weights, matters mercantile, swells the streets. Goods of all kind are borne to and fro. In his blindness, what must the Apostle think? He is as one bearing a candle flame. What readiness he might have to meet the jostle of the traders is nothing to what he needs next when they are arrived at the square. For here, in clusters tight and disparate, are gathered preachers, mentors, masters and followers, domini of varied belief. Here the trade is creeds, and the stock measured in disciples. Men call out for custom, promise reward, promise the favour of God, promise a place at the right hand. Some, in extravagant dress with red sash, with purple stole, or covering of snakeskin, make high drama, dance steps, drumbeat. All is clamour. All seek the attention of each passerby, make urgent claim of knowledge. Here seem assembled all those who inter-locute between man and God, who have been variously touched by light, by fire, by vision. As the disciples move among them, their sleeves are pulled by youths in day employ to bring listeners.

'Come, come hither, listen to my master. Save your soul.'

'Here, hear the great Athos. Hear the salvation of the world.'

'Do not touch us, let go.' Lemuel spins back to see a youth try to drag the blind apostle to where a number of men stand in brown robes. With two hands Papias knocks the youth forcefully back.

'Stop! Stand back. Do not touch him!'

'Come, come to hear the word of John,' the youth says, and points.

'Of John?' Papias asks, startled.

'Of John, yes, John, come,' the youth nods.

And the Apostle and the disciples move across to stand then in stunned amaze and listen.

'Learn of the water of life,' cries one of the men. 'Unless you be baptised of the water of life you cannot enter to the kingdom of God.'

A man, wizened, gum-shrunk, approaches, upon his cheek a constellation of sores.

'All can be saved and given eternal life in the name of John the Messiah.'

'John was not the Messiah!' Lemuel cries. The crowd stirs about to consider him. But the baptiser is not deterred; he is used to all manner of objection, the goldsmiths have decried him, all and sundry.

'Yes, John was the Messiah. John came from God,' he calls down, 'came from the right hand of God to show the way to heaven. In his ministry here on earth he performed many miracles. Made the blind to see, the lame to walk. Often in the waters of the Jordan came healing, came salvation thanks to John.'

The old man drops to his knees. The crowd that has gathered presses forwards. Some who have been attending less dramatic presentations hurry over for the spectacle. Something may happen. You never know the hour. The sun burns hotly. There is brilliance of white light.

'John was not the Messiah!' Lemuel cries once more. 'John came before. To bear witness. He was sent by God to bear witness to the light that was to come.'

There are murmurs and the crowd presses to see, a swathe of sun-browned faces and dark beards. Is there to be a fight? Which tells the truth? Will they wrestle each other for victory of God?

The disciple is prepared to elbow forwards to further argue, but John says, 'Lemuel, come away.'

The Apostle turns and tells Papias to lead them to a quieter place in the square.

'Come back and find salvation!' the baptiser exhorts.

The disciples in a loosened knot slip back from the crowd. Some shake their heads at them for cowardice or remaining unclean of spirit. Then another has stepped forwards to be baptised and takes all attention.

In the square there are everywhere islands of proclaimers, about them small gatherings that stand and disperse as interest or boredom decide. Here are loud hollerers, ones who beat their chests across with thorned sticks and cry out to the blue sky, here others in heavy chains, so long worn as to have enwreathed the flesh with running calluses, red and purple and yellow. So, too, are small assemblies in attendance to doctrines obscure, prophets from distant lands whose names are unfamiliar but were, too, emissaries of God. There are desert gods, mountain gods, river gods, gods of rain, gods of particular places, particular months, days. Gods who demand sacrifice, payment, service. At one larger gathering there is proclaimed a great god of insects; those who would be his disciples may take inside them the very body and spirit of their god who is come on earth in the low form of beetles, centipedes, such. A man with great wool of hair and whiter-than-white of eye blears about, chants in tongues, then dips his hand into a timber bucket and draws from it the long wriggling body of a horned insect. Fine black antennae twist in the air. 'Take inside you the body and spirit of God!' he cries out, then opens wide his mouth and drops the insect inside. There is chorus of mixed admiration and revulsion both. He chews roundly, shuts his eyes, and intones some manner of prayer.

'Come, partake of the body of God. Eat and be made holy!'

The disciples move on. The crowds flow fickle, this way and that; about their edge, with condemnatory regard, those passing to and from the synagogue. See what happens, they seem to say, when the doors are opened, when anyone can be called God.

The hot sun boils down. The air is crisped. The Christians cross the sunlight to the further end, not far from the stalls of the gold and tinsmiths.

'Here, here is quieter,' Lemuel says.

They look to one another. None has been prepared for this. None has imagined the world so and in their dismay wonder what the Apostle has understood of the scene before them. How will their faith be adequate to the world?

'We should go back,' Meletios says. 'It is too crowded, too dangerous. There is no place for us here.'

'For this we are come,' John says.

His face is composed, his manner unperturbed. What depths of belief are in him cannot be imagined by the others. What sustains him, what remains not only undefeated but even undiminished by human weakness, capriciousness, by time itself, is outside their understanding. How is it he is not dismayed? How is it, with the jabbering range of religions arrayed before them, he believes still in beginning here, now? Who will listen to their quiet Word? The opposition will be outrageous. The odds against them making headway so great that to all but the Apostle it seems a doomed enterprise. Yes, spread the Word, but to those ready to receive it, to those in their own houses, where the disciples will not be troubled by clamour and jeering and ridicule. This is the easier path. Then, too, because of love, because they love the one who has been at the centre of their so long, they would not see him attacked and belittled. Because of love, they urge him once more to go back.

But John is of another mind. His resolve such that neither argument nor age nor force will impede him. The world will not obstruct him from the place he is to come. No pain, no rejection it can offer, will dissuade him, for he believes he has long ago been taken from himself, that the one who should have died many times ages since is not the one who remains. He is become the instrument. And this, in the scope of his understanding, is what love has made of him, what love wants, and to which he has submitted his being entire. For this he is here. To tell of love.

'Be not afraid,' John says to them. 'The Lord is with us.'

He raises his blind eyes to the light. He holds out his hands not far from his body. He begins.

28

Fools of a fool. Of an old fool. Of a blind old fool. In the State Agora, Auster says, preaching to no one. They should have stayed on their island, let their bones whiten on the shore.

This is the time of the Divine. Not a carpenter's son.

The world is more full of fools than wise men know.

My hour approaches.

On the third day of preaching in the square, their audience small and temporary, there comes before the Christians a file of figures in coarse shrouds, their faces smeared with dirt. They are at first no different from others of bizarre practice who cross there. But one among them stops when he hears John say the name of Jesus.

'Jesus was a prophet,' this one calls out.

The few who are gathered turn back to look.

'Jesus was a witness to the Son of God,' the dust-faced says, 'to the great Lazarus, who rose from the dead.'

'Lazarus was raised by Jesus,' Danil shouts. 'It was Jesus, of Galillee, who prayed at the tomb and brought Lazarus back from the dead.'

'Blasphemy! Lazarus sent word to the mind of Jesus that he come and bear witness to his resurrection. Jesus came because he was sent for. To tell the world of the greatness of Lazarus. Pray to Lazarus that ye might all be resurrected!' the Lazarean cries. From the ground he lifts a handful of dust and pushes it to his mouth. 'Dust to dust,' he shouts out, chokes. 'We are dust lest we be resurrected again to new life by Lazarus. Come, follow.'

The man, with dust mouth and dirt face, leads the file like ghosts away, and some, attendant on the Christians, follow.

In ways they have been no different from others trafficking there, but in their aftermath the Apostle is quietened in himself. It is as though a cloak of weariness has been left on his shoulders. It is past the noon. Papias asks him if he will rest on the steps, if he will take water.

'Yes, Papias. I would drink now and gladly.'

He sits into the shade of a porch. The others continue to preach to whomever delays before them.

Lazarus. Because of Lazarus you returned.

We had gone beyond Jordan into the place where John first baptised. And there abode.

And there were many who came and believed in you there.

I thought: we might remain. We might continue here in safety and love.

It was a place of peace. Our needs were simple. We were free of accusers and hatred. Might we not have remained there? The twelve and the others that came. A first community. Might we not have lived thus, sitting between the olive trees to hear your teaching?

To build a church even there, to live in example of love.

Might that not suffice? I thought. That we might live so in your presence.

Then came the figure out of the sunlight.

I saw him first, a shape moving in a wave of heat. He approached steadily across the burnt ground, small dust of haste in his wake. I went to meet him.

'I bring news to Jesus of Nazareth,' he said.

I did not want the news. I confess it. I did not want the world to come and find us. To find you.

'What news?'

'I am to tell Jesus of Nazareth,' he said, and went past me.

I felt the cold of death then. As foreknowledge. I understood submission but did not want to submit. Understood sacrifice but did not want you to be sacrificed. I am a man only. And knew and feared what must come.

When I followed after already, you had risen and walked to make easier his finding you.

'Lord, the one whom you love is sick,' the messenger said. The one who was sick, he told, was Lazarus from Bethany, brother of Mary and Martha. They sent word that you might come, for they believed in you and prayed you might intercede.

You withdrew into a quiet place.

We were left with argument.

'We should not go, it is dangerous,' James said.

'Why can we not remain here?'

'They will take him if he return.'

A chorus of consent then among us.

'How take him when he is the Lord?' the question of Judas.

Two days.

For two days you did not go.

For two days you remained apart and did not eat and did not speak and took but little water.

I sat not far distant. I wanted to tell the messenger return, tell them he cannot come. Tell them it is unsafe and he will be killed for this Lazarus. Tell them we are at peace here, that there will be no more signs and miracles. This time is now for our community of love, here, and we will welcome who will come to us.

There was no need to go. If it was your wish, you could heal Lazarus from afar, I thought, simply by saying it should be so. You could stay and cure both.

From where I sat, I prayed it would be so. I prayed another figure might come out of the sunlight with word Lazarus was healed.

At the dawning of the third day, you shook my shoulder. Had I slept? How had I slept when I wanted so to remain awake?

You woke all the disciples, in the thin light said, 'Let us go again into Judea.'

The protests were quiet but firm. Voices about the mystery. 'Master, they have of late sought to stone you, why should you return?'

'Are there not twelve hours in the day?' you said. 'If any man walks in the day he stumbles not, because he sees the light of this world. But if a man walks in the night he stumbles, because there is no light in him.'

We did not understand of night and light and of what you answered. You said, 'Our friend Lazarus sleeps, but I go that I may wake him out of sleep.'

'But if he sleeps, Lord, he shall be well,' Philip said. 'We need not go.'

In your face a cloud.

'Lazarus is dead,' you told plainly. 'And I am glad for your sakes that I was not there, to the intent ye may believe.' You looked away into the sun rising. What pity was in your eyes. For pity is love.

'Nevertheless, let us go unto him.'

You moved away to make ready.

Thomas said to us who sat in puzzlement and fear, 'Let us also go, that we may die with him.'

A quiet return we had of it. None there were who spoke. The messenger run ahead of us.

The end begun.

And Martha came out the road to meet us. 'Lord, if you had been here, my brother would never have died. Even now I am sure, whatever you ask of God, God will give you.'

'Your brother will rise again,' you told her. 'I am the resurrection and the life, he who believes in me, even if he dies will come to life. And everyone who is alive and believes in me shall never die at all. Do you believe this?'

'Yes, Lord, I believe you are the Christ, the Son of God, come into the world.'

And Martha went and brought Mary, and those who were in the house consoling her followed. And Mary fell at your feet with weeping. 'Lord, if you had been here, my brother would never have died.'

And you were moved with deepest emotions, your spirit troubled.

I never saw such before and was afraid.

You wept.

And those thereabouts said, 'See, how he loved him!' But others, 'He opened the eyes of the blind man, couldn't he have done something to stop this man from dying?'

Even troubled so, even with tears falling, you went then unto the tomb.

And after, some believed because Lazarus was again in life. And others went to the Pharisees, and the chief priests gathered the Sanhedrin to ask, 'What do we? For this man does many miracles. If we let him thus alone, all men will believe in him and the Romans will come and take away both our place and our nation.'

And from that day they planned to put you to death.

We went from there after into the wilderness. And to the city called Ephraim. It was the time near Passover. And many asked if you would come up to Jerusalem for the feast.

The high priests had issued commandment that if any knew where you were, they must show. That they might come and take you.

So there was no more the peace as was before Lazarus.

All was changed. For this I wept. To accept what must be.

The time that was coming. The time was coming when you would be gone.

The end begun.

There is the sound of trumpets. Shrill blasts flourish above the noise of the crowd. And again they sound. Do they come out of the dazzling sunlight, out of the white heat above? Does the sky open its folds to revelation? There flows a wave of murmur then hush as the trumpeting approaches. Three notes, then three more herald arrival. The fanfare makes stop the square entire. It comes not from the sky but the eastern corner, and there is a parting of people then as first a tall insignia is borne forward. It is a symbol O, a great silvered circle on a high pole, carried by one with shaven head and garment of pale blue. Behind him come a pair likewise attired and bareheaded carrying placards aloft on which are written 'The Divine' and 'The One.' Following these are the trumpeters. They blast again, make clear of birds the upper ledges. Into the brilliance of the light, with a manner no different from the approach of a Roman column, come more of these figures, beardless, head erect, in palest blue. Their clothing uniform, their identities are masked at first. They come in file with fixed expression. There are a dozen of them, then more. The crowds part for them as they cut across the square to its centre. The trumpets ring out. Men, women, children push forward to see what is arrived amongst them.

There are further banners, insignia obscure painted in red, then two figures bearing drums. Behind these comes Diotrophes, august, chin-tight, upon his chest a silver O. Then other drummers follow. At what signal is unclear, but now they quicken the beat. Hands flash and the sound thunders. The trumpeters enjoin in a music of urgent annunciation. All the crowds in the square are arrested, all other claims made deaf. Then enters, at last, Matthias.

The blue-robed disciples in front have formed a large O in the square. It is into its centre Matthias now walks. He, too, has shaven head and eyebrows, is moon-faced serene, seems not to see those who press forward to see him. The tempo of the drumbeat quickens to match his ingress, stops to silence when he stands in mid-circle.

It is high theatre, and the crowd responds. From other holy men, teachers, those who were listening move away to catch this instead.

'Children of God,' Matthias shouts, 'bow your heads!'

And as one the entire circle of disciples about him does. Some in the crowd do likewise, momentarily unsure if something blinding is about to descend. Soon enough they are eye-cocked back, peering in at the performance.

'Children of God, bow your heads and give thanks. We are come to bring you the good news. The good news of the One. Who made you. Whose children you are. The One from whom all goodness flows.' Matthias raises his hands skywards, and as the sleeves of the robe fall back, the arms and fingers are whiter than flesh, as if he has reached previously into immaculate light. He calls out, 'O Divine, who has chosen me for thy message, give me power to bring it to these your children!'

He shuts his eyes, lowers his head to his chest, then, as though the power he asks is granted, he raises it quickly and proclaims, 'The Divine One is the Father. We are all his children. This is the message he instructs me to bring to you.' Matthias turns his eyes about him – one blind, one seeing – discovers the Apostle and his disciples not far distant by the steps. 'Do not believe you are sinners. Why should you be called sinners? The children of the Divine are not sinners. Would God make sinners? Would the Creator make imperfect children? If so, then he would not be the One who made heaven and earth, who made all things, and gave to all things a perfect soul. No, heed not those who speak to you of sin. Heed not talk of imperfection. You who hear my word are children of the One and can through following the Father's ways return at death to his side. This he has told me. This is the truth and the way. We are things of light. We are the essence he created. Be not afraid of your own perfection. Your own light. Come and follow us. This way is heaven. The Divine has said. Has come to me even on an island, where I prayed for him to enlighten me, to show me what was truth. He brought me light and power, power to heal, to bring to him the elect, those of his children who will sit at the front rank in heaven.

'Children of God,' Matthias cries, 'we are made for his glory. Come and follow. Heed not those who preach to you of men, of the Baptist, of Lazarus, of Jesus; these are but lesser teachers, prophets, yea even holy men, whose message was misunderstood and is now proclaimed for advantage by the unscrupulous. Follow not them. They are dealers in mistruth. Darkness apt awaits them.'

'You lie!'

The voice of dissent is heard in Matthias's pause for breath.

Papias has left the others and come closer without meaning to. He has been drawn by a potent conflux of anger, fascination, and shame. He knows he should walk away. He knows the Apostle will not wish him to speak out, but the words are from him before he can stop them. Heads in the crowd turn his way.

'Jesus is the Christ, the Messiah, is the Son of God,' he shouts. 'You are Matthias, one of us, who lived among us on the island of Patmos, who believed in our Lord Jesus Christ.'

Matthias's eye finds him, the familiar head between the shoulders of the others.

'Behold one whom I brought back from death!' he cries out. 'Was it not so?' He turns to the circle, wherein now Papias sees Auster, Linus, Baltsaros, Phineas.

Cadmus steps forward. 'I was witness to this miracle,' he says.

'And I,' calls Auster.

'I, too!'

The voices chorus, and the crowd murmurs their approval. 'From death,' one says. 'Verily, a miracle,' another calls.

'You are Papias the Ingrate,' Matthias says, 'who lives in darkness. Who comes to block the way to light. A follower of Jesus, a man who you call God. No man is God. Am I God? No. Are any of you? Who here is man and God? Raise your hand, step forth.'

The crowd cowers, shakes its head.

'Jesus was come from God,' Papias shouts, 'was the Son of God! He came down from heaven.'

'Indeed? Came down how? In a golden chariot? With phalanx of angels? Where came down? In Ephesus? In Rome? In what great city? And God had one son only? Why one only? Why not many? Surely if God could have one son, he could have many, being almighty? Only one son, truly? And God's son, what, was a lowly carpenter? Was not even a good carpenter! Have you God's chairs and tables?'

There is soft laughter. There is mild concord. How outlandish this young objector, Papias the Ingrate, seems. The mind of the crowd like a tide is turned against him.

'No, you twist the words,' Papias shouts.

'It is blasphemy to call Jesus the only Son of God!' Matthias roars out. 'It is outrage against the true Divine! You will be damned to perpetual darkness for it!'

'No, no, you are the . . .'

The hand of Danil grasps Papias back. Further words die in the young disciple's throat. He looks into the face of the other, anguished. But Danil says nothing, only beckons backwards his head. When Papias doesn't move, Danil reaches and draws him by the hand. They move back through the crowd while Matthias speaks on, his voice swollen with triumph. 'Light will come to light, and darkness be expelled,' he calls. 'All who are of light, who would be children of the Divine, come to us. We will show you the way.'

He is speaking still when Papias is returned to the Apostle, who sits on the steps yet. His face betrays no anger, no hurt, but only an impossible calm. He raises his hand for Papias, who gives his arm.

Without discourse from any, they leave, moving into the fly-swarmed shade of a side street, unnoticed, and are as a remnant of a dispersed defeated army, outrageously wounded, retreating.

29

Why did the Apostle not come forth? Why did he not speak out?

Papias turns restlessly on his bed mat. They have moved to a dwelling house belonging to one Levi, a Jew who is drawn to them but will not say so publicly and risk expulsion from the synagogue. There are others of like mind who believe in Jesus but still think themselves Jewish. Proclaiming this, they have been expelled from the temple. Though Levi told Danil they could live in the house for free, he pretends a rent. So they are come there in the night and have each made a quarter of privacy for rush mat and prayer. From years on Patmos they are most comfortable with insularity.

Papias does not sleep. He turns about on the thorns of disappointment in the one he loves. He must reason to himself why the Apostle's actions were right. He must come to an understanding that is still far distant.

I was humiliated. We were disparaged, all, jeered. Why did he let Jesus be jeered? I would have rushed forth and wrestled Matthias to the dust. Are we not to defend our Lord? Would not the Holy Spirit have burned within us if even we few fought against so many? Would he not have seen us to victory?

This meekness he showed. The world is too harsh for it. We win no favours for meekness.

And why why why did the Apostle not speak out? Are we to let the world laugh at us? To be made the fools of such as Matthias?

Matthias did not bring me from death. I was not dead. I was not. He has no power.

We should have done something. There were a hundred, two hundred, more, gathered. It was time to act.

But what is our action?

What are we to do, being so few? Who will follow Jesus when there are so many others? What are we, a small number of the meek?

Unless the Apostle speak out. He is our testament. He is the living miracle, the beloved disciple, who lives on undiminished by time, who remains until our Lord come again. He endures. No sickness takes him. He is proof himself of God's love. No harm will come to him. His faith is a shield. But must it not also be a spear? Must we not go forth and defeat the enemies of Christ?

Why? Why did he not come forth? Why did he let them jeer?

Papias turns about in ropes of moonlight. The more he turns, the more tightly bound.

There is no sleep. He lies on thorns he thinks, and grows hot to fever. His ear stump burns, as if elsewhere Matthias speaks ill of him. Across the bright night sky a flit of bats. All the commotion stilled, all the voices of the city of Ephesus quieted now. What traffic might be is of spirits and thieves only.

Papias reaches over shoulder to scratch at his back. He has done so before he has thought not to. The rash sings. Swiftly his back entire is aflame. He thinks it even worse than previous and in the moonglow opens his garment to see if he can look behind him.

He does not need to. For in the fall of light it is revealed that the angry rash has travelled further and from his left side now crosses in blisters toward his heart.

The Christians find a practice of sorts. In the dwelling house of Levi, Lemuel rings the bell at sunrise. They rise and pray as before, their island now this house, the city about them the sea, in which they go like fishermen. The Apostle leads them in prayer, then after instructs who should travel to which house. Within a short time they have discovered there are, thereabouts in Ephesus, various that are inclined towards Christianity but are not yet believers in all the disciples teach. Some there are who yet attend the synagogue, others who themselves have been expelled from it. There are some of great age who remember a chance encounter years previous with a travelling Apostle, a figure standing in the square, a voice worn rough from preaching and the still eyes of the saintly or mad. They listened a time and walked away. But did not forget. Unknown, embedded, was a splinter of doubt that is the beginning of faith. Though the skin grew over it, it remained yet, and now near the age of death, it rises. In such grey-bearded elders, one foot stepped inside the cool of the tomb, the question of the Christians troubles still. What is the truth of it? What if truly it happened so? If the one that time was lit by God? If my crossing the square that day into his path was not chance? What if tomorrow I die and learn what he spoke was true? Will I see his martyred face again, too late?

On the threshold of death, such elders send word to the house of Levi that they can be visited in the evening time. John agrees. Eli, Danil, Lemuel go by turns to call on various of these.

But not Papias. He the Apostle keeps close to him. In the quiet of the house he sits sometimes and teaches to the young disciple. The summer heat blazes outside, but the stone house is cool. John can begin anywhere. He can, without apparent prompt, commence by saying, 'It was six days before the Passover and Jesus came to Bethany, where Lazarus was, who had been dead.' Or later that same day, 'Jesus went over the Sea of Galilee and a great multitude followed him.' Or at another time, 'There was a marriage in Cana of Galilee.' And in listening, Papias begins to realise that in the mind of the Apostle there is no exact chronology. The events of his life with Jesus are as epiphanies, each so illumined as to dim all around them. So Papias comes to understand that he cannot ask the question *What happened thereafter?* Nor can he ask the many others that rise in his mind. After Lazarus lived again, did he speak to Jesus? And what did he tell of what he had seen in the hereafter? And when did Lazarus die at last? Was he martyred? Did he rise up? Was he chosen? Is each one of us *chosen*? How did

Lazarus seem after his resurrection? What had changed for him? Was the earth itself differently understood?

There are a thousand questions unasked.

Sometimes John speaks of Judas Iscariot. 'He cared not for the poor, but was a thief. He had the bag and bore for himself what was put therein.' And says this as though Papias has asked of him, or carries an opinion that needs correcting.

The young disciple merely listens. In his own mind he tries to order the events. He fits the pieces into a fractured whole. In the telling he notices smallest changes in the timbre of the Apostle's voice, and from these interprets grief and loss and regret and what comes to seem to him the living history of love. For love is measured in hurt here. Love is what has remained, a grieved longing that has outlasted time, that keeps the image of love untarnished, unchanged, as yet in the same youth and beauty, with the same imperishable mystery. When the Apostle speaks the name of Jesus, his face does not change. He retains ever the serene composure that makes the world about him seem an elsewhere. He cannot be known as others. He cannot be Papias's friend or father, but can love him nonetheless. This is the very strangeness the young disciple comes to realise in the days and nights he sits attendant on the Apostle. He moves from thinking *John loved Jesus* to *he* loves *him*. It is not passed.

Then he comes to the realisation: the telling is a way to keep it present.

For four weeks of summer, there is nothing else. The disciples go into the city, Papias stays with John. He lives in the constant teaching. He hears things he has heard before, but now the Apostle is at greater pains to be certain that he has understood the import. For his pupil he tries to clarify, time and again, as if he draws a line in the sand, then smudges it away with his sandal and tries again, as if there is one absolute and true, and endlessly he fails to delineate it exactly.

'He who says he is in the light and hates his brother is in darkness even until now.

'He who loves his brother abides in the light, and there is no occasion of stumbling in him.

'But he who hates his brother is in darkness and walks in darkness, Papias, and knows not whither he goes. You understand?'

'Yes.'

'He knows not whither he goes,' he says, 'because that darkness has blinded his eyes.'

Papias looks at him. The blind face is unchanged. Never once has Papias known him to speak against the loss of his sight. Nor does he seem to here. It is strangely the opposite, as though he is the one who sees.

There are small victories. Danil reports a family of a wealthy trader who has come to believe Jesus is the Christ. Josiah on his deathbed has asked for the unction of the Holy Spirit and Eli has administered to him. With the gentle gladness of his character, Meletios tells that one Tobias wishes to take the Eucharist.

'We will go to him,' John says.

'His house is beyond the city, Master. A far distance.'

'We will leave in the morning.'

The disciples exchange looks of concern. They have come to know more closely the hostility of the city. They wish the day when Matthias appeared had not happened, and that Papias had not drawn attention to them by speaking out. They want no public. It is safer and easier if they go unnoticed, as if they are bearers of a secret faith. They are happier that the Apostle remains in the house, unseen.

'Master, the city is dangerous for you,' Danil says.

'I have no fear, Danil. We will visit good Tobias and share Eucharist with him.'

'Perhaps Meletios and I should go only.'

'Yes, two of us – or three even, say Eli – is sufficient surely?' adds Danil.

The Apostle raises his face to him. It is a face pale and calm, the skin soft with an appearance of thinness almost to translucence.

The eyebrows are faint wisps of white, the eyes still and impossibly distant.

'Why do you fear? Why do you fear the world?' he asks.

'We do not fear it for ourselves, but for you, Master. The city is full of noise and commerce and pagan creeds. There are thieves, rough figures that think nothing to slit a throat and look after for the purse. We fear for you, Master,' Danil says, his thin face furrowed in earnestness.

'Why fear for me,' says John, 'when I have none for myself? I am not come to be killed in Ephesus. My brothers, look not to the world and fear. I know the world. You need not think to hide it from me. I know the time that is and what people are in it. I know all these things, and I say to you, fear not. We will go and visit Tobias and share Eucharist with him.'

They dispute no further. The daybreak following they leave. They bear with them little, but in sacking cloth an antique chalice the Apostle has since before Patmos. Their route follows the archaic processional road leading to the Temple of Artemis through the Magnesian Gate. There are groves on either side. Their footsteps are on the trodden dust of ages where in legion petitioners and worshippers have come. There are some such about them on the road. The sun is rising. Their fellow travellers consider them, this curious collection of quiet men who have not dressed in fine robes to go to beseech the goddess. What chance their prayers? Some, wealthy, borne on litters and flanked by servants, bring golden artefacts for offering, likeness of themselves, coins with brief messages stamped, busts of Artemis herself. They pass the slow-walking Christians with mild scorn, losers in the day race to the Divine. Others there are, figures in poor and ragged finery, who walk the route clutching a single coin or token, their heads low, weighted with desperation. By and large none converse with other pilgrims. All work at a private reckoning, an inner calculus whereby as they approach the portal of the gods each is already measuring how much better their world will be hereafter.

Wordless, the Christians pass on. They pass where others turn for the way to the temple. On the road, one, lame and old, hobbles towards them from the opposite direction. Shortly they come to him. When they are alongside he turns a scowl their way, then blinks quickly some sun-blindness and licks at blistered lips. He calls out.

'Strangers, stop.'

They do.

'Why do you not visit the temple? You walk past.'

'We go elsewhere,' says Danil, and turns to move on.

'The ancient one, I know him,' says the old man. 'Who are you, Ancient?'

'He is our friend,' replies Danil quickly. But John stands.

'I am John, son of Zebedee,' says the Apostle. 'How does thou know me?'

'I know thee. Though I know not how.'

'Why do you go to the temple?'

'Why, to pay homage. To give thanks, to ask for favour.'

'What favour?'

'My leg fails me.'

'How does thou know me?'

'I know thee.'

'Where have you been?'

'In the world. I am old.' The man palms the wrinkles of his brow, sweated dust. He studies the Apostle. 'In Symrna long since, you . . .'

'Tell.'

The man searches in imperfect memory.

'No, I cannot. But I know that I know you.'

'We are believers in our Lord Jesus Christ,' John says. 'The Son of God, who sits at the right hand of the Father. Who will come again soon. Go not into the temple. Go home to thy wife and children.'

'Christians.'

'Yes.'

'As many I saw crucified on these very roads. There, there, even beyond there to the rise.' He points about him.

The Apostle does not turn.

'Even so,' he says, and it seems to the others gathered there that in his blindness he looks not at, but within the other.

The man blinks in puzzlement. 'How do you know of my wife and children?'

'Go in peace,' says John, 'go in the peace of our Lord Jesus Christ, who loves thee.'

'Who loves me? How loves me?'

'Verily he does. And thy wife and thy children, too.'

The man's mouth is fallen open, his brows lowered in bewilderment. He scratches his head for memories. Where was it he saw this one before? Vague clouds of mind he sifts through, tries to find the image. Was it this man he dreamt not three nights since coming to meet him?

The Apostle offers his hand. The man takes it.

Then the Christians pass on, leaving him standing so in the mystery of things, not yet aware that when they are in the distance and merest specks on the road, he will discover the strength returned to his leg, his lameness gone.

30

In the night they return, their spirits lifted. The moon shows through cloud. Tobias has given them good welcome and has professed his faith in Christ. They have shared in the Eucharist and feel each one a cleansed serenity, as if a white linen cloth has been unfolded in their spirits. They come back the starry way into the city.

Is it to be so? Papias wonders. Will it be one by one they win disciples to them? How long is left in the world? How long is there for sinners to repent? For the lost to find the way? The walking makes his rash burn. He lets his elbow chafe against his right side as he goes, but the relief is brief. He walks face-upward a time, looking into the stars for revelation. When the itching worsens, he fights it with prayer, amasses a legion of them, then loses to the sudden darting of a night creature crossing their road.

They come across a low place where the river water seeps out into marshy ground. Hereabouts are snakes. The thought of them, ceaselessly writhing in the soft wet dark, is enough to disband the next column of prayer. How can a man be holy in this world? How can he keep himself to higher things? Lord, help me.

They come, unscathed, through, and are back on the sunbaked ground when the moonlight is swiftly shut away. Cloud darkens all. The stars are taken as if within a fist. The road vanishes.

Meletios cries out, 'What is happening?'

'It is a storm,' Danil shouts. 'It comes quickly.'

'What storm? It was calm a moment since.'

'Master, it darkens to storm,' Papias tells. 'We must take shelter.'

Wind blows at the Apostle where he stands. He raises his face to it, his hair blown awry, his blind eyes flickering. He holds outwards a hand as if touching.

'Come, come, Master,' Papias says, but in looking about can see nothing. Darkness is absolute. It is a storm unlike any – no rain falls, but hills and land are blackness scoured with wind. They cannot see where they might go for cover. All, by instinct and fearful hope, look above and see only the darkened world. The air blows a howl. No bat or bird moves, the sky emptied of all but wind. The disciples can go nowhere. Lemuel takes the hand of Eli; he, Meletios; and so the others, until they are a thin linkage on the bare earth, themselves only as shelter. Fearful of what contagion he carries, Papias does not give his hand to the Apostle, but his robed arm. They stand in the dark, the gusting fierce enough to make quiver the flesh on their bones. It is occasion for faith only. There is nothing in the night to protect them. They are some distance yet from the city on a flat plain. Moon and stars are so obscured as to make their return unimaginable in the darkness above. Light is out and with it quiet. A prayer would go unheard.

They stand, blown about, attendant on what will happen.

Then comes the first shudder.

The earth beneath them moves. In the gale each is unsure if it is he alone who has lost balance. In the dark they shoulder against one another, reach for support. Again the ground shudders, and they fall.

But not the Apostle. He stands with Papias, the earth quaking about them. There is rumble and groan and noise such as a beast might make in grave pain. It comes from within and without both, is uncertainly sourced, as if creation itself aches and buckles and bursts the bounds of its form. Air and ground alike are torn. What cries the disciples make are unheard in the howling. The great shuddering shakes out ribbons of dark in the dark. There is the sound of cracking, as though the world were round like an egg and its shell fissured by the beak of a beast coming to be born.

The disciples are fallen to the ground that opens thereabouts. They cannot see beyond their hands, and the land may
be all fallen away from what they can tell. Perhaps all is already
fallen, all from Judea to Africa to the eastern lands, already
returned to the nothingness from which begun. They themselves may remain the last island, and their time, too, be about
to end. They do not know. They dare not look above for the
arrival of the Almighty, but in the wordless prayer that comes
on the instant of imminent death they pray it may be so.
There may be vast illumination in moments. In moments the
sky may part like a cloth and the angels descend. Have faith.
Hold on.

For first the earth buckles once more. Once more there is a vast
shuddering, a sundering of iron ground with rough exhale of heat.
Those with face in dust feel the urgent, plotless exodus of creatures
from the crust, wild scuttle of hundred- and thousand-footed
insects seeking refuge in the hair, the ears, the crevices of the
human islands. In the darkness all are unseen.

'Be not afraid!' the Apostle cries out. 'Be not afraid!'

But they are nonetheless. What reckoning comes they fear then.
They fear each a private failing that will be illumined in instants.
They have been but men, and have the weaknesses of men. Their
faith and love has been inadequate, and the knowledge is a
scorching along the rims of their souls.

So it is in that time as the earth quakes beneath them.

Do not come yet, is their prayer. Do not come yet.

Down the dark howls the storm. The Apostle's head is upturned.
Papias cowers down, looks up to see the starred white hair, the
outreached hands. How can he not fear it? How can he be certain
of unhurt? Papias holds his arms tightly about himself. He clings to
his sides, as if they, too, might give way. Do I believe well enough?
Do I believe well enough that I am loved? Is it love that comes
now?

He screws tight his eyes, clenches his teeth against fierce
embrace. His head is lowered as if to be split by lightning.

Then, without his knowing, the Apostle steps away from them into the black.

The ground falls from the ground. It is as though the earth is transmuted into water and a great wave rolls through it. In the dark it is a terror dream. Bodies tumble, are rolled forward in the dirt. The disciples cry out in horror. Here are legs, hands clutching at dust. The world is being broken. From below rises the noise of rupture, of resistance and collapse. The wave passed, the ground is stilled a moment. Then earth parts from earth with crack and roar, a formless vocable ripped from beneath creation, a sounded agony as in the surface great lesions appear. An instant and they burst open.

If a beast from below rises, none sees. All fall along the ground. There is a gaping dark. There is a scream above others.

In Ephesus stone topples from stone. Columns sway as if scrolls of papyri. Great porches collapse. From Roman mosaics gods fall.

Matthias stands in his chamber. Auster rushes to him.

'We should go, Master. We should find open ground.'

'Go you. I will stay.'

'The house will fall.'

'Go, I say, go!'

When the other still does not leave, Matthias turns to him in rage. 'You fear. Follow your fear. Run. I stay. I fear nothing.'

'There is fire, Master. The streets shake.'

'Good. Let the world be shaken. Let the world burn, and all within it that do not believe in the One. Let all perish. Let only the pure remain. So the world is cleansed.'

Auster bites at his lip, twists his hands, studies the profile of the other, whose blinded eye is a weal of white.

'Go, come back later if it be his will that you live,' Matthias says, without turning. 'Go!'

The sandals leave, a quick-slap down the steps.

Alone, Matthias attends the plot of revelation in mid-chamber. I will not die.

I will not die.

I will not die, because I am your son.

A creature of form indistinct, Papias scrambles wildly across the ground. The earth has stopped. In the dark he makes out the figure of Danil, then Lemuel.

'Where is he? Where is he? He left me. He walked away when I . . . I had let go of him in fear. I . . . Where is he?'

Lemuel is dirt-blind. He fingers into his eyes roughly, blinks to see what world they are in.

'The Apostle is gone?'

'I didn't realise he . . . It is my fault, he . . .'

'Papias, stop! He is gone?'

'Yes.'

They are on their feet.

'Gone? How gone?' Danil asks. 'What did you see?'

'Nothing. I saw nothing. I was afraid.'

'We were all afraid, Papias. You have no blame,' says Meletios gently.

'Master!' Papias calls. 'Master!'

'Careful! The ground is split. There is a . . .' Danil does not say 'hole'. But as he and the others make out the great fissure that has opened there beside them, all think the same thought.

It cannot be.

Papias feels his insides sicken and gags on vomit. His body buckles. Lemuel grasps his shoulder.

'We will search for him,' he tells.

But still cloud keeps the moon and her stars behind. There is such dark as to blind everything that is beyond the span of a man. The disciples go feelingly in the broken world, calling. They get no response, their search burdened with despair.

Papias cannot keep himself from thinking. What if he is gone? Risen to the heavens and none of us saw or knew. How could he leave us so?

The pain of this question is easier than the one that shadows it:

what if he fell into the opening? What if the ground split here at his feet and he fell within? What if that is what happened?

Then nothing.

Then nothingness is.

Then all is made nothing.

It cannot be.

'Master! Master!' Papias calls. But the dark returns no answer.

They search a small circle, then Lemuel says, 'Beyond we cannot see. We must stop and await the dawn.'

'We cannot stop.'

'It is dangerous, Papias. We may all perish.'

'We must continue looking.'

'We can see nothing.'

'I would rather perish than stop.'

'We must be for one another. If he is gone, we are what remains. We must be of one voice.'

'He is not gone!' Papias cries. 'He has not left us!'

He turns from them and goes into the dark.

'Wait, Papias!' Lemuel says, and when the younger disciple pauses, tells him, 'We will all go. We will hold to each other, be bound like a vine.'

He offers his hand. Papias seems to hesitate in taking it, but does. Each takes the hand of another and they go forth over the ground slowly, calling for the one they have lost.

It is an hour.

Then another. Pink dawn fringes the horizon.

Then they find him. He is fallen between the earth and the world below, his hip and leg twisted, his head bloodied where it struck a rock. He has the stillness of death.

They rush to him. Papias cradles the beloved head.

There is breath. He lives still but is badly injured. He is too weak to speak.

None say a word. Their spirits are too busy with prayer.

With such tenderness as cannot be told, they bear him from the ground.

31

The house of Levi is undamaged. There the disciples return and lay the Apostle on layered bed mats and a goatskin cushion, the property of Levi. John is weak, speaks but little. Sometimes he says the word 'children', and Papias is unsure if he asks for the children of Martha or refers to the disciples. He drifts away in sleep. Martha is sent for and comes with a cousin, Ruth, to attend to him.

The disciples sit in an outer room, mute with shock. The quake, the Apostle's fall, seem redolent with meaning, but none want to translate it. They cannot deny how near John has come to death, and may die still, and how that thought moves all to a precipice. But they do not want to ask why, why such might happen, and why now. They cannot bear what seems to approach. Is it the will of God that John will die? And if it is, who are they to try to divert it? And yet divert it they would. Is the Apostle's work done? Is it to die from a fall in Ephesus that he has lived so long? Where comes Christ? Where is the revelation?

His hands knit, Papias rocks himself slightly back and forth as he prays. Lemuel's head is bowed, Danil's brow a furrowed field.

The women come and go from the Apostle with oils and ointments. He is bathed, his wounds cleaned. He lies three days while the house is filled in every corner with white birds of prayer.

On the fourth day Martha tells that he asks for them.

The disciples come into the room with the abashed timidity of men about an infant. John appears to all a changed figure. Is he more frail, or is it only the frailty of their hope that is more apparent to them now? His thin hair is combed away from his face; his beard runs to his chest.

Papias weeps to see him. He cannot stand a moment but rushes forwards and kneels by the bed and lays his head down by the Apostle's hand. It rises to comfort him.

'Weep not,' John says. 'All is as should be.'

'You are hurt, Master. You fell. I let you leave.'

'Be consoled, Papias.'

But poisons of guilt and loathing choke the disciple's spirit. In the terror of the quake his hands have touched them all; he may have passed disease to each, and death be quickening toward them. Christ must come. Christ must come now or Papias will have killed them all. In spasms the fear and longing bursts from him. He weeps bitterly.

The hand of the Apostle is upon his head.

'Be consoled, Papias.'

John thanks them for their prayers. All wish to ask why he had walked from them, whither was he going? What purpose did he have? Did he go to encounter whom? What? In his blindness did he *see* something they did not? And if not, what did it mean? What meaning was in the earth splitting so? What is the meaning in catastrophe?

The questions remain unasked.

'There must be many hurt,' John says.

'We have not gone outside, Master. We have been worried here.'

Thought flickers in the pale face.

'You must go, all of you. Go and help who needs help. Be of good charity.' His tongue he touches to his lips. 'The God of patience and consolation be with you. Papias rise up. Be not afraid. May you all be like-minded to one another in love according to our Lord Jesus Christ. Go and be the glory of our Lord made manifest. My children, love not in word, neither in tongue, but in deed and in truth. Love, this is the commandment we have. Love. Go, and peace be to thee. Go.'

The Apostle's hand rises in salute and blessing and farewell.

None move away. Briefly they are affixed to the scene. For it is a moment before the world rights itself in their spirits. Is he returned to them then? Is all to be repaired? There is a difference felt but not yet understood. Some change has occurred, but the defining of it is to be left for later. Now they are each, in the core of their souls, *consoled*. It is as if into the solitary space of each spirit has come a companion.

This, companionship, the nature of consolation exactly. And of love.

The city has suffered worst in its poorer quarters. In the outskirts are narrow streets where cheap dwellings crowd. Some have fallen entire, a spillage appalling of stone and bodies. Furnishings, tables, beds, are broken, scattered into the street. Some buildings are one side fallen and gape aghast with strange, naked vulnerability. Now, the fourth day, there are still everywhere cries, wailing. Everywhere there are figures scrabbling at the dirt. The disciples part from one another and go amongst the people. The day is boiled hot, but no sun shines. Rather, an opaque skin covers the sky and makes bleary the air. No wind takes away the scent of death and destruction.

On the threshold stone from which her house has fallen away a woman sits lamenting. Danil goes to her.

In cavernous ruins where fire has taken a family, Lemuel finds two children. Eli and Meletios come to the aid of an aged tinsmith who has lost his wife. Husbands, uncles, cousins, grandmothers, wives, children, all are missing and prayed for. The disciples come amongst those whose hope is snapped like dry bread, who bewail the horror and cannot be spoken to of consolation. Instead, Danil and the others offer their presence. What skills they have are in quietude, and these are plentiful. They sit on the floor of those in mourning, listen to the pain of ones lost in the mystery of suffering. They are its witnesses.

It is practice that Papias finds at first most difficult. He wants to preach God's love. He wants to tell that Christ is coming, that they must just believe. But even he, too, comes to this understanding, that it is a time of silence and action. In one house a trader who has lost his father gives him salted fish for thanks; this Papias brings to another not far distant who starves. A scorched morning when the birds of prey wheel lower a woman rushes from a ruin, clutches at his robe. 'Help me, help me, my daughter.' She pulls him to an inner courtyard of stone and sand and broken timber. 'She lives. I know she lives!' she says. 'I hear her.'

'You hear her?'

'She doesn't stop calling. Listen. You can hear.'

Papias hears nothing. It is days since the quake. None can be living still.

'Help me. Please sir, help.'

Papias looks at her as at a memory. He looks away and throws himself into clawing free the rubble. The sun burns at his back. Beneath his robe he can feel the sores ooze. For an hour, two, he pulls away the collapsed building. He hears no sound of any child, only the woman sobbing prayers to all gods and any gods that will listen. Shreds of cloth, shards of vase, remnants of all manner, he pulls from the dust, then finds large stones that have crossed one another in falling. Beneath he hears a whimper.

'It is her! She lives!' The woman falls prostrate.

Papias runs to the street for help, and then there is a crowd gathered, and with angled poles they pry open the sealed place, and Papias brings forth the living girl.

I thought you came out of the heavens, the earth breaking.

I thought the hour at hand, our waiting over.

What light I saw I went towards. What light was and was the light to ever be now that time was ended.

I thought.

The earth breaking, I fell.

Now do I come to meet you.

I have little breath left in this world.

We prepare the way. Imperfect as we are.

Come, Lord. Come.

In the stillness of the bed where the women attend to him, John remains. He takes but little water. He waits.

Frail and gaunt, he breathes with great gaps between breaths. There are long absences in which Martha fears another breath will not come; then, as if an afterthought, it does. This, the stillness with which he reposes, and his blindness, makes it seem he is elsewhere, or that his spirit comes and goes from his body on airlike wings. When the disciples return each evening, they return with the same face, the same question in their eyes. Martha answers that he is unchanged, and they go to him; he holds out his hands, and they take them and tell of what they have met in the city. They wash and break bread together in the small room and pray thanks.

'Will you teach us, Master?' Papias asks.

'The Master is too weak, he should not,' Danil says.

'Rest yourself, Master,' urges Lemuel. 'There will be time for teaching later, Papias.'

'I am sorry, forgive me.'

But John moves forward to angle himself upright and is assisted then until he is facing them. 'Papias is right. I will teach until the last hour,' he says. 'I will teach of when the Lord knew he was to leave us. When he knew that his hour was come and that he should depart out of this world unto the Father, having loved his own who were in the world, he loved them unto the end.'

He speaks slowly, the words are placed like the timbers of a bridge. He finds each with clear deliberation and tells of the Last Supper. It is plain as he speaks that he speaks toward suffering, that in the telling itself he revisits the very place of which he tells, and is in truth *there*. He is there as Christ moves amongst them to wash their feet, there as Peter objects and Jesus says, 'If I wash thee not, thou hast no part with me,' and Peter answers, 'Lord, not my feet only, but also my hands and my head.' He is there as his own hands are washed, and he looks down at them, his hands in the hands of

Jesus, the water flowing over them and no word spoken. In the telling John is again by Christ's side at the table. And so, too, then, are those who listen.

The voice of the Apostle is quiet, barely more than a whisper. The room is small, and in it the disciples and the two women do not move. Night is fallen outside as it is in the telling when Judas leaves the table and goes out, and John says Jesus told, 'Now is the Son of Man glorified, and God is glorified in him.' John says this so quietly, it seems he might say no more. In the pause is love and loss absolute. In the movement of his throat is swallowed grief. His blind eyes pulse. It is clear to all the spirit pain he encounters, how *near* the telling brings him, and yet, at the end of some phrases, a pause in the account, and his body reminds him how far.

He regains minor strength, tells until he falters again to say, on the edge of the audible, 'Jesus told, "In my Father's house are many mansions; if it were not so, I would have told you. I go to prepare a place for you. And if I go and prepare a place for you, I will come again, and receive you unto myself."'

Again he pauses. His chin trembles. Immensely he struggles to speak. His tongue wets his lower lip.

They should tell him to rest himself, that they will leave him to rest now, but they are afraid of what feeling seems to course through him now. They are afraid this may be the last time. Every utterance is at the point of revelation.

' "And if I go",' John says again, very faintly. ' "And if I go and prepare a place for you, I will come again and receive you unto myself. There where I am, there may you be also."'

He stops. He lets his head rest back.

Silence falls.

The day following, Papias comes to the Apostle before he is to go about in the city. He comes to seek blessing only, but John seems to him stronger than the night before, and he cannot keep himself from asking.

'Master, what you teach . . .'

'Yes, Papias?'

'I would record it in scripture. I have not the hand of Prochorus but would endeavour well. I would make faithful copy.'

'What I teach you teach,' John says. 'You are the scripture living. There is no need.'

'But I am imperfect, Master, and forget and would have it written that . . .'

'There is no need, Papias,' John says with surprising force, then is quieted to say, 'We are in the last time. There are many Antichrists, are there not?'

'There are.'

'So it was written. So we know it is the last time. So we know he comes. We will be living scriptures to the end. It will suffice.'

Papias presses no more. He goes into the city as before. In the aftertime of the earthquake have come into Ephesus the soothsayers, fortune-tellers, dealers in tokens to dispel disaster and bring back the dead. Out of desert, mountain, and plain have come bearded nomads bearing potions, scrolls, effigies, bones, the skulls of creatures slain by lightning, such things. They trade on the fear of survivors. They broadcast fevered interpretations of the gods' displeasure and how favour is to be regained. Crowds flock to them. The city streets fill with flushed faces. Homewards hurry those who have bargained new immunity, while others rush out afraid they are too late. It is a city aswarm with prophets. Some speak in tongues urgent and profound and untranslatable; others quote scriptures of sages un-known, figures from distant lands who scribed the secret mysteries of the world. Fair copies can be purchased at good price, bargains all. Protect yourself with the holy words.

Papias hastens on. He is travelling down a shaded street to call on the mother whose daughter he rescued when a figure steps into his way. He does not recognise Auster at first.

'Papias!' The voice is a hoarse whisper, with shaven head, the face a moon. 'It is I, Auster.' He waits a moment as if to allow the other to consider the glory of himself. 'The One would speak to you.'

'The One?'

'He would speak with you. He sent me to bring you.'

The One? There is a chill in hearing it. 'Go from me,' Papias says. 'Tell him I would not go. Tell him I would not speak with him ever.'

'You will want to speak with him. You will want to come.'

'Go from me. I have urgent business.'

'The woman will wait.'

'What woman? What do you speak?'

'I know. I know all you know and do. I say again, come, follow me, friend.'

'I have nothing to say to Matthias.'

'But he has much to say to you. Come.'

'I will not. Go, be gone from me. You are an Antichrist.'

Auster smiles. 'O how you sting. You are in the dark, friend. I know. I have come from that dark. You live a lie.'

'I do not. I am in the light of Jesus Christ, who comes again. The hour is at hand. Be gone from me.'

Auster is unchanged. He stares from within a studied calm. He says, 'He would speak with you, you must come. You will come. For he will show you proof your life is a lie. He will show you proof because yet you may be saved, and he has decreed it so that you be offered this chance. You he elects. You will come. It will be revealed to you. Friend, he will show you proof that you follow a fool, proof that your John is not John.'

32

They go an unfamiliar route, Auster to the fore, Papias some short distance behind as if he follows not. The journey is not long, but the heat oppressive. At an august building with round doors carved in a single large O, Auster awaits his charge. He smiles to see him come.

'Blessings to you, friend. You will see.' His eyes glitter like nothing in nature. 'Come.'

He opens the door on to air thickly fragranced. In an antechamber Papias waits. He should not have come, he thinks. He should have driven him off as an evil spirit. Should have been deaf to any words the other used. Papias paces this thought until it finds a contrary: he was among us. He was one of us, and for so long believed as us. So, too, may not he believe again? And Matthias, too. May it not be this chance is come for Papias to return them all to the fold? Is this not the mystery of the Lord, how all things fit and find place?

'Now. Come, come and cleanse here,' Auster says.

He leads the way to a font and folded cloths.

'Friend, shall I wash your feet?' he asks, smiles at the refusal.

After, Papias is brought along a hallway where a figure stands with silver bell. He is none the disciple knows, a newer follower.

'I leave you, friend. You will thank me, you will see,' Auster tells softly and retreats.

The bell peals, a bright tingling. The door is opened from within. Papias goes into a broad room unfurnished but for a great standing silver O similar to that he saw in the house of Diotrophes. There is a like couch on a raised platform, a pair of tall urns, long-stemmed white blossoms. There is the scent of frankincense. For some instants Papias is in the room alone. Who opened the door left by it as he entered. It is theatre of high order, the space prepared and allowed its play before the protagonist. Reverence, awe, respect: such are the prizes sought. The great circle of silver is ornately crafted, a masterwork without seam. From where Papias stands, he looks through it to the staged couch, the altar where now Matthias arrives. He wears a robe of palest blue and comes with hands flatly before him, palm-to-palm, as if he bears in miniature a church of one. He steps up, turns, looks down at the disciple through the O. Again an instant, then he looks above him and opens his hands to cup shape, to catch what invisibly falls. This he gathers until filled, and then opens both hands in a gentle gesture of throwing outwards and sharing the bounty he has just received. Matthias bows in after-thanks, opens wide his arms.

'Papias, welcome. May Divine God be with you.'

The disciple has lost his words.

Matthias comes down the side of the altar, his bare feet sound-less. He stands before the visitor, surveys him. 'My heart is warmed. I am glad you have come,' he says.

'I did not want to come.'

'Nonetheless I am glad. Come and sit.' Matthias gestures a hand to his right. All in his manner is practised, the movement of hand in air a soft curve, as though it flows or mimes the supposed ease of angels.

Papias does not move. 'I will not sit.'

'Just so. You are afraid.' Matthias nods. 'You need not be afraid of me, Papias. I am a holy man. I will bring you no harm, only blessing. I am a man of God. As are you. Should we not sit and discuss?'

'I will not sit.'

'Ah. Do you wish to drink? Are you thirsty? You appear hot.'

'I want nothing. Tell me what you want to tell me,' Papias says shortly. He is hot and thirsty, his ear stump pulses painfully.

'So many things, my friend, so many things.' Matthias takes a step closer. His eye has never recovered, the lid only closes partly over it. There is an out-turned weal of pinkish white. His breath is near enough to smell, a sweet wine.

'We have lived the same life, you and I, Papias. Have we not?' he asks. 'Both of us seeking to find the truth. To find the Divine. Both of us servants of this quest. And is this not the best of a man? Is this not the highest ambition of a soul? To know that this life is but a shell of another eternal one, and that it is to be spent in the service of the Creator; is this not what you and I have understood?' He pauses. Papias does not answer him. 'We have both known this, and have both been seekers. We have both sought to serve, to have our earthly lives mean something to the Divine, to the One, to God, whatever name we have called him. It matters not. He is the same. And you and I, Papias, in our seeking both came to the same place. Both of us heard the preaching of a great preacher, an old man who might have been our father, who might have been the fathers we had each lost, and who spoke to us of a heavenly father and his son. A father who loved his son.'

Matthias's mouth is at Papias ear, his black beard touching; his voice he drops to a whisper. 'It's true. You know it. You know it for I know it. We are alike. We came to him for this reason and surrendered all else. We lived on Patmos, you and I both, and forgot the world. What did it matter to us? We did not care for this world, we cared for the love of the Father. We thought to have found what we sought. What hardships were on the island mattered not. We could live so for ever – until called to the next life.'

Matthias steps back, as if to consider where he has climbed, how far to above, how far to below.

'Dear Papias, good Papias, we have been alike, you and I, seekers of the truth, servants of the Creator. "O God, my soul thirsteth for thee, my flesh longeth for thee in a dry and thirsty land, where no water is." Have we both not prayed so? And has the Almighty not heard us? He has, Papias. The Almighty, the Divine, the One *has* heard. And answered me.' Matthias is close enough to kiss. 'And you also,' he whispers. 'You have been heard – and answered, Papias. Answered. I know. You have been chosen. You, of all, chosen, to be my right hand. Neither of us can deny it. You were dead. You were cold as dust. I asked for the Divine to intervene that you might be saved, that you might live to bear witness. And you were saved. Think on this. Think. Why do you live now when you were dead? Why do you live, Papias?'

'I live to praise God.'

'Indeed.'

'I live to follow the apostle John, the disciple of Jesus Christ, the Son of God.'

Matthias opens his hands as if to catch and crush the creed that comes at him. He might give a short response but thinks better of it and slowly brings his palms together before him. He looks at Papias with pity. His lips are tightly pressed.

'Good Papias,' he says at last. 'Good Papias, loyal and true Papias, my heart is full of love for you. You know this. I bear you the love of the Creator who has chosen you. And what I must tell I know will hurt, and I would not hurt the one I love. But,' Matthias sighs, opens his hands in a gesture of helplessness, 'from blindness to seeing is not easy passage. Many prefer the dark. But not a seeker such as you. You, good Papias, wish the light, wish the truth.' Matthias indicates a couch by the wall. 'Sit to hear.'

'I will stand. Tell what you tell and I will be gone for ever.'

'You see? You stay when already you could be gone. You seek the truth; this consoles me in the pain I must deliver. Papias, you have been blind. I, too, have been blind, I confess it. We mistook a messenger for the Messiah. It is not our fault, we had the conviction of an old man who said he was himself a witness, who said he himself had touched the hand of this Messiah and walked with him, who himself had seen miracles. O vanity and iniquity! Wickedness and conceit! I must tell you, Papias: this John you follow is not the same that followed Jesus of Nazareth. He pretends it only. Perhaps in his dotage he believes it having pretended so long.'

'It is not true! I will not listen!' Papias says, and turns towards the door.

'It is outrage, yes. It is painful, yes. But it is true, yes. I can show you the proof.'

Papias stops. His back is turned. Should he leave now? Should he deny Matthias another moment to spread his lies? His face is crimson. His hands shake.

'What proof?'

'I grieve to see you wounded, dear Papias. But wait, I will show.' Matthias leaves the room.

Papias is aware of his heart racing. Beneath his robe his flesh is awake, the creature of contagion crawling. He presses his hand hard against his chest, but it is not contained. With his nails he scratches deep.

'Here! Here, come, sit, Papias, and see.' Matthias is returned and holds in his hand a scrolled papyrus.

'What is it?'

'Come, sit, read for yourself.'

'What is it?' Papias asks again, as he takes the scroll.

Matthias wears a pained look as he delivers the blow.

'Dear Papias,' he says, 'good Papias, it is the true gospel of the apostle John.'

Papias sits without knowing he sits. His spirit is fallen. He holds the scroll opened before him. Matthias is beside him on the couch. He reaches to steady the young hand that shakes.

The scroll is ancient and wrinkled and frail. A delicate thing that has survived by miracle peril of sea and land, storm and fire. It is some part torn, some part stained by blood or wine or oil. Papias's heart is pierced to read it.

Here, in the Greek language, is written an account of the life and death of Jesus of Nazareth by one who was by his side. It tells of his meeting John the Baptist and of I, John, who followed him then. It tells of the wedding at Cana where Jesus taught the lesson that water should be considered wine, and by this meant our life on earth is water to the wine that is the world hereafter. It tells of his travels in Samaria with John and other disciples that grew so many until they could not be fed and turned angrily from him. Here is told that Jesus was a teacher and prophet, who spoke of God as the Father of all. 'But his message was mistaken by those who feared he was too favoured by the crowd. They told he called himself the Son of God that they might bring the law against him. This Jesus never said,' it is written. 'He was of us, a Gallilean. A man.'

Here, Papias lifts his head from the scroll. He finds his throat has closed and he cannot swallow. He finds his chest is constricted and will not allow air. He should put the scroll aside. He should read no more. But there is in the scripture a fierce hold. He is compelled by a sense of its authenticity. This is the truth, it seems to say, is the fact of what was. It is history and science only. There is nothing else.

The hand of Matthias lies over his own, the face is near enough for the sweet breath to feather against the disciple's cheek.

'Read more. Read all,' Matthias says.

Papias should not, but does. It is not true. This is not true.

But what if it is?

The larger portion of the gospel is an account of the capture, the scourging, the trial and crucifixion of Jesus. The writer spares no detail. Jesus is taken by Roman soldiers, who knock him to the ground and beat him though he does not resist. John stands back in fear. He follows when they drag the body off from the Place of Skulls. In a single phrase he tells of the trial, then moves to his main subject, the torturing of the body. Here is told each cut, each wound that opens in the face and body of Jesus. The writer glories in it. Jesus falls and is beaten. The dust clings to his wounds. Others on the route take turns to throw stones, pots, what comes to hand. The writer John tries to intervene but is driven back. Jesus is lashed. Jesus is stabbed between his shoulder blades with a knife and cries out.

Papias pushes the scroll back from him.

'It is sad, I know,' Matthias says softly. 'My heart was moved, too. The brute facts of it.' He pats Papias's hand. 'Who would not feel sympathy for such a man?' Matthias turns his face fully to the disciple; his eye wound jumps minutely and he raises a hand to still it. 'But read, read on, good Papias. It is important. You will see.'

The attacks continue all the way to the hill of Calvary. The writer is skilled in horror. The flesh that is torn away, the fluids that leak to the dust, the thousand scourges, all depicted. Then the crucifixion. Nails being driven, a darkening sky. The body mounted on to the cross.

Then, as the gospel nears its end, toward the bottom of the scroll, this: 'The body of Jesus hung on the cross until dead. When the soldiers had gone, the body was taken down and borne from that place and buried in a tomb. But fearing the wrath of the people and that they might come to desecrate the body in the morning I, John, and others of his disciples, took Jesus from the tomb and buried him elsewhere that we alone might know the last place of the teacher, Jesus of Nazareth.'

Papias lets the scroll fall.

'An account of love,' Matthias says. 'Clearly this John loved this Jesus. An account of hatred. Clearly this John hated the Romans and those who did not share his love.' He moistens his lips, purses some words he would say next. He must choose carefully.

'Papias, dear friend Papias, this script is old. It was traded in the market by an ancient who had come out of Antioch. He had many other like scrolls, testaments of various sages; he had a gospel, too, of one Matthew.' Matthias wrinkles his nose a short sneer, but quickly sees the disciple is not ready for such. Not yet. 'But this testament of John, I enquired of. He said he had it of a woman who traded it for salted fish. Truly. She was herself old and ragged, he told. She was alone and wandering and half mad. She said she knew the mother of this Jesus of Nazareth and had an account of his living written by one who loved him.' Matthias moves closer still. His voice he drops to a whisper, 'One John who hanged himself thereafter in guilt and love and was buried in Judea.'

245

Papias cannot speak. He cannot rise and run out. He cannot make the time go backwards and unhear what has been said. The silver O that stands in the room wavers in the glass of his tears. All along his chest the blisters speak. He shudders. Matthias lays an arm across his shoulders.

'We must not blame ourselves for believing an old man. I believed, too, a long time until the light. Until the One. But you have been chosen, Papias. You were dead, remember, and I asked that you be brought back, and you were. You are the elect, as am I. We cannot deny our calling. This other is in our past, was a false way, a way of darkness, but you are come here to find the true.' Matthias presses the disciple close to him, but Papias shakes violently. He brings a hand up to claw at his chest. He scratches through his robe.

'Calm yourself, it is all right. Calm,' the voice whispers at his ear.

But the shaking worsens. His body burns. Such heat as rises he thinks must burst aflame. White sweat leaks from his face. He scratches again fiercely, and again, twists in the embrace that holds him.

'What is it, Papias? Calm yourself. I am here. You need fear nothing. You are in the company of love, dear Papias.'

That he might still the troubled disciple Matthias doubles his embrace. He holds the other, who shakes wildly as a tree in storm. His cheek he lays against the chest of Papias.

And here he sees, in the opening of the robe, the angry red contagion.

'What? What is on you?' Sharply Matthias pulls back. He stands.

White-faced, shuddering, in the violent throes of an inner struggle, Papias stares outwards.

An instant, then Matthias reaches and with both hands rips open the disciple's garment to reveal a torso covered entire in rash and blister, blood and crust and ooze. He cries out in revulsion, looks at the hands that have touched the disease. He spins back, staggers, calls for Auster, who comes at once and clasps his hand across his mouth.

'Get him out! Get him from here! He is unclean! He is cursed! He would not come to us, and so now is devoured. Get him out!'

With a hand still across his mouth, and the other sleeved, Auster prods at Papias with his foot. Papias goes, and falls into the street, and lies there, shaking still and tearing at himself until the time later when Kester finds him.

33

Now.

Now might you bring the world to end.

Your servants wait.

John ails. What fortitude and changeless health he had on the island are no more. Martha and Ruth attend him. He is cleansed and wears a fresh white robe where he lies on the bed. For many hours of the day, while the disciples are elsewhere carrying the Word, he remains in a cave of silence. Sometimes, hearing the whispered voices of the children, he raises his head from stillness and tells Martha to let them come to him. They stand by the bed and he is changed by their attendance. His hands take theirs; he smiles as if at this proof of innocence in the world yet.

'Who am I?' he asks them.

'You are John, son of Zebedee, disciple of our Lord Jesus Christ.'

The days are long. The summer burns itself in brilliant heat, but in the stone room where he lies it is shaded and cool. There he waits. Is each breath he draws numbered? Is there an appointed time when the Lord will come? What moment marks it? What configuration of stars, what height the sun, heralds the opening of the heavens? Or will there be no notice, no annunciation but one instant in ordinary time when the sky parts and he is there?

'I will not leave you comfortless, I will come to you,' he remembers.

Then he says this over soundlessly in his mind. *I will not leave you comfortless, I will come to you.* And again. His thin, dry lips move minutely. His blind eyes are turned away, angling to the right, to the space above him, where he can see then the face of Jesus as he said the words.

Kester comforts Papias. The disciple pulls back from him and tries to hide himself and the disease, but the mute sees and is unafraid. At his side he has a bundle in which he carries the things he steals. From this he takes a pouch. He gives Papias lemon water to drink, sits in the street a long time with him until he is calmed.

Having drunk, Papias will not return to him the water pouch. 'I am unclean, you must not take it. You must not drink from it after me.'

He puts it on the ground. Kester the thief picks it up.

Papias clings to his knees, rocks himself in desolation. Where should he go now? What can he do? The gospel he has read sickens him in his spirit. He does not believe it. It cannot be true. That was not the gospel of the true John. It was written for sale, for trading to the credulous. The beloved disciple is in the house of Levi. He is the apostle John. I believe it. I believe it. I believe it. That was nothing. It was deceit and lies.

But still his spirit sickens. The contagion eats further inches of his chest. He thinks his skin smells of death. How can he go back to the Apostle now?

At sunset the others note that he has not returned. But it is supposed he accepts the hospitality of a Christian and will be back in the morning. Nonetheless, the Apostle is concerned. With assistance he sits upright. 'Where was Papias going?' he asks.

None are certain. 'To the east of the city,' Danil tells.

'We pray for him,' says John.

After a deep quiet full of disquiet, John asks the news of Ephesus then lies back to listen. In the telling he hopes for signs, but cannot say so.

The discourse is quickly impassioned. The disciples speak of the splintered world. 'There are a thousand creeds, and more each day,' Lemuel says. 'Everywhere there are ones obscured by darkness.'

'I am sad to confess, the world hates us still,' Meletios says.

'But there are believers in Jesus,' Danil argues.

'Yes, but what Jesus?' Lemuel asks. 'They number him no different from other prophets. He is another they can petition, no more than this.'

'But is not this a beginning?'

'No. They understand nothing of what we teach.'

'And the scribes and the chief priests, they speak against us still no different from before,' Meletios says.

'But there are some in the synagogue,' Danil says. 'I have met with Chiram and one Eben, who confessed to me they believed in Jesus but could not say so in public for fear of being driven from the temple.'

Lemuel shakes his head. 'We must teach otherwise. They prefer the praise of men to God.'

'Yes, but . . .' Danil shrugs at the old bell ringer. 'The work to come is still long.'

'That Jesus is a teacher is most easily understood. But this is not belief. They sit to a sacred meal but do not understand the Eucharist. Our gains are small.'

'Should we not be content that they receive us?' Meletios essays hopefully. 'That some there are who listen?'

'But what comfort is in this?' Lemuel asks. 'I can number on my fingers the ones who believe truly: Gaius, Demetrios, the young follower Polycarp, who asks that he come to see the Apostle.'

'Let him to come,' John says.

'You are weak still, Master. You should not be taxed with visitors.'

'Let who would come, to come. I would see all my brothers in Christ. We are a communion. We need not walls to keep others out.'

The discourse falls quiet. The sun has set. The disciples sit enlarged by their shadows. In what they are engaged seems enterprise of vast dimension and they are small and human only.

'Let us pray,' John says.

They do. Their praying is old solace, comfort ancient as time, as man's first petitioning into the first night.

An hour passes, another. They say the words of psalms, of scriptures in usage immemorial, lines once chanted in desert and plain, in the dust wherein grew cities that now are dust again. A single voice rises and the others join. A pause follows. Then, without indication, another amongst them begins a new prayer. So the dark is measured. They do not conclude. None move away to sleep. The Apostle is awake and prays with them.

And in that time, between dark and dark, when there is nothing but the bare bowed spirits of these men, there comes to John a frail light. He is moved by love. It comes to him at first as the deepest pity, that these have not seen Jesus as he has, and yet they follow. Their faith near makes him weep, and he feels for each one an unsayable love, within which is gratitude, pride, admiration, wonder, mystery, sympathy, surprise, all tender variants of affection. It wells up and floods the chambers of him as an inner tide. He is overcome. In his darkness then an epiphany: *such love he must not fail.* It is as simple as this, for epiphany is foremost marked by simplicity, by the condition of *claritas.* He sees as he has not before. Such love he must not fail.

Into the silence, he tells, 'Brothers, my brothers in Christ, unto the last hour, yea, unto the last moment of the last hour, you will teach the Word that others may be saved. In this is the love of God, that you teach the love of God. That you show the way, the way will be shown to you, and to all who find you. Though it is the last hour, we do not labour less, but more.'

He pauses. His voice is strengthened.

'I would that one of you would write these words,' he says.

Startled, as if from dream into the thing dreamt, the disciples bestir themselves. Danil lights a candle, Lemuel brings papyrus and stylus, offers these to Meletios, whose hand is fairest.

251

Then, to instruct, to clarify, to lead into light, to assist those he loves in their labours, which labours he knows will continue to the end of time, John dictates his great epistle. He writes to the world. He speaks clearly, with certain pause, each thought delineated with care.

'That which was from the beginning, which we have heard, which we have seen with our eyes, which we have looked upon, and our hands have handled, of the Word of life . . .'

His voice is clear, his manner calm.

'These things write we unto you that your joy may be full.

'This then is the message that we have heard of him, and declare unto you, that God is light, and in him is no darkness at all.'

John speaks on in the candlelight until it burns low and another is lit. He speaks without fatigue, telling, urging, teaching what numberless multitude in the unseen world might yet be Christian. He thinks of it as a last act, a summation of what is, a last offering out of his life that those he loves might use in their labours. For he has understood that in Ephesus there is much darkness. 'The whole world lies in wickedness,' he tells Meletios to write. And the writing, the telling, is an act against this. It is both warning and promise. 'Believe in the name of the Son of God,' he tells, 'that ye may know ye have eternal life.'

The dawn comes and he is speaking yet. His throat is grown hoarse, and Meletios looks up from the scripture, fearful that the Apostle will speak himself to his last breath. 'You must rest,' he says, 'we have the Word. We will bring it forth.'

The disciples are rapt, in-spired. How is this the aged one they feared dying after his fall? Danil brings him water to drink. John sips at it. He falls silent; in the after-hush asks, 'Is Papias not returned?'

34

How long is love? How long is love when there is nothing? When there is no other? When there is none to touch or see or hear? How is love then to endure? What hope for human love when it is sustained only by belief? How can a man love God? How can he love what he cannot see, cannot touch, cannot feel? And, more impossible yet, how can he feel that God loves him back? Does the air love? Does the sun? Does the dust of the plain?

I am not worthy to be loved. My very flesh dies.

If we are loved, why is our way not made easier? Why does evil and pestilence prosper? Why do our enemies thrive? Why does the Lord not help us when we have carried his Word for so long? Where here is love? Where is the love in these blisters, in this disease that eats to my heart? Where is the love in this pain that wracks my body? O my soul is black with anger.

I am not worthy to be loved. My very flesh dies.

But O if you would come.

If you would come, I would be healed.

If I could see you, I could love.

If I could touch you, I could love.

If you would come.

John is the Apostle. I do not believe the scripture. Matthias twists the world for his own vanity. The Apostle rests in the house of Levi. I would I could go to him. I would I could kneel by his bed and his hand lay upon my head.

But I will not see him again now.

He it is who loves. He it is who remains true. Does his love for you not die? Does it remain a lifetime? Though it is yet ages past since he saw you, does he see you still? What can he feel that I cannot?

I feel only grief.

I confess it. I feel only grief and loneliness and anger.

By my sins I am cast out. I am elect to death.

Where is the love for me? Where is the mercy?

I crave it. I crave to feel love.

O my heart bleeds. My soul is black with anger.

Lord, have pity.

In a quake-toppled house where remains a room partly roofed, Kester the thief attends to Papias. The disciple is lain in a corner on a wooden pallet with a coarse covering of camel hair. His arms he crosses to scratch at his sores. Shakes wrack him. Now he trembles violent as a leaf in the last gale of autumn, now he is still as death. Such sudden visits make his body weaker still. If he would sleep, he might have respite, but he cannot. He lies with eyes baleful opened. All day and all night he stares. The vacant air lit and darkened, he studies as if for transport of angels. But none such come, only further sores. These, as though his blood resists less or extends welcome, bloom swiftly. There are sores built on sores. Rough ridges of flesh rise and burst in yellow pus. His nails flail. His lips swell as though by sinister kiss. Blisters at the edges will bleed if Papias opens wide his mouth, so Kester dribbles water from a cloth. He sits by. Sometimes in the day he is gone into Ephesus and returns with what he has stolen – foodstuffs, cloth, the makings of fire.

From a stall in a market, whether by theft or bargain, he brings herbs for a cure. These he mixes to a brew, lets cool till thickened to a paste.

'Why? Why do you bring this? I am to die, go away. Do not touch me. Save yourself, leave me,' Papias says, and turns from him to the wall.

Upon the raw exposed back, Kester lays the paste.

But the cure does not take. The sores climb the disciple's throat to meet those that travel out from the lips. On the bed, Papias shakes like the toy of a distempered child. He cannot still himself. His hands tremble wildly; his arms fly about; he lets out a long, pitiful moaning; tears at his hair. The pain become unendurable; he crawls to chafe himself against the wall, blood and poison running, as he cries out, 'Take me! O Lord, I beseech you. Hear me!'

35

The disciples are heartened. Within a day they have learned the epistle by heart; through them it will multiply. They preach with emboldened spirit by the basilicas, in market squares. Tireless, they go all the streets of the city fishing for souls. There is concern for Papias but not yet alarm.

The young man with eyes of piercing blue who is called Polycarp is brought to meet the Apostle and becomes one of them. On good reports of the faith of Gaius, John dictates to him an epistle, gives it to Lemuel to bring.

'Is there no report of Papias?'

'We seek for him everywhere, but he is not known.'

'Seek still. I will pray for him.'

The Apostle angles his face upwards, as if to interrogate the sunlight. In the stillness of the day his strength ebbs. Having so long forgotten his body, having lived without thought of its health for many years, now he finds he is reminded of frailty. This stiff movement of his fingers, this seized joint of elbow, labour of lungs, grind of anklebone, intervals of deafness, heart-race, numbness, cold unfeeling toes, such things as recall him to his humanity. His body fails. Having long since considered time immaterial, he does not know what age he is, and this is of no concern. Only that he abides matters. He must remain until the Lord comes again. That is all.

He lies on the daybed and prays for Papias. He fears the disciple is gone to Matthias or that Matthias has enacted some evil, and he sends his prayers against this.

In the days that follow, the disciples return from the city to report their number grows. In their voices John can hear the timbre of hope.

'There are others who would come see you,' Lemuel tells. 'They ask that they might see the one who touched the hand of our Lord.'

The apostle John hesitates. He does not want to be the reason for belief. He does not wish reverence or awe for his own person.

'Blessed are they who believe without seeing,' Danil says.

'Agreed, but all men are weak. And if it should increase the faith of some, then where is the wrong?' asks Lemuel.

'They have the Word, what need the person?' Danil replies quickly, then seeing Lemuel's eyes realises what he has said. 'I am sorry, Master. I did not mean . . .'

'It is the truth, good Danil,' John says, and seems to think on this some time, then decides, 'But if there are some who would come and pray with us and share the Eucharist, then all are welcome. Tell them to come in the truth of our Lord Jesus Christ.'

The evening following, there are twenty. A week later, and from other small communities further distance, there comes more. They are too many to fit into the room and some stand bowed in the street outside. The Apostle is moved. To this church of two score and ten he speaks the words of the epistle. They are a small sect only, a minor assembly among the many others that gather in the city of Ephesus, where heresies flourish, but in their attentiveness and devotion is significance; in their number, too.

In John light breaks. When he speaks his aches are forgone. His voice is raised. He lifts his arms wide, and is then like a figure of olden time whose soul sings, whose testament is burnished with fire.

'These are the last of days,' he tells. 'Behold, we prepare the way.'

But in the aftertime, when the numbers are dispersed again and the night fallen, he is revisited by infirmity. His humanness declares itself in pain. Though he does not tell the others, such aches, such

257

effort to find breath in his chest, are new to him. He lies in his own dark, aware of the air that seems harder to draw now. His thin lips are dry. He would ask for water, but it is night and the others sleep. Instead he suffers a thirst that tightens his throat. The effort for breath exhausts him. Is it now? Is it here in the night alone that he will see love coming? Along the hallways to his heart a fierce pain hastens. In the absolute aloneness of suffering he tries to make his mind accept what his body feels. The hurt is immense, his face grimaces as it arrives with iron blade in the centre of his being. But he does not cry out. His mouth opens, an O of anguish, and his eyes weep. He is impaled and cannot breathe. His two hands he brings to his chest and holds tightly, as though in battle to keep life from being cut out.

Is it now? Is it here?

The disciples sleep. He has not strength to call out. His chin he presses to his chest, his legs he draws upwards. He is small as a child.

And in the wrack of the pain, in the throes of his agony when dark upon dark he suffers, when he is brought even to the furthermost edge of living, there must come yet the hurt of bewilderment. For in hurt speaks humanity and John is mere man. If the very many near encounters with death in all his ancient lifetime had taught him to believe a coat of care was about him, that countless times he was protected, spared, even to the earth-quake, miraculously enduring, then here now it seems is an ending. Such pain he has never felt. The coat is drawn from him and he is naked. And what comes to his mind, not yet in words, is *why*.

Why here, now, alone, do I die?

There is no light. Of Jesus there is no herald. No fold in the dark opens, nor do angels descend.

36

Light. Light. Light.

Sunlight on the road shining. Heaven light making golden the sand. Light. In Andrew's fair hair. In the pale body of the Baptist in the river water. Light. In thee, O Lord, do I put my trust. Behold. Upon the crest of a sandhill. Behold the Lamb of God. I saw a spirit descending from heaven like a dove, and it abode upon him. The beginning. What are you looking for? Light. Rabbi, where are you staying? Light. Come and see. We have found him, the Messiah! We have found him! O Lord Jesus. In thee, O Lord, do I put my trust. Light. And seven golden candlesticks. And his hairs were as white as snow and his eyes as a flame of fire. Light. The Lord is my rock and my fortress and my deliverer. On the road to Cana not a word spoken. We walked to revelation. Unto thee, O Lord, do I lift up my soul. The stone water jars. The bird trapped. Light. His praise shall ever be in my mouth. And his feet like unto fine brass as if they burned in a furnace. Wings beating, the bird trapped. The awning shade. Shall I not rise and free it? And his voice as the sound of many waters. Light. I waited patiently for the Lord, and he inclined unto me and heard my cry. See the bird above us. They have no wine. Light. There was a man of the Pharisees named Nicodemus. I will praise thee with my whole heart. And in a city of Samaria, which is called Sychar. And the sheep market by the pool, which is called Bethesda. Light. And he had in his right hand seven stars. And the Sea of Galilee, which is the Sea of Tiberias. Bread of heaven. I am the bread of life. Light. And out of his mouth went a sharp two-edged sword. And as Jesus passed by he saw a man who was blind from birth. As the deer longs after the water brooks, so longs my soul after thee. Light. And he spat unto the ground and made clay of the spittle and anointed the eyes. Go wash in the pool of Siloam. And his countenance was as the sun shineth. Light. And he laid his right hand upon me. How were thine eyes opened? There was a man called Jesus. Saying unto me, fear not. Light. Whosoever believeth in me shall not abide in darkness. O my Lord. Light. Bring light. I fall in darkness.

The sun rising, a bell is rung.

Meletios it is who goes to the Apostle. John reposes in such stillness he seems barely a man. His chest does not rise. The disciple is afraid to stir him. Surely he heard the bell, but perhaps prays so fiercely, is so portioned into the world of the spirit that his body is the lesser part and responds not. The disciple attends some moments, uncertainly. Then fears crawl free. Is he living? Meletios leans closer. From the Apostle there is not the slightest movement. It cannot be. It is unthinkable, and what cannot be thought cannot be believed. He reaches out his hand to touch John, but leaves it quivering in the air. Dread saddles coldly the back of his neck. The room is damp, heavy, the stones glisten.

'Master?' he says softly.

There is no response, no movement in the blind face of the Apostle.

'Master? It is Meletios.'

Again nothing.

He lays his hand upon the thin, thin frame of the old man, frail assemblage of bones in a white robe. His action is too slight to be called shaking; rather he touches tenderly the arm and presses there.

Into the room small light falls.

'Master?' His voice, though a whisper, betrays the first thick clots of loss. The lumps of grief rise in him. He moves his hand to the ancient face and feels it cold, and he cries out.

And from what furthermost edge, from what dark or light, by chance or design, John returns.

Very slight, he moves his head to one side, speaks softly the disciple's name.

Meletios drops to his knees, takes the Apostle's right hand in both of his and presses his head to it. 'Master, Master.' He can say nothing more at first. He hears John draw a slender breath.

'You are cold, Master. I will bring you more blankets.'

'Meletios?'

'Yes, Master?'

'I am here.'

It is not a question, or is it? Is he confused?

'You are here, Master. Yes, in the house of Levi in Ephesus.'

'Yes. But . . .' The Apostle raises his right hand, it floats trembling in midair, pale uncertain bird, and then moves across to where it alights upon his left shoulder. John pats his own shoulder, then the upper arm, and forearm.

'I cannot feel this side,' he says. There is no fright in his voice; he tells it because it is. 'My arm, my leg.' Then, in mild interrogative, 'They are there?'

'Yes.'

John lies still. His breaths are long between.

'I cannot move them,' he tells.

'It is tiredness, Master,' Meletios offers, lineaments of love in his face 'You have not your strength. Rest, rest now. We will pray for your well-being.'

John does not reply. He lies in the heart of the mystery while Meletios goes to alert the others.

I am here, he thinks. But I cannot see and cannot feel that I am. How then do I know?

It is as though he has been partly taken.

In the day that follows, he turns the question over: why is it so? Does the Lord speak to him by this language of dying? Does he near take him each time, in the sea, in the quake, and by this, too?

Does he tell something by sickness? What message is untranslated here? Why does the Apostle near death and not die? To now John has supposed the reason: that he prepares the way, that he remains spreading the Word until he comes again. It is the Lord's love for him, and his for the Lord.

But in the blind, dark stillness of the bed when one half of himself he cannot feel, he thinks there is something other.

He is a sign that he himself does not understand.

Teach me, he prays. Where do I wrong? Teach me to live as you wish.

That night Lemuel lies on the floor by the Apostle's bed. He cannot tell if he sleeps or not. He listens for each breath. When he rises in the dawn, John is awake already.

'We must find Papias,' he says.

'We have searched, Master.'

'You must bear me to Matthias.'

'But you are weak, it is not prudent. The city is . . .'

John raises his right hand. 'To Matthias, bear me there. We will find Papias.'

'Let Danil go, or I shall. There is no need for you. You are weak . . .'

'There is need for me yet.'

'I did not mean . . .'

'It is all right, Lemuel. I am to go. Will you bring me thither?'

He is borne from the house in the early morning on a litter lain with a blanket of sheep's wool. The disciples all go with him. The way is crowded and already filled with traffic of commerce. Seabirds are come ashore in forecast of storm; they pilfer and squawk. Criers already rend the air with prices. The Christians then are a quiet caravan, aloof, privately purposeful. They cross from the district of alleyways and crooked lanes into the broader thoroughfare. The key of season is turned; the sky blotched with cloud. Small gusts of salt wind blow. Watchful of the heavens, traders lay stones on their wares, lower their prices a fraction.

Ephesus has seen all the world, its oddity and grandeur both, and pays little attention to the litter-borne apostle. Those who take notice think only it is one being carried to a tomb.

There are as ever in the streets the proclaimers, the soothsayers, the testifiers, and the priest. The weather changing is apt topic, the storm approaches. Here one points to the sky with force and conviction, declares he sees the seam rendering; here another tells the talk of the wind. The Christians press on. But on the edge of the square they are blocked by a crowd gathered for the spectacle of the gospel seller. The others have seen him before, but have not told the Apostle. He is a bearded, long-haired crier who waves a clutch of scrolls.

'Here, here, come gather and listen! Here is told the bloody crucifixion of Jesus of Nazareth.'

For better market, he has a youth in loincloth and crown of thorn bush standing head-bowed alongside.

'Read, read the suffering of the carpenter's son!' he cries. And then commences by striking at the youth's bare back with a knotted lash.

An O from the crowd draws him on. He lashes again. The youth withers.

The seller knows his tale by heart. He knows what moves his audience, what vanity and righteousness make of man, and tells, 'Here, see he who thought himself a second God. Read what was his punishment. Read the words written by those who were witness. Read the gospel of Boas for each lash told. The gospel of Judas, who loved Jesus, here the very nails driven, look! A bargain. Truly. A reminder to all the sin of pride.'

What sorrow it is for John to hear cannot be imagined. Love is grief and anger.

The disciples call out to make way, and he is brought past and away. But already in the after-moments, in the strange bumped floating of the litter through the streets where John is borne like a last remnant of truth, something is happening. It happens with suffering. It happens as the sky clouds quicken and the light moves dark and bright and dark again. The wind from the east comes. The birds like torn things scatter and return. The air is made bitter. John says nothing. He lies in the first vision of new knowledge, in the place where it is first nothing but light without shape or form, a candescence that makes wince. He knows but does not know what yet. The thing that happens is whiteness only, is brilliance and illumination neither tender nor comforting but such as to cause pain. For in light is former darkness shown. There is something that happens. It is an inner blinding. But of it nothing can be spoken yet.

The litter is borne out from the city to the house of Matthias.

'Are you well, Master?' Melitios asks, for the Apostle has made no movement or sound. 'This is the place.'

'Tell we have come for Papias.'

Danil knocks. The disciples wait. A sinewy shaven-head figure with pale eyebrows that they do not at first recognise as Linus opens the door. He wears a blue robe to the ground; his hands he cups before his chest.

'We are come to talk with Papias.'

'Papias?' The name is like sourness in Linus's mouth. He tongue-tips his full lips. 'Papias is not here.'

He goes to close the door against them, but Danil stops him, seizes his arm. 'We have come to see him, where is he?'

Linus shrugs free, smoothes the fall of his robe. 'We are holy men here,' he says in distaste. 'None stay who do not wish it. Papias is not here. He went off. He is unclean.'

'Unclean? You who were one of us now call us . . .'

'He is diseased. His flesh rots. You knew and sent him to us, Auster says. That you might strike at the Holy One.'

'He is . . . you lie.'

'His skin falls off.' Linus presses forward his head to spit the phrase. 'He is dead now.'

Danil must keep himself from striking him.

'Bring us to Matthias,' John says.

Linus wets his lips. There is authority in the Apostle he fears yet.

'The Holy One is in the sanctum. He fasts. He is not to be disturbed.'

'Bring us there,' John says, and the disciples push past the remonstrations of the other and go through the building, opening doors, until they come to a place of candles and incense and a stone altar upon which lies Matthias. He remains perfectly still.

'Matthias!' Lemuel calls.

Still the other does not move.

Lemuel approaches. 'Matthias, where is Papias?'

Very slowly, with such deliberation of movement as to be considered grace, Matthias raises himself, to the air above makes a circular blessing with his right hand. Then he steps down from the altar.

He smiles to see this ancient man come before him.

'Old man,' he says. 'Do yet you see the light? Are you come to confess the true way?'

'We are come for Papias,' Lemuel says stoutly. 'He has been here?'

Matthias stands some way back from them.

'He has, but I could not save him. He was eaten with contagion.'

'Where is he?' John asks.

'He is dead.' Matthias smiles. 'Your Christ did not come to save him. He knew this and came to me. He confessed himself unclean, and I cleansed him of the sin of ignorance.'

John raises his voice. 'You are an Antichrist. You are the evil that is in the world.'

'Old man, it is you are the corruption. This Papias came to know. I see he did not tell you that he was a leper. He feared to. Why? Why did he not come to you? Why did he come to your charity and love? I will tell you. Because he came to know you are nothing but a useless old man waiting to die. What else are you? I showed him the true gospel of John I bought in the market. Have you one? They have many. Papias read it and knew you were nothing. Even in the gospel your Jesus is only a prophet. You are a vain old fool who has lied himself to importance. Who believes what you say?' Matthias glares about at the disciples. 'These old men? These who went out from their own people and made outcasts of themselves? Papias came to know. To understand. He came to ask to follow me. To be one of us. Already once I had brought him back from the dead. But he had doubted the One too long, too long he had turned his back on the Divine, and so his own back was eaten first. His flesh . . .' he scowls in disgust, '. . . was putrefied.'

'You are lying!' Danil shouts.

'O stout Danil, stout in ignorance to the last. On his knees Papias begged that I heal him. Yea, there where you stand he wept and pleaded, kissed my hand.'

'Come, let us leave this evil,' John says, 'we have no business here.'

As they bear him from there, Matthias calls, 'See how at last he withers? The old man will be dead soon. Fear not, you can yet repent like Papias. You can yet come to see the truth. When the old man is buried in a week, in a month at most, you will come then. I know.'

They reach the doorway.

Matthias calls his farewell, 'I will pray for you all.'

Then they are gone. He stands looking at the doorway some moments. The confrontation has inflamed his heart, and now the rash on his chest stings again. He closes his eyes against the urgency to scratch. Then he steps back to the altar and climbs on to it, lying prostrate, hands crossed on the contagion, as he prays for a cure.

37

The disciples bear the Apostle back. None speak. The sky darkens
with storm that is not yet come. Wind whips the awnings; ropes on
masts whistle a lash song. Above the streets wheel seabirds with cry
plaintive and urgent. John is carried back to his bed. What is
happening within him happens still. But the action is inchoate yet,
a turning of hurt and anger and grief that in one man's spirit are as a
blade working, paring, incising. From the raw and tender stuff of
love and its disappointment is painfully fashioned enlightenment.
How is he to change the thinking of a lifetime? The world is rotten
with soft credence. Man twists belief for his own purpose. Each day
a new messiah. A hundred years he is, and the most of that he has
been a voice, preaching the word in desert towns, in hill villages, in
Roman cities. But as he returns from encounter with Matthias, a
hundred years seems too long to have lived. The world does not
improve but worsens. How hard to keep faith in it. What effort,
what hardship, has been his for so long, so long he has remained
believing that soon, soon faith would be rewarded, that now
through infinite weariness he must find strength to turn around
his mind. The terrible news of Papias, the memory of the gospel
seller, how fiercely Matthias and the others had turned against
them, such things are deep wounds.

'Lay and rest, Master,' Meletios says. 'The journey has wearied
you.'

And John has not the strength to answer him.

★   ★   ★

Do I die now? Do I die now when the world is thronged with evil?
One side of my body I cannot feel.
How am I, an old man, to turn back the Antichrists?
My heart shakes with rage.
I would the world were ended already.
Or that I were young and strong again and could strike your enemies down. I would be as a fierce sword.
But I am weak. My breaths are numbered.
I sin of despair.

You crossed the brook Cedron, where there was the garden you had oft visited. The last of times. We knew and did not know. The night falling in the olive trees. They came with lanterns and torches and weapons.
'Whom seek ye?'
'Jesus of Nazareth.'
'I am he.'
Then Simon Peter. Then Annas. Then Caiaphas. Then Pilate.
'Art thou the King of the Jews?'
'My kingdom is not of this world.'
I followed. I could not weep.
The last of times.
Already you were gone.
'Away with him! Away with him!'
The cross.

The storm proper comes in the night. The sky over Ephesus booms with thunder. Such noise as is makes shake stone jars and statues. The moon and stars are taken. The sea comes inshore on a high tide, throws boats like toys, makes mud of dust and slides it elsewhere. In the dark all huddle and pray. The night breaks up. Thunder deafens again. A crash and then another, then another still. In the streets and alleyways, in the square, out the Magnesian Gate, no man or beast moves. It is tempest too fierce and keeps from sleep the thousands who stare at the dark. Boom, the thunder breaks again. What is thrown about but entire kingdoms? one tells. Here in the heavens is battle engaged. How the sky holds it is mystery. Something must fall through.

And at first this is lightning. A rend is cut and forth flashes a white spear. Of jagged edge a sky javelin flies. The city is illumined, made small by the vastness of light; its antique history, its fabled greatness are as nothing beneath the force loosed from the dark.

Again the thunder. Now with it further javelins. A first sheet of rain pelts down. Drops larger than the eyeballs of camels. Wind whips, takes down what is upright. Cloths, coverings, poles, lengths of netting, rope, stools, crates, all fly.

The storm does not stop. Unabated in the dark is the fierce conflict. A hundred crashes of thunder, more are counted. Lightning whitens the arrows of the rain.

And in this broken night, the disciples come to the bedside of the Apostle. They, too, are fearful and seek assurance.

What happens? Is this weather only? Or is it now at last that the end of time comes?

The thunder crashes. The lightning illumines their frailty.

'Master?'

'We pray,' John says.

They pray then the Introit of their community. The words that may be their last in this ending of the world.

'In the beginning was the Word,' John says, and the others are enjoined. 'And the Word was with God, and the Word was God. The same was in the beginning with God. All things were made by him; and without him was not anything made that was made. In him was life, and the life was the light of men. And the light shineth in darkness, and the darkness comprehended it not.'

If the ending is now, it will come on the words of the beginning. If it is now, it will be on their profession of faith.

They pray the Introit a second time. 'In the beginning was the Word.' Their voices are raised in the thunderous night. They cry out the words above the roar and the lash and all the bruited dark. And in the action of the praying itself the voice of the Apostle grows stronger. Gradually he loses age and weariness, and though the storm continues wild and wracks the world thereabouts, he has no fear. He is before them as one in rapture, and here, in mid-prayer, he finds his feeling returned to his left side, and he raises up that hand to the other, and can move then from the lain position to stand amongst them. He is marvel and revelation. But none declare it, for the world may be nearly done now, and with the Apostle standing before them they pray only. Their prayers have the intensity of another form – not words but flame perhaps – and burn their foreheads where they are turned upright in expectation and yearning.

The storm crashes yet, the dark more dark still, all the world bowed and blinded.

And now, here, in John, is again revelation.

Here is vision of time itself, of all things temporal and not.

He knows.

He knows as he has not before what is finite and what infinite. He knows that for light darkness is needed and that his hundred years is not an end but a beginning only. He raises up his hands, and it is as though to word sent long ago response is now received. His voice cries out a prayer. And here in the illumined room of his spirit he sees a church, a vast lit place to which keep coming men, women, and children innumerable as stars. The church fills and further fills, its walls expanding; his spirit rises like an eagle and sees the throng stretch into the greater distance, yea on to the horizon of sea and sky itself. 'Hall'luyah, Hall'luyah,' he cries, and the disciples look to one another in awe and joy of what immanence is made manifest. Here is rapture and revelation. 'Hall'luyah, Hall'luyah!' Here is an ecstasy of soul, a condition out of ancient scripture, a purity of communion not known nor considered actual in their old age of the world. But here it is. Here is man with God. Here are all things made new.

John sees.

Returned to him is every moment from the first to the last and beyond. Returned to him in perfect clarity is each instant he spent by the side of Jesus. Each word spoken is in his mind. The teachings are as scribed on fresh papyrus. All is recollected. In those moments while the storm beats and flashes, he himself is the book being written. Here are things he had forgotten. Not the detail of sunlight nor the scent of the olive trees, not the salt slap of the Sea of Tiberias nor the close heat of Cana, but words, ways of saying. Everything taught, each phrase Jesus said is here now. And in that moment John knows the testament is not himself but the Word, and that what remains and what will remain to the last is just this, the word he carries. What gift he bears is not a narrative, is not a telling of what happened, but something other; it is a vision for all time, it is the very cornerstone of the vast church that looms in his mind.

He sees.

He sees and is humbled and uplifted both. He sees as if from a great height and is consoled.

The storm raging still, he lowers his arms. He speaks the names of the disciples gathered there and tells them not to fear.

He says, 'The Lord is with us.' Then he asks that one of them write what he will tell.

He sits. A light is lit.

In voice clear and strong, he begins to tell of the Baptist: 'There was a man sent from God whose name was John.'

38

He speaks on through dark. He does not stop. His manner is composed. Though outside the night is still broken, the disciples have no fear. Each has heard the Apostle teach pieces of the whole before, but here verse and chapter follow as though the words are already written. John does not grow weary. Into his voice comes sometimes anger at the world, sometimes sorrow, and sometimes nothing but the suffusion of love. Hour follows hour. He speaks long passages of the words of Jesus, and while he does, to those attending it seems a truth absolute, that these *exact* were the words spoken and by miracle in this man here preserved. In such a way is time overcome. There is no tarnish of age, no lack of clarity or pause for recall. The words are there, and are as an argument full of reason and logic. Phrases are balanced, built. Time and again certain words ring out. Love. Beloved. Friend. Truth. True. Glory. Command. World. Hour. Darkness. Light. And amidst these is all manner of the verb 'to remain'. *Abide. Dwell on. Stay.*

The composition continues. None can say for how long. Does the dawn come and the day pass and another night fall? Is it even on to the third day, as some will tell? Does the storm blow all the while? It does not matter. From this all else will follow. From this will be accounts numerous, versions of how and where and when that will continue even for thousands of years. There will follow scholars and sages, legions of the learned who in the coming history of the world will unearth possible traces of the gospel's genesis,

272

what comes to be added after, what versions followed what and to what purpose in the unfolding of the early church. There will be one John, and then another. There will be argument and debate as to who wrote what and fragments of antique testimony offered in frail proofs. But none will matter. The words themselves will outlast all such. They will last to the very edge of eternity.

And this John knows as he says them. He knows the beginning and the end. He knows what work is his now, and that the world will not finish here, only his. He himself is already disappearing. He tells on. His spirit soars. He sees what is to come. He sees the numbers of the Christians grow. He sees the churches and thereafter the great cathedrals, the psalms, the songs, the composed Masses, the raptures and revelations of centuries of art divine yet to come. He sees the lives to follow of those about him, of Polycarp, of Lemuel, Meletios, and the others. He sees that on Patmos, Simon and old Ioseph are not dead but even now recover. As, too, in the fallen room in Ephesus where Kester tends to him, does the disciple Papias. The blisters retreat, the flesh is made new. In a day Papias will come to place the Apostle's hand upon his head. But already John will be near to discover that death is a doorway an instant long and beyond it is life everlasting. He sees this, and sees, too, how Papias will in time become bishop of Hierapolis, near Laodicea, and there himself write five books in his old age wherein he will tell of the apostle John, 'whose voice yet lives and remains.'

On and on it continues.

Vision is without end.

John tells his way to the resurrection. He tells it as now it will be told for all time. He tells it as testimony that God loves. And as he does, all feel the movement in their spirits from emptiness to fullness complete.

For here he is running to the tomb now and arriving first. Here he is, the sunlight in his hair. Here he is, little more than a youth running down the road, believing. The dust flies behind him. How swift he is. He sees the tomb opened and he cannot keep himself

273

from joy. His hands he brings to his mouth. He would cry out. He would cry out with joy for ever now. The light fills in him as pure water that flows and flows. Love is resurrected.

He is risen. He is risen. He is risen.

My Lord, you are come.

AUTHOR'S NOTE

I did not intend to write this novel. I intended only to find out the answer to a question that arrived in my mind one afternoon while I was working on another book. The question came to me out of the blue. It was: What was John doing the day before he wrote the gospel? I was not working on a religious theme. I had not been thinking of John or anything biblical, and had not at that point read all of the John gospel. But I had this question. What I wanted to know was something of the man. I supposed then that some basic research would answer the question and began a year of reading.

I was guided to the exhaustive work of Raymond E. Brown, one of the best-known Johannine scholars in the world. I read his translation of and commentary on John and the John epistles, as well as his study 'The Community of the Beloved Disciple', which attempts to reconstruct the history of one Christian community in the first century, and I would urge anyone seeking an in-depth historical perspective on the Johannine community to read his work. Through Brown I was led to other commentators, to Edwyn Hoskyns, Charles Kingsley Barnett, Robert Lightfoot, Willem Grossouw, Alan Robinson, Rudolf Schnackenburg, and many others. It quickly became apparent there was a vast Johannine literature, and within it were whole cycles of interpretation.

There are theories of all kinds surrounding this gospel. There was extreme scepticism; by some the gospel was dated late, even late into the second century. There was no connection between it and John, the son of Zebedee. For some there was no connection between the John gospel and the John epistles. Some commentators argue for three Johns; others that John is merely a name attached to the work of a community of Christians in the second century. It is only in more recent times that the author of the gospel is having his status as an orthodox Christian restored, with some commentators suggesting he may in fact have something to do with John, son of Zebedee. I have no doubt that there are already as many challengers of this interpretation as there are supporters.

A year in research and I was no closer to answering the question. There were few facts. It seemed a John had been exiled on Patmos. A John is believed to have died in Ephesus. But outside of these glimpses, I had begun to sense a man. As a novelist, I write not to tell what I think, but to find out what I feel. I began imagining a man. This was a very old man who had met Jesus of Nazareth when he himself was still a youth. What would it be like? What would it be like to have the most profound experience of your life when you were that young, to have witnessed what he had witnessed and then be left alone in the aftermath?

Slowly I began to understand that what drew me was the idea of faith, and that portion of it that is doubt. *What if it was so?* is the novelist's proposition, not *It was so*. So any questionable interpretations are my own, and should not be imputed to any of the sources listed above. This is a novel, not history nor biography. I hope it offers the rewards of a novel in depicting the inner life of a man of faith and doubt, and, most important, perhaps, what it might be to love for a lifetime.

A NOTE ON THE TYPE

The text of this book is set in Bembo. This type was first used in 1495 by the Venetian printer Aldus Manutius for Cardinal Bembo's *De Aetna*, and was cut for Manutius by Francesco Griffo. It was one of the types used by Claude Garamond (1480–1561) as a model for his Romain de l'Université, and so it was the forerunner of what became standard European type for the following two centuries. Its modern form follows the original types and was designed for Monotype in 1929.